D1442828

Whirlpool

*Also by Lorena McCourtney
in Large Print:*

Bridal Trap
Escape
Top of the Moon

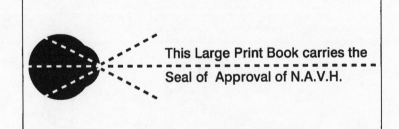

This Large Print Book carries the
Seal of Approval of N.A.V.H.

Whirlpool

THE JULESBURG MYSTERIES: BOOK ONE

Lorena
McCourtney

To Eva -
with best wishes
from your writer friend
in Oregon - 2 Thessalonians 3:16
Lorena McCourtney

Thorndike Press • Waterville, Maine

Published in 2004 by arrangement with Baker Book House.

Thorndike Press® Large Print Christian Mystery.

The tree indicium is a trademark of Thorndike Press.

The text of this Large Print edition is unabridged.
Other aspects of the book may vary from the original edition.

Set in 16 pt. Plantin by Christina S. Huff.

Printed in the United States on permanent paper.

Library of Congress Cataloging-in-Publication Data

McCourtney, Lorena.
    Whirlpool / Lorena McCourtney.
        p. cm. — (The Julesburg mysteries ; bk. 1)
    ISBN 0-7862-6246-X (lg. print : hc : alk. paper)
        1. Arson investigation — Fiction.   2. Divorced women —
Fiction.   3. Oregon — Fiction.   4. Large type books.
I. Title.
PS3563.C3449W48 2004
    813'.54—dc22   2003068710

Mightier than the thunder of the great waters, mightier than the breakers of the sea, the LORD on high is mighty.

Psalm 93:4

As the Founder/CEO of NAVH, the only national health agency solely devoted to those who, although not totally blind, have an eye disease which could lead to serious visual impairment, I am pleased to recognize Thorndike Press* as one of the leading publishers in the large print field.

Founded in 1954 in San Francisco to prepare large print textbooks for partially seeing children, NAVH became the pioneer and standard setting agency in the preparation of large type.

Today, those publishers who meet our standards carry the prestigious "Seal of Approval" indicating high quality large print. We are delighted that Thorndike Press is one of the publishers whose titles meet these standards. We are also pleased to recognize the significant contribution Thorndike Press is making in this important and growing field.

Lorraine H. Marchi, L.H.D.
Founder/CEO
NAVH

* Thorndike Press encompasses the following imprints: Thorndike, Wheeler, Walker and Large Pr int Press.

1

Stefanie Canfield shouldered her way through the throng of people streaming in the opposite direction. Down on the beach, a fireburst of red stars exploded, followed by raucous whistles of appreciation from the crowd. Beyond, the surf boomed in the darkness. Fog muffled the roar, but from farther out echoed the rhythmic bong of a buoy.

Not an ideal night for Fourth of July fireworks, but Stefanie felt exhilarated anyway and glad she'd come. She smiled and returned a greeting from Eliza Ganzer, the nurse who with an iron hand ruled the office of the town's lone doctor. A friendly wave to Lisa Benedetti reminded Stefanie that she should get her hair trimmed at Lisa's shop next week.

"Hey Mark, the fire truck looks fantastic!" she called to Mark Higgins, chief of the local volunteer fire department. The old fire truck was on display near the announcer's stand, red paint polished to a showroom gleam. The compliment brought a shine to Mark's leathery face that rivaled the sparkle of the truck's brass trim.

Stefanie had skipped the previous two years of the small-town celebration. The year before last she'd been beside her mother's hospital bed, gripping her mother's thin hand and praying. Two weeks before last year's celebration, Hunter had dropped his devastating news on her. But those dark days were behind her.

"The Stars and Stripes Forever" blared with a squawk from the town's ancient sound system, a squawk that had been there for as long as Stefanie could remember. The tangy aroma of wood smoke rose from bonfires on the beach, and a scent of barbecuing ribs drifted from the busy Do-Si-Do Square Dancers Club stand.

Stefanie paused at a strip of plastic tape marking a reserved parking space and scanned the crowd for her friend Val's bright auburn hair. She and Val were supposed to meet there under the street banner proclaiming that these were Julesburg's "Celebrate Our Century Days."

A car nosed into the reserved space, and old Ben Mosely in his police uniform gestured it to the curb. Dismay jolted Stefanie as she recognized the silver Porsche. She tried to push her feelings aside. The

Porsche's occupants were *not* going to undermine her enjoyment of the night.

But that did not mean she had to put herself through a face-to-face encounter with them.

She turned and tried to melt into the crowd, but curious onlookers had bunched around the car and formed an impenetrable barrier, pinning her against the cold fender. Hunter's blond head and tall frame emerged from the far side of the car. He, busily gladhanding people, didn't see her. *Or perhaps he's just choosing to shut me out of his line of vision. Smooth, Hunter, very smooth.*

The gaze of the woman stepping out on the passenger's side did not sidestep Stefanie. Her eyes met Stefanie's with silver-blue malice. She added a pointed glance at Stefanie's hip pressed against the car. With a peculiar feeling of guilt, as if she'd been caught trying to claim something that was not hers, Stefanie managed to open a few inches of space between herself and the fender.

The woman didn't speak. *Does the eagle speak to its prey? Well, maybe an eagle isn't the best comparison.* The lift of eyebrows and the superior smile spoke predatory volumes, but honey-haired Trisha Duvall's unscrupulous manipulations fell far short of that noble bird's character. Even now, Trisha angled her ring finger so that the streetlight shot the diamond's glitter into Stefanie's eyes.

Stefanie wanted to take cover in the throng, wanted to stomp the moment into insignificance. Yet her muscles seemed frozen, her body impaled under Trisha's chilling gaze. *She's enjoying this moment,* Stefanie realized. A sudden surge of anger propelled her through the barrier of bodies lining the sidewalk. She ducked around the corner of the nearest building and leaned against it, breathing hard.

Stop it! It's not as if Hunter and Trisha's relationship is some shocking new revelation. Stefanie had learned about the affair and moved out of the house a year ago. Trisha had been living there for months. *I'm long over him.*

So why am I standing here breathing as if I'd just run a marathon? Was it because Trisha was flashing that diamond ring, the official symbol of a coming marriage? Hunter had made the not unexpected gesture of giving Trisha a far larger diamond than the stone in Stefanie's old ring.

Is that *upsetting me?* Stefanie tilted her head and pressed it against the cold concrete. *No. I don't care. I really don't.* Seeing

10

them together was nothing new in tiny Julesburg. She remembered sweeping by Trisha without a second glance on the day she and the lawyer and accountant confronted Hunter at the Cougar Creek Timber Products office.

Yet her earlier sense of exhilaration felt contrived, like something huffed and puffed into a hollow shell of herself. She shook her foot, absentmindedly trying to revive circulation that seemed to have slowed.

Was her agitation at seeing Hunter and Trisha together caused by a subconscious guilt for not trying hard enough to save her marriage? *Oh, but I did try!* True, her first instinct when she found out about Hunter's betrayals was to throw a suitcase at him and end the marriage on the spot. *Go, Hunter, I don't want you anymore.*

But she'd not said the words. Instead, she'd looked to the Lord. She'd studied and prayed. About marriage. About forgiveness. She'd believed giving up on the marriage was not what the Lord would have her do. She'd vowed to fight for her marriage. And, of course, back then she'd still loved him.

There was counseling. The marriage seminar in Eugene. The marriage-manual, revive-your-relationship strategies: gourmet meals, negligees, specially planned "dates," determined efforts to communicate. And the prayers, so many fervent prayers.

She clenched her fists as she remembered Hunter's indifferent response. *And you, Lord, you were indifferent too . . .*

Let it go. It's over. Forget it. Just slip through the crowd, walk back up the hill to the house, and watch the fireworks from there.

No! She straightened her spine against the gritty wall and dug her heels into the hard ground. *No, I will not run. I'll find Val and we'll sit and watch the fireworks from right here by the beach, exactly as planned.*

But as Stefanie started to push herself away from the building, a wave of light-headedness washed over her. She leaned back against the wall. She hadn't had an episode in months. *Oh, Lord, please, not here, not now. Don't let me collapse and make some weird scene.*

The prayer came unbidden. Instantly she pushed it from her mind and instead drew on what the doctors had instructed her to do when she felt an attack coming on. Take deep, calming breaths. Open eyes to help retain balance. Relax each muscle individually. Stretch out the arms. Don't panic.

Easy for them to say. The dampness of her palms chilled against the cold concrete. She couldn't stretch her arms, but she moved

12

her hands a few inches. Her fingers trembled. How could she *not* panic when claustrophobia tightened her throat and numbed her hands?

And the worst part, not knowing what might come after this lightheaded claustrophobia . . .

"Stef, what's wrong?"

Stefanie hadn't realized her eyes had closed and her jaw had clenched until she heard Val Halstead's voice. With relief, she opened her eyes and felt the gathering tide of the attack weaken and recede.

"Stef?"

"Present and accounted for." Stefanie managed a smile. She rotated her shoulders to relax them. "I'm fine."

"*Fine?* If you clutch that wall any tighter, you're going to come away with concrete in your fingernails." Val stepped closer, peering at Stefanie with shrewd green eyes. "Uh-oh. I recognize the symptoms. An ex-husband sighting, right?"

Stefanie stepped away from the building and busied herself by dusting grit from her hands.

"And it wasn't just the ex, was it? You saw them together, the Plywood King and his Liposuction Queen, playing the royal couple."

In spite of her shakiness, Stefanie had to laugh. Wouldn't Hunter and Trisha both have purple fits if they knew what Val said about them?

"And I noticed they arrived in the royal coach, of course. I wonder how the Queen will feel if the royal coach gets repossessed?"

Stefanie had kept the details of the mill's financial problems to herself, but rumors were rampant. She did not intend to add to them, not even to her best friend, Valerie. She brushed her hands against her pants. "C'mon, let's go find a place to sit —"

"What are they doing here anyway?" Val stepped out to the sidewalk and peered at the floodlit announcer's stand. The streetlight brought out the red in Val's auburn hair. "I can't imagine Trisha being eager to dash out here and mingle with the peasants. Or is this some civic duty Hunter does every year?"

"No, not if he can help it." Early in their marriage, Stefanie had dragged Hunter to a couple of celebrations, but he'd never come on his own. *So why are Hunter and Trisha here tonight?*

Stefanie and Val moved with the flow of the crowd toward the grassy slope overlooking the beach. The Fourth of July celebration of this small town on the Oregon

14

coast always drew an astonishing number of people. Outsiders as well as locals came to enjoy Julesburg's friendly old-fashioned atmosphere. Stefanie was pleased that she felt not even a twinge when she spotted Hunter and Trisha together in the announcer's stand, blond heads tipped intimately together.

"I'll bet that between them, they're wearing enough hair spray to anchor a battleship," the ever-loyal Val observed.

The top of the rock wall overlooking the beach was already lined with people. Stefanie and Val found a good spot below where they could lean back against the wall, under the dangling feet. Val, ever prepared, had brought blankets and vinyl cushions.

The announcer, Wally Greer, president of what passed for a Chamber of Commerce in Julesburg, was making chatty comments over the microphone about the origins of the upcoming pageant. "This is our thirty-fifth year, and in case you didn't know it, folks, I'm proud to say that yours truly was one of the original 'Indians.' " Wally had taken over the announcing job after Stefanie's grandfather died and would no doubt have it until his own passing.

"You okay now?" Val asked.

"Sure, I'm fine." Stefanie draped a

15

blanket around her shoulders and scooted the cushion into a more comfortable hollow. "Couldn't be better."

"You really did look a little strange back there. I thought I might have to drape you over my shoulder and haul you off to Dr. Halmoose."

If necessary, big-boned, determined Val could have done exactly that. Stefanie started to make some flippant remark, but changed her mind. A good friend like Val deserved a real explanation.

"Since that car accident I had before you moved here, I've had several of these . . ." Stefanie hesitated. "I'm not sure what you'd call them. Episodes, I guess."

"Of . . . ?"

"They're hard to describe."

"You're talking about the time your car went over the edge of some mountain road?"

Stefanie nodded. She pulled the blanket tighter around her shoulders. Thinking back to that frightening time still made her edgy. "I'd driven out there after a terrible argument with Hunter. I needed to get away for a little while. But the road was muddy, and on a slick curve I just skidded over the edge. The car rolled several times before it hit the bottom of a ravine. I was trapped there with the car wrapped around me like a . . . metal coffin." Her throat closed up as she remembered the helplessness of being trapped. She flexed her fingers and waited a moment for the feeling to pass. "The steering wheel was jammed so tight against my chest I could hardly breathe."

Val reached over and squeezed Stefanie's hand under the blanket. "Oh, sweetie, I'd never realized it was that awful."

"A couple of hunters found me a few hours later, but it took a crew with the jaws of life even longer to get there and extricate me."

"You must have been terrified."

"Yeah, I was. And after that I started having these . . . episodes. Sometimes they come without warning, but usually I get this strange, light-headed feeling first. Then I get a feeling of claustrophobia, as if I'm about to suffocate."

"As if you're trapped in the car again."

"Exactly like that. A few times, early on, I physically collapsed. More often, it's simply several minutes or a half hour later, and I have no memory of the time in between. It happened once at Fit 'n' Fun. Tina said I got a glazed look on my face and sat on a bench for a while." Stefanie swallowed. She focused her eyes on a sparkler someone was twirling down on the beach. "But another

17

time, I found myself here on the beach, which was a shock, since last I remembered I was talking on the phone at the house. Another time I went into a storm of cleaning and threw out everything, from old photos to the bride and groom figurines from my wedding cake."

"Well, it's one way to get housework done. Sometimes I wish I could just go into a trance when I have to vacuum and dust." Then Valerie's tone turned earnest. "Stef, this really does sound serious. Shouldn't you see a doctor?"

"Oh, I did. An army of them. Dr. Halmoose first, then specialists in Portland. I think they put me through every test known to modern science."

"And?"

"Nothing definitive. They finally decided it was possibly something called a 'dissociative reaction,' in which some mental processes split off from the main body of consciousness, due to shock or stress."

"And stress is something you've had more than your share of."

"They gave me tranquilizers and told me I shouldn't drive for a while. They said the episodes would probably fade away, which they have. Until I started to feel . . . odd tonight."

"Was there anything, you know, suspicious about the accident? Did the police investigate it?"

The questions startled Stefanie because she saw the implication behind them. "Are you suggesting Hunter —"

"Sweetie, the guy's a scumbag," Valerie stated. "Wouldn't it be convenient for him if you were just out of the way?"

"Yeah, maybe. But even if our relationship is hostile, I don't think it's *that* hostile. Both Ben and his deputy came out, but there wasn't really anything to investigate."

"Personally, I wouldn't trust our local police force — Which is, what? Two guys with a water pistol and a '73 Pinto? — to solve a dognapping."

"They're okay. I've known old Ben for as long as I can remember. And the patrol car is a *little* newer than '73."

"Well, whatever." Val paused. "Hey, how come you never mentioned anything to me about these 'episodes'?"

"I guess I didn't want you to think I was weird."

But Stefanie knew there was another reason she hadn't confided in Val earlier. Their friendship had started with a definite wariness on Stefanie's part. *Do I want a friendship founded on the fact that we both had straying husbands?* she'd asked herself. But in time, they'd gotten past that hurdle and had become good friends.

"Hey, look," Stefanie said, pushing away the bad thoughts, "I think the fog is lifting. I can see Lighthouse Hill."

"Good. Let's get this show on the road."

As if Val's word were command, the microphone suddenly squawked to life. "Okay, folks, we're about to get going now," Wally Greer said with his usual air of self-importance. "But first I want to introduce someone I'm sure most of you already know. One of our leading citizens, Hunter Blackwell, owner of Cougar Creek Timber Products, has volunteered to help with the program this evening. So let's have a big hand for Hunter and his lovely fianceé, Miss Trisha Duvall!"

After the applause died down, Hunter's smooth voice glided through the microphone. "I'm delighted to be with you folks here tonight. I'm proud to be a longtime member of this fine community and happy to be carrying on its traditions. I'm looking forward to the pageant, and I hope you are too."

He sounds uncharacteristically folksy, Stefanie noted. His tone was warm and intimate, as if the audience members were his

20

good buddies. Stefanie's thoughts circled back to Wally's words. Hunter had *volunteered* to participate tonight? How strange, totally unlike him.

Stefanie focused her attention on the pageant, a reenactment of an early battle with the Indians in which Roman Jules heroically saved the town. Indians in costume shot flaming arrows. An Indian princess shaded her eyes and looked out to sea. Settlers' guns boomed with make-believe smoke. Wally narrated each detail with deadly seriousness. "And at this point, with our brave settlers marooned without food or shelter on the Hill, all appeared lost."

Val doubled over, hooting with laughter in spite of glares from a couple of onlookers. "Oh, this is fantastic, Stef. It's so incredibly awful, it's good."

"The actors *are* just amateurs from here in town," Stefanie retorted, feeling defensive about her hometown's pageant. But, as two "settlers" collided and sprawled in the sand, she had to admit that it was closer to a Keystone Cops skit than high drama. Ruefully, she told Val about the role she'd once played in the pageant.

"I was the Indian Princess years ago. I was supposed to climb up on that rock down there," she pointed to a dark blob on the beach, "but a sneaker wave rolled in and swamped me, and there I was, sloshing around like an oversized mermaid in buckskin. My hair got caught on the rock, and I was coughing and gasping. The whole pageant screeched to a halt." She managed a laugh, although memory of her teenage embarrassment still touched a tender spot. Later, she'd found out via overheard whispers that she'd been awarded the coveted Indian Princess role only because of her grandfather's status in the community.

"I still can't picture you seventy pounds heavier." Val turned her head to appraise Stefanie in the dim light. "I'd swear you've always had those elegant cheekbones and been slim and willowy as a model."

"Then let me tell you about the miraculous benefits of working out at Julesburg's finest health club, the appropriately named Fit 'n' Fun!" Stefanie crowed with the infectious enthusiasm of a late-night infomercial host. "Come one, come all; all you have to lose is your unwanted pounds!"

Val grinned. "I don't hear the fine print that Fit 'n' Fun is also the *only* health club in Julesburg, and you own it, but you've sold me. Sign me up for another lifetime or two."

The pageant ended with the bang-up conclusion of a simulated firing of Julesburg's old cannon. As the smoke cleared, Hunter took over.

"Well, folks, wasn't that great? Let's show our hardworking actors and actresses how much we appreciate their efforts." He started clapping, then waited until the applause died down. "Now, as you probably know, the fireworks display is financed by donations from you loyal citizens out there. We'll be announcing dedications for those donations from time to time. And this opening shot of the fireworks is dedicated to my very own sweetheart of a fianceé. Trisha, this one's for you!"

A triple explosion of red, white, and blue lit the sky. Appreciative oohs and aahs from the crowd followed.

No ooh or aah from Val. "What someone ought to do," she muttered, "is light a couple of firecrackers under that adulterous oaf and his greedy 'sweetheart of a fianceé.' "

The fireworks continued, though the drifting fog often softened the colorful explosions to pastel blurs. There was a dedication from Police Chief Ben Mosely to his wife, Twila, and Wally honored his deceased wife with a burst of gold stars. The local bank sent a noisy blast of lime green to its good customers. Stefanie had given a donation from Fit 'n' Fun, but she hadn't asked for a dedication.

Then, in a lull between fireworks, a murmur swept through the crowd. It started in the parking lot and moved like a rolling wave down the slope. People began to stand up and exchange questions.

"What is it?"

"What's happening?"

"Is it part of the fireworks or something special?"

People turned to the north with a shuffle of feet and more murmurs. Stefanie and Val stood up, blankets still wrapped around their shoulders. The night sky had lightened and taken on an odd reddish tint. An acrid scent, stronger than fireworks, stung Stefanie's nose.

"What's going on?" Val stood on tiptoe. "Can you see anything?"

"No. . . . Yes, there!" Stefanie pointed. A reddish glow filtering through the fog at the north end of town looked like some special fireworks effect. But the odd light hung on too long, and it brightened instead of fading.

The strange reddish glow expanded, covering the entire northern horizon. Stefanie's skin prickled as the eerie infusion of color deepened.

A shout went up from someone standing on the raised announcer's stand. "I can see flames!"

But it was Hunter's hoarse voice blaring over the microphone that galvanized the crowd. "It's the mill! The mill is on fire!"

2

Stefanie thrust the blanket at Val.

"Hey wait, Stef —"

Stefanie didn't wait. She ran, dodging on-lookers, colliding into them. "I'm sorry! Excuse me, I have to get through —" She skidded and fell on the grassy slope. Someone stepped on her hand while she was down, but she ignored the pain and struggled to her feet.

The siren at the firehouse wailed, calling Julesburg's volunteer fire-fighting force to duty. Stefanie knew most of its members must be there at the celebration. Mark Higgins's voice roared over the siren and the noise of the crowd. "C'mon, let's move it! We gotta get the truck out of here!"

Stefanie scrambled over a dip in the wall. People and cars already filled the street. The fire truck, siren also wailing, inched toward the exit of the parking lot.

"Okay folks, let's keep calm and —" The squawk of the sound system drowned out the last of Wally Greer's words.

Honking horns and the shriek of the town's police car joined the din. Red and blue lights flashed an eerie counterpoint to the glow of red fog.

People already streamed in the direction of the mill. Those on foot passed the vehicles stalled in traffic. Stefanie caught a glimpse of Hunter dragging Trisha toward the Porsche. A fireworks explosion added a boom and shower of blue stars to the confusion. It went unnoticed; no one cared about the festivities.

Stefanie had outdistanced much of the crowd by the time she passed the town's long-closed movie theater. Tongues of gold and red flame shot into the sky, and clouds of black smoke swallowed the red-stained fog. The wail of the fire truck moved slowly up the street.

Can that old fire truck put out fires anymore? Stefanie wondered. She momentarily had to slow to a walk and clamp a hand over the stitch in her side. She knew the conflagration went far beyond anything the town's amateur firefighters had ever fought. How had the fire gotten so big, so bad, so quickly? The mill had a modern sprinkler system. Her father had always been vigilant about safety.

Unless Hunter had cut corners there too.

The Porsche crawled past Stefanie just before she reached the bank building. Hunter blasted the horn as he wove in and out of traffic. The tires squealed when he found an opening and gunned the engine.

Stefanie cut across the school playground. The narrow wooden bridge spanning Cougar Creek shook as she pounded across it. The shallow pools below reflected the red stain in the sky. Burning ashes fell around her, smoking in the wet grass, sizzling in the water.

Stefanie's shortcut route brought her to the back side of the mill, where the logs were stored before being peeled into veneer to make plywood. She paused, gasping for breath. She'd always loved the woodsy scent of the logs, but the acrid smell of the burning mill covered that now. She coughed as smoke filled her nose and throat. Her tongue burned and her eyes watered with it. She circled the log deck, and the heat from beyond it blasted her. She threw up a hand to shield her face. The fire truck was already in action, but the spray of water looked puny as a Water Pik against the mountains of flame. Two pale-green Forest Service vehicles that usually fought blazes in the woods arrived, a state police car behind them.

Oh, Lord, please don't let anyone be inside! Don't let this cost any lives!

But Stefanie told herself that there couldn't be anyone inside. The mill had been closed for several days, making a week-long holiday of the Fourth of July to conserve the company's dwindling supply of logs. Which also meant that the veneer dryers and hot presses, where small fires usually occurred, were shut down. So how had the fire started?

Stefanie spotted Hunter near the fire truck. The flames gilded his blond hair as he frantically helped tear down the chain-link fence around the equipment yard. She saw none of Hunter's usual cool and polished demeanor, none of the faintly amused, detached calm with which he greeted most crises. Including, she remembered, the time she confronted him with his infidelity. His shirttail hung loose, and his carefully groomed hair fell in a tangle across his face. A sudden swoop of wind enveloped him and several firefighters in black smoke. In spite of the hostilities between her and Hunter, Stefanie felt a spike of fear for him. *Keep him safe, Lord.*

He emerged from the smoke, carrying the limp form of another man, his face blackened. Stefanie ran toward him. *I can help!*

I've had CPR training! But the ambulance arrived before she did, and Hunter handed the man over to the medics.

Ben Mosely had arrived too. "Time to move back, folks," he said in his gruff voice. He swept his arm in front of him as he strode along the edge of onlookers. His manner was calm and unhurried. "Let the men do their job. Move back now."

Everyone moved back, including Stefanie.

More fire trucks arrived from the small towns north and south of Julesburg. Yet within minutes, it was obvious the mill could not be saved. Stefanie saw efforts change from trying to put the fire out to trying to keep it from spreading to surrounding businesses and houses. Nearby homeowners were hosing down the roofs of their homes.

Even knowing there was nothing she could do, Stefanie couldn't walk away and go home. With some other onlookers, she climbed steep Clyde Street to a vacant lot overlooking the mill. The foggy mist had turned to a drizzle, which was a blessing to keep the fire from spreading, but the wet drops and smoke joined to form an unpleasant moldering smell.

Stefanie slumped to a promontory of wet rock. *That's my family's history going up in flames down there.* The thought was numbing. The company her grandfather and father worked most of their lives to start and grow — all going up in smoke and ashes. She'd worked at the mill too, but it hadn't truly been a part of her as it had been of them. Even though there was a certain stage-set unreality to the scene, Stefanie felt gratitude that her father and grandfather weren't alive to witness it.

The roof and walls were gone. The metal skeleton of the main building still loomed within the flames. *Will it stand? I want something left standing.* Then one dark beam crashed, and others caved toward it. Ashes drifted down around her. An ember landed on her hand, and the pinpoint of pain made her vaguely aware of the ache of her stepped-on knuckles.

Stefanie tried to focus on something other than her own pain. *Hunter's family history is burning too,* she reminded herself. She found a tissue in her pocket and wrapped it around her oozing knuckles. How did he feel, watching the spreading destruction? He'd been much closer to the mill than she had been in recent years. Close, too, to the grandfather who had helped pioneer the company and groomed him to take it over.

Onlookers glanced her way frequently.

31

Many had known her father, some even her grandfather. She overheard questions and answers and theories about the origin of the fire.

"Isn't Pete Dooley the guard? Where was he?"

"Knowing ol' Dooley, probably sleeping."

"I'll bet something's been smoldering in the dryer ever since the mill shut down last week."

" 'Course, there's the rumor that Blackwell —" A glance at Stefanie and a jab in the ribs from his neighbor cut the rumor off in midsentence.

Lisa Benedetti came over to Stefanie and squeezed her hand. "This is terrible, Stef. I don't even know what to say." Then a retired foreman took off his hat in front of her and said gruffly, "Your grandpa would be heartbroke, wouldn't he? I kinda am myself."

Most of the crowd, Stefanie knew, were more than curious onlookers drawn by a spectacle of destruction. Their jobs were burning up too; the livelihood of much of the town depended on Cougar Creek Timber Products. She wondered, as they must be wondering, how they were going to keep up mortgage and car payments, feed their kids, pay their property taxes? Almost as an absentminded afterthought, more personal questions struck her. *How will this affect my future? What will it mean in my dealings with Hunter?* Such thoughts seemed petty, almost irrelevant at the moment, and she pushed them away.

She moved farther back on the vacant lot, taking shelter under a scrubby pine. She caught an occasional glimpse of Hunter. His blond head stood out among workmen's caps and the firefighter's sloping yellow hats. He seemed like a different man than the one she had always known. Heroic even, as he took an exhausted firefighter's place by the hose. *At this moment I admire you, Hunter Blackwell. This is the man I thought you were when I married you.*

Eventually, the flames began to recede. The fiery tongues licked lower. The roar diminished. People began trickling away. But Stefanie stayed on, sitting under the pine, shoulders hunched against the drizzling rain, until, with a sense of shock, she realized she was alone. She stood up stiffly brushing twigs and grass from her damp pants. *How long have I been here?* She was just about to step out of the shadows of the pine tree when a vehicle turned onto Clyde Street. She drew back, too emotionally frazzled to encounter anyone. A moment later, she realized the vehicle was one of Cougar Creek's tan-and-brown pickups. Hunter stepped out of it.

He walked toward her. She thought he meant to speak to her. Then she realized he hadn't seen her. He was simply heading for the rocky promontory overlooking the mill. Smoke smudged his face, and one shirt sleeve hung loose, ripped at the shoulder. His bare knee showed through a hole in his slacks. Her heart filled with unexpected compassion. *I'm sorry. I know the despair you must feel.*

She started to step out of the shadows. *Surely, in spite of the hostility between us, we can share a few words of comfort and consolation —*

She stopped, foot poised, as a sudden flare from below lit his face.

While fighting the fire, his handsome features had shown grim determination. Up close, she could see the tired slump of his shoulders, the dark line of a cut on his arm. But his face . . .

Not horror, not defeat or despair or heartache.

Satisfaction. Even, in a small twist of his lips, a smile of triumph.

I must be wrong! That can't be what he's

feeling! She froze in the shadows, unmoving as a mouse avoiding a cat. Disbelief conflicted with the reality of what her eyes saw. *Satisfaction? Triumph? No, I'm wrong —*

The emotion lingered on Hunter's face only a few moments. Then, as if he were deliberately censoring his expression, the strange smile left his mouth, and grim determination returned. He climbed back in the pickup and drove down the hill. A moment later she saw him rejoin the men keeping vigil at the mill.

Feeling almost as if she were coming out of a trance, Stefanie collected herself enough to head home. She began to think beyond the scene of leaping flames that felt branded on her brain. Her mind swirled with the questions she had asked herself earlier that evening.

Why were Hunter and Trisha in such high profile at the fireworks? Why had Hunter so uncharacteristically volunteered to help with the program? Was it some newly acquired sense of civic responsibility? A character switch to caring about small-town causes?

Or was it an alibi?

Because if Hunter was at the celebration when the fire broke out, and hundreds of people had seen him and heard his hoarse cry of shock over the microphone, well, then obviously he wasn't at the mill setting the fire.

Oh, come on, Stef. She grabbed the back door key from the hook under the steps of the old Victorian house. *Where do you get such crazy ideas?*

Hunter had huge flaws as a husband. He had his faults as the manager of Cougar Creek Timber Products. He was greedily trying to grab her share of the company out from under her. But surely he was not a match-happy firebug!

And yet . . .

Where did Hunter stand, with the mill destroyed? Wiped out financially, his future shattered? Not necessarily. With a big insurance settlement, he could pay off the huge debts entangling the company, debts her accountant was only now uncovering. He could get Stefanie out of the way with a cash settlement. He wouldn't have her part ownership of the company complicating his business dealings. And all the mill's financial records were ashes. Incriminating details her lawyer and accountant suspected but hadn't yet uncovered were destroyed.

Stefanie realized that the fire might well be financial salvation for Hunter. The solution to all his problems.

In her upstairs bedroom, Stefanie skimmed out of her clothes. She wrinkled her nose — the scent of smoke permeated everything from jacket to underthings. She slipped into a robe and carried her clothes and sneakers at arm's length down to the laundry room. Then, wearily she brushed the acrid taste out of her mouth and showered the ashes and smoke out of her hair and skin. She also covered her two most painful knuckles with Band-Aids.

A curve of hillside hid a full view of the mill from her house, but a faint reddish light from the fire lingered in the bedroom even with the drapes closed. The oval mirror on her old-fashioned dressing table shimmered a ghostly reflection of silver and shadows. Outside her window, a breeze gently clattered the wind chimes.

After she had washed up, Stefanie lay in bed, bone tired but sleepless. *Do I honestly think Hunter could have done this?*

He had maneuvered some tricky deals during their marriage. He had gotten her signature on various papers that were not what he'd told her they were. His financial tactics at the mill stretched creative accounting beyond ethical limits. But those maneuverings, unscrupulous as they might be, fell far short of wanton destruction.

She pulled the covers tighter around her neck. *So am I convinced he's innocent, that he had no part in this?*

No.

3

In the light of morning, Stefanie's suspicions seemed less believable.

A smoky pall hung over the town, but to the west, sunshine glittered on a calm blue sea. White surf scalloped the offshore rocks. A seagull perched on the porch railing and squawked for the bread crusts Stefanie often tossed out.

Stefanie sat on a tall stool at the breakfast bar, which was a modern addition her mother had made to the old-fashioned kitchen. Sipping black coffee and eating cereal topped with yogurt and strawberries, she thought about the night before.

Actually, Stefanie had to admit, her middle-of-the-night suspicions about Hunter now struck her as suspicious in themselves. *Paranoid delusions of the discarded wife? How can I possibly know what that expression on Hunter's face really meant? Just drop it.*

It was her usual day to go to the nursing home up in Dutton Bay, and she saw no reason to alter her schedule because of the fire. She dressed in casual leggings and added a pair of costume-jewelry daisy earrings. She poked around in the cluttered jewelry box, as she always did, hoping that somehow her mother's jade cameo necklace would turn up. She hadn't been able to find the necklace when she and Hunter separated. At the time, she'd hoped the cameo was tucked in some box she'd already packed and would show up later, but she'd never found it.

She stopped in the laundry room to sniff her clean clothes. Good. The smoky scent was gone. She tossed everything but the sneakers in the dryer. Outside, the smell of smoke still hung heavy in the air. Soggy ashes littered the walkway to the garage.

The morning at Laurel Cove Nursing Center was, as always, rewarding. Her mother had spent a few weeks there after one of her surgeries, and Stefanie had seen how physical activity brightened the lives of the residents. Her time at the nursing home had been strictly volunteer at first, but they'd eventually put her on the payroll.

Her exercise class was waiting in the activity room when she arrived. Stefanie talked with the group before beginning the exercises, offering hugs and teases and encouragement.

"Bertha, are you ready to add a half pound to your ankle weights today? Dan, look at those muscles!" she said with a teasing squeeze of Dan's stringy but still-working bicep. "Millie, you got a new perm, didn't you? Looks fantastic."

She spent several minutes chatting with a new woman, Gracie. She asked about Gracie's grandchildren and drew her out until Gracie shyly confided, "What I'd really like to do is surprise my granddaughter Annie by being able to touch my toes."

Touch her toes? Stefanie eyed the tiny lady. "We'll work on that," she promised.

She put a CD of Glenn Miller music in the player and led the group through various exercises, tailoring them to individual abilities. Gentle aerobics, light weight lifting, easy bends for flexibility, ball tossing for coordination. Gracie was a long way from touching her toes, but by the end of the session she was tapping those toes to the music.

None of the class members mentioned the fire to Stefanie, but a couple of the older members of the staff asked about it. "Just a terrible accident," was the only response Stefanie knew to make.

Back in Julesburg she drove by the mill but found the street cordoned off. A cleanup crew was still spraying stubborn hot spots. Smoke spiraled from the debris, but it no longer billowed in black clouds.

Stefanie didn't head to work immediately. Her hopes to add a snack and juice bar at Fit 'n' Fun were still at an insufficient-funds status, so she ate a salad at the house before going to lead an aerobics class. Afterward, she called a repairman about a malfunctioning treadmill and set up a special training program for a girl with Down Syndrome. When she could avoid it no longer, she tackled the bookkeeping. She groaned as she looked at the computer screen. *I hate numbers. Which is no doubt one reason my financial affairs with Hunter and Cougar Creek Timber Products are in such disastrous shape.*

She heard scraps of conversation about the fire all afternoon, but it wasn't until late in the day that Tina, Fit 'n' Fun's receptionist and girl-of-all-trades, peered into the office.

"Got a minute?"

Stefanie glanced up from the computer screen. "Sure, c'mon in."

Tina was petite and trim, with a freckled face and long brown hair her husband didn't want her to cut. She'd been working out on one of their new exercise machines so she could demonstrate it to clients. She toweled sweat off her face. "Great machine. My abs feel strong enough to bounce a wildcat."

"Good. I'm glad to hear buying the machines wasn't wasted money."

Tina dropped the small talk. "Will the mill be rebuilt, do you think?" Her husband was a glue spreader, and her tone was anxious. "That would mean construction jobs. Otherwise . . ." The lines between Tina's hazel eyes said it all. She and her husband had three kids and Tina's wheelchair-bound mother to support.

Stefanie shook her head. "I don't know. I haven't talked to Hunter yet." No jobs at the mill could have a domino effect in tiny Julesburg. *I don't know what this might do to Fit 'n' Fun's future either.* But she didn't want to lay that additional worry on Tina.

After finishing her paperwork, Stefanie picked up her mail at the post office and unlocked the door to her house just after 5:00. She'd return to Fit 'n' Fun later to lead a couple of evening classes. The doorbell chimed while she was browsing through bills and advertisements. Still wearing the blue leotard and draped overskirt in which she'd come home, she opened the door.

Ben Mosely stood on the porch, his police car parked in the driveway. "Miss Stefanie,"

43

he said. He'd called her that since she was a little girl playing with his polished badge. His weathered face sagged with weariness, and red lines webbed his eyes. He held his police officer's hat at chest level.

"Ben! Come in." Stefanie tilted her head and scolded him lightly. "You look as if you didn't sleep more than ten minutes last night."

"That's about it, all right. Terrible thing, the fire and all. A real tragedy for the company and the town."

Stefanie motioned to her sofa, and, in spite of his beefy frame, Ben perched almost daintily on the edge of a cushion. He turned the hat back and forth in his big hands as if he felt awkward or uneasy.

Stefanie offered the platitude she had heard many times that day. "At least no one was injured or killed. We can be thankful for that."

"Mike Orland is in the Coos Bay hospital with smoke inhalation. But he'd be a lot worse off if it weren't for Hunter carrying him out."

Stefanie nodded. "Things might have been much worse all around if the mill had been operating and full of workmen when the fire happened."

Ben jumped on the comment as if he'd

44

been looking for an opening. "Yep, that's true, and that's what makes it a puzzle, you know. How it got started with everything shut down."

"Wasn't a watchman on duty?"

"Pete Dooley is usually there, but he's got a bunch of grandkids, you know. Hunter let him take the night off so's he could go to the fireworks with the kids."

"How thoughtful," Stefanie murmured. And how totally unlike Hunter. She couldn't imagine him dealing with the watchman personally. The suspicions she'd earlier discarded flickered at the edge of her mind.

"Could I get you some coffee or tea? A soft drink?" she offered.

"No, thanks. I'm fine." Ben ran his thick fingers through his bushy thatch of white hair. "You were there last night?"

"At the fireworks? Or the fire?"

"Both, actually. We're just trying to find out where people were and what they saw."

"My friend Valerie Halstead and I went to the fireworks."

"Together?"

"No, we met there, under the street banner. I was standing just a few feet away when you opened the car door for Hunter's fianceé."

Ben didn't acknowledge seeing her, and

he probably hadn't. Trisha's charisma tended to dazzle males of any age.

"You said your friend's name is Valerie? Halstead?"

"Yes."

He took out a small notebook and wrote Valerie's name in it. Surprised, Stefanie added, "Val comes to Fit 'n' Fun. She works for Volkman Laser Systems."

"Ah," he said. He wrote Volkman in parentheses after Val's name.

"She lives in one of those new condos up on Lighthouse Hill."

"Ah. And then you and this Val went to the fire?"

"No. I heard Hunter yell over the microphone that the mill was burning. I left Val behind and ran over there by myself."

"Did you see anything unusual when you arrived? Notice anyone or anything unfamiliar or suspicious looking?"

"No . . . Although I did notice that the sprinklers weren't running on the log deck. I don't think they'd be turned off just because the mill was shut down." The logs were continually kept damp. Otherwise they'd dry out and crack and not be usable for peeling veneer to make plywood. "But maybe by the time I got there, the fire had already burned through the control system."

46

Another line in the notebook. "Before going to the fireworks, you were . . . where?"

"Here at home."

"Alone?"

"Yes. Fit 'n' Fun was closed for the holiday. I was just catching up on a few things around here."

He eyed the Band-Aids on her knuckles. "Hurt your hand recently, did you?"

She flexed the fingers on her injured hand. "When I was running to the mill, I slipped on the grass down below the wall. Someone stepped on my hand before I could get up."

Another one of his noncommittal but somehow meaningful "Ahs." He tapped the ballpoint pen on his thigh.

Feeling a sudden need to lighten things up, Stefanie smiled. "So I don't think I'll be going around socking anyone in the jaw for a while."

Ben didn't smile. Was he maneuvering her to reveal her suspicions about Hunter and the fire? And feeling uneasy about doing so?

"I suppose you still know quite a lot about the mill." Ben's words hovered between statement and question.

"I worked in the mill office for several years after I dropped out of college. You remember that, I'm sure. But I haven't been around there much in recent years."

"I understand you stayed quite a long time watching the fire from that vacant lot on Clyde Street."

The remark surprised her. How did he know that? His tone of voice almost made it sound like he thought her actions peculiar. Like she was some unsavory voyeur hanging around until the last flame died.

"I did stay a long time. It was 3:30 in the morning when I got home. It was . . . strange, watching the family history go up in flames."

And even more strange was the odd, triumphant look that had been on Hunter's face. Stefanie looked away toward the fireplace in the corner. *Should I tell Ben?*

But how could she suggest something so appalling when all she had to go on was a dimly lit facial expression? Although there was also Hunter's high-profile appearance at the fireworks and his equally unlikely action of offering the watchman the night off. And the fact that the company was in a financial tangle . . .

I'll just confide my concerns to Ben. Yet when Stefanie looked at Ben, his steady blue eyes regarded her with a guarded watchfulness. His big hand held the pen poised over the notebook as if to capture some incriminating statement.

Incriminating?

With a jolt that jerked her spine ramrod straight, the truth hit her.

4

"Ben, you think *I* started the fire at the mill?" Stefanie gasped. She looked down at her fingers again. "You think I hurt my hand while I was setting the fire?"

A deep red suffused Ben's face. His gaze shifted to her feet, and his own big feet shuffled on the carpet.

Stefanie shook her head. "Ben, this isn't some gasoline-toting arsonist, it's me, Stefanie, remember?" She jabbed a finger at her chest. "You were the one who taught me how to drive! How can you think I had anything to do with this?"

Ben's gaze lifted to meet hers. His weathered cheeks were still red with embarrassment, but the jut of his jaw said embarrassment wouldn't stop him. Ben Mosely was not one to shirk his duty just because an old friend was involved. He'd hauled in his nephew for a house break-in. He'd arrested his brother-in-law for drunk driving. Ben made no exceptions for personal relationships where the law was concerned.

"I'm sorry, Miss Stefanie, but we have to check out all the possibilities."

"Then you'd better start checking out Hunter!"

Ben nodded. "We're doing that. And other people too."

"Such as?"

"There've been layoffs at the mill. Could be someone holding a grudge. Or maybe a transient passing through, a firebug who just likes to see things burn. Or could be it was just an accident."

"But how could you have even a smidgen of suspicion I'd burn the mill? It was my grandfather's life's work. My father's too! It's the lifeblood of the town. What would I have to gain by burning it down?"

"Nobody's accusing you, Miss Stefanie."

"This sounds awfully close to an accusation!"

"It's just that sometimes people don't act rationally when it comes to . . . affairs of the heart." Ben stumbled over words that were not in his usual vocabulary. "Sometimes people do strange things and don't think about the consequences when they want to get even."

"So you think this is all about Hunter and me and Trisha Duvall. That I'm furious because he left me for her, so I'm

51

going to get back at him by burning the mill."

"What Hunter did was pretty terrible, Miss Stefanie. Everyone knows that —"

"If Wally Greer's speech to Hunter and his 'lovely fianceé' last night is any example, most people in town are quite willing to welcome the next Mrs. Blackwell with open arms!"

Ben didn't comment on that but simply added, "Some people wouldn't blame you for wanting to do something drastic to get even."

"Believe me, if I were interested in getting even, it's Hunter or Trisha I'd go after, not the mill," she said.

She shook her head, and her fingers absentmindedly smoothed the edge of her wraparound skirt. As an adolescent she'd sometimes had vindictive thoughts about calamities happening to classmates who ostracized and teased her. She'd hoped Bucky Anderson would get eaten by a shark. She'd wanted the arch of roses to crash down on Debbie Olsen when she was crowned Prom Queen. She'd wished an earthquake would open the ground and swallow everyone who called her "Porky Princess." But even before she became a Christian, she never saw herself actually committing acts of vengeance.

Not even against Hunter and Trisha for what they'd done.

"What happened between Hunter and Trisha and me doesn't matter anymore," she told Ben with a firm confidence. "We're all moving ahead with our lives."

"There are rumors you're still battling over the mill ownership. Getting a chunk of insurance cash could be pretty convenient for you," Ben suggested. "Easier than trying to split Cougar Creek Timber Products."

"More convenient for Hunter too!" she countered.

Ben nodded, but she saw the crease deepen between his thick eyebrows, as if he disapproved of the comment. She could see how the situation might look to him. Hunter had been out there on the front lines the night before, heroically fighting the fire and rescuing people. And what had she been doing? Nothing. Standing on the hill. Watching too long, like some mesmerized firebug. Showing up with a hurt hand.

Then she realized what was behind Ben's comment about her knowing quite a lot about the mill. *He's speculating that I know my way around the mill well enough to burn it down.*

Stefanie jumped to her feet. "Is this all

53

Hunter's idea? Did he suggest I started the fire?"

"No." Ben held out a hand, palm down, as if to soothe her. "He thinks it was an accident. Something electrical."

That didn't quiet Stefanie's suspicions. Making accusations wouldn't be a smart move for Hunter. To avoid complications with an insurance settlement, he'd want the authorities to think it was an accident.

"Like I said, right now we're just checking out different angles." Ben stood and closed the notebook. "The county sheriff's office will probably take over most of the investigation. Someone from the state fire marshall's office is coming. The federal Bureau of Alcohol, Tobacco, and Firearms may get involved. Randy and I don't have the manpower or know-how for an arson investigation."

"I'll help any way I can. I have nothing to hide."

"The sharpest investigative guns may come from the insurance company. This is going to cost them a bundle if they have to pay off. So you can bet their investigators will be here with a magnifying glass and a fine-tooth comb."

"Just let me know if there's any way I can help."

He picked up his hat from the sofa. "Twila says she hasn't seen you in church much lately."

Twila, Ben's wife, was the backbone of Julesburg Community Church, but she had never been able to convince Ben to share her spiritual convictions. Ben probably didn't know it, but a lot of people prayed for him. They were probably praying for Stefanie too, because Ben was right. She hadn't been in church lately. Twila had called several times.

Lightly, she said, "Is that part of your investigation, Ben? Whether or not I'm a backslider at church?"

A twinge of embarrassment returned. "No, of course not." He put the hat on his head, briskly switching to officer-on-duty mode. She wondered about his granddaughter, who had cystic fibrosis, but it didn't seem the right time to ask.

"Just one more thing. . . . Do you remember what you were wearing last night?"

"Jeans, a Fit 'n' Fun sweatshirt, purple jacket, sneakers. Why?"

"Would you mind if I take a look at the clothes?"

The request puzzled her, but she saw no reason not to cooperate. "I'll get them out of the dryer —"

"The dryer? You've washed them already? When?"

"Last night, when I got home."

"You did a washing at 3:30 in the morning?" The question was almost a yelp. "Even the sneakers?"

Under different circumstances, Stefanie would have laughed at how old-fashioned Ben sounded. Oh, this younger generation! Washing at 3:30 in the morning. Blithely throwing all sorts of things in together. Not something Twila would ever do. But then she realized he was shocked because he saw the possibility of ulterior motive behind her hasty laundry work. *He thinks I could have washed everything to get rid of any trace of something flammable I used to start the fire.*

"Everything was so damp and smoky." Her explanation sounded limp and weak. Stefanie felt dazed as she slumped into the wing chair. *I'm a suspect.*

"Do you still want to see the clothes?"

"No. That won't be necessary."

She straightened in the chair. "Am I under arrest? Don't I have a right to have a lawyer present when I'm questioned?"

"You're not under arrest. We're just trying to interview anybody who might know anything. But if you don't want to answer questions without a lawyer present, that's your right."

He had earlier asked what she'd been doing before the pageant and fireworks. The reasoning behind that question was clear now. The fire could have been set earlier, before the celebration. If the fire started where it could engulf much of the windowless interior of the building, it could have burned for some time before becoming visible outside.

"Have you investigated Hunter's activities earlier in the evening?" she demanded.

"Hunter and Miss Duvall had dinner at the Singing Whale, with drinks in the lounge first. They were there for some two and a half hours. The waitress and bartender remember serving them."

Two and a half hours during which Hunter was making sure he and Trisha were highly visible. Hours during which she had no alibi at all.

Ben turned toward the door. "Well, I think that's all for now. You're not planning to . . . uh . . . leave town in the near future, are you?"

"I can check my calendar, but I don't think there's any 'disappear to deserted island in the Caribbean' scheduled on it."

Her lame attempt at a quip fell flat. Ben didn't smile when he said, "Good. And it might not be a bad idea to think about getting yourself a good lawyer." He paused at the door. "If you don't mind, we'd appreciate if you'd come in and get fingerprinted as soon as possible."

"Fingerprinted? Why?"

"If we do find any usable fingerprints at the mill, we can check yours against them and maybe settle this without any more fuss and bother for you."

He made it sound as if comparing fingerprints was solely for her benefit, to remove suspicion from her. She saw the opposite possibility lurking within the request; fingerprints could incriminate rather than exonerate her.

But incrimination was impossible; she wasn't involved in the fire in any way.

Still, she hesitated about complying. She was reasonably certain Ben couldn't demand her fingerprints without something stronger than suspicions, and she suspected a lawyer would tell her not to do it.

Stefanie hedged. "From the looks of what's left of the mill, there isn't anything *to* fingerprint."

"You never can tell."

Stefanie made up her mind within minutes after Ben's departure. After all, she was innocent. She had nothing, including fingerprints, to hide.

She drove down to the tiny police station first thing the following morning. It was located in the same building as the water department and the town library. A scent of coffee came from a back room. Randy Wilson, Ben's partner and the only other person on the Julesburg police force, came to the counter. Stefanie asked for Ben.

"He's out at the mill." Randy was considerably younger than Ben. Late twenties, good looking in a slick, Burt Reynolds sort of way, mustache and all. He had a reputation as a ladies' man. "Guy from the state fire marshall's office is here."

"Ben asked me to come in for fingerprinting."

"I can do that."

As if it were an important ceremony, Randy got an ink pad and cards from a drawer. He carefully rolled each of her fingers across the pad and transferred the prints to a card. There was a separate space for each print.

"This is the old-fashioned way, of course," Randy said. "The big police departments have a computerized system that scans the prints in."

Her hands felt oddly disconnected from

her as she watched Randy work with them. Inanimate objects. Pieces of evidence.

"Not often I get to fingerprint such pretty hands." Randy grinned as he held her ring finger longer than necessary when transferring the print to the card. "Would you believe they actually pay me for doing this?"

His mild attempt at flirting did not ease Stefanie's discomfort. *Am I making a big mistake doing this?* She believed that in spite of his flirty ways, Randy would happily nail her as an arsonist. He was known to be considerably more ambitious than Ben. There was talk that he might run for county sheriff in the fall, and she could be an upward step on his ladder of advancement. He moistened a paper towel with some strong-smelling fluid and handed it to her.

"There, that's all there is to it."

She stared at the prints as she wiped her hands. There they were, unique symbols of her, fingerprints unlike anyone else's in the world. A special identity God had given to each of his children. Another one of his strange and marvelous wonders.

At times like this, Stefanie saw such potent proof of the Lord's powers of creation. He cared about the tiniest of details. She remembered a Bible verse that had always touched her: "Even the very hairs of your head are numbered." Yet at other times God seemed so distant and uncaring. . . .

"Now about that hair sample," Randy said briskly, as if her thoughts about hair had reminded him.

Stefanie lifted her head sharply as she tossed the paper towel into the trash. "What hair sample? Ben didn't say anything about a hair sample."

"Oh? Well, yeah, we gotta have a hair sample." Randy reached in another drawer for a pair of scissors. "I can take a snip from right here on the side, and it won't even show."

Stefanie jerked her hair away from his hand. She needed a haircut, but she was not thrilled with the idea of Randy taking a whack at it. "Why do you want a sample of my hair?"

"Police procedure." Randy stated the nonexplanation with a lofty superiority, as if it were a matter beyond her comprehension. "Of course, it's voluntary." He paused, then added, "At this time."

Stefanie hesitated. She knew refusal would no doubt imply that she had something to hide. *What does hair reveal to an expert? DNA, hair dye . . . bad hair day resulting in an uncontrollable urge to burn something down?* It all seemed wildly preposterous, a bad joke.

But her hair surely couldn't reveal anything incriminating, because she had nothing to do with any of it! Yet a feeling of being herded into a trap suddenly swept through her.

"No," she said faintly, then more strongly, "No!"

"No? You're refusing to give a hair sample?"

Stefanie didn't answer. She simply turned and fled.

5

Julesburg. Pop. 1,450.

A line had been slashed through the zero on the sign, and a "1" had been scrawled in. Ryan Harrison braked to let a calico cat dash across the street in front of him. Was the cat included in the population count?

Years ago when he lived in Julesburg, the number on the sign read an even 1,000. People said the only way to get the number up that high was to include every critter in town. "A goat just gave birth to twins," the old guy who owned the bait shop on the dock quipped when someone replaced the last zero with a "2."

Ryan shook his head, not knowing whether to be amused or exasperated with a town that refused to let a tired joke die.

He drove slowly, the window of his Blazer open. A few new buildings dotted the main street, the hint of progress offset by other buildings boarded up and vacant. The movie theater with its enigmatic name, the Nevermore, now had a weathered "For

Sale" sign nailed across the double doors. A few letters still clung to the marquee. Did the old theater still have its somewhat mysterious reputation?

Traffic apparently warranted three stoplights, although there was little evidence of any traffic at that hour of the evening. A convenience store called the Calico Pantry stood where a second-hand store had once offered old sofas and tarnished toasters. A new two-story motel with adjoining restaurant appeared to be the centerpiece of town. A sign in the shape of a frisky whale above the restaurant identified it as the Singing Whale.

In spite of the shabby downtown, many more houses clung to the wooded hills to the east. The all-glass front of one oversized structure glinted like a sheet of gold in the last rays of the setting sun. Angular new redwood-and-glass condos climbed the steep side of Lighthouse Hill.

Ryan pulled into a parking space in the empty beach-overlook area at the south end of town. Waves blasted around offshore rocks before crashing on the sandy beach in an endless roar. A handful of fishing boats bobbed in the shelter of the rock jetty to the north. The scent of seaweed and damp sand and faintly fishy seawater reminded him of hours spent in barefoot beachcombing. He'd seen gray whales from that very spot and captured agates in the froth of retreating waves.

The water had darkened to blue ink now, but Technicolor flares of orange and gold and red stained the sky. Gulls swooped. "They sound like little lost kids," his sister Angie had once said. He watched until the flamboyant sky gentled to softer pastels.

Nice show, Lord!

He looked back at the quiet main street. A car passed. A fish-shaped windsock twirled in the breeze beside a gift shop. A boy bicycled by, cap turned backwards. Seen like that, Julesburg was the quintessential hometown. Ryan could almost feel nostalgic about it.

If it weren't that his two years there had been the most miserable and unhappy of his life.

Only one person had made those years bearable.

He squinted, picturing her there on the beach. Barefoot. Rescuing some stranded starfish. Wild tangle of brown hair. Light-up-your-life smile. Hazel eyes sometimes full of mischief, more often guarded. He felt a rush of affection for her, even though it wasn't romance they had shared back then,

65

not even the puppy-love variety. They were friends, buddies, coconspirators. Two against the world of Julesburg Junior High. Some people thought small-town schools were all one big happy family. Ryan, familiar with the unenviable position at the bottom of the junior-high food chain, knew better.

Ryan's friend was at the bottom too, so they stuck together. They shared lunch in the cafeteria. Huddled together in study hall. Skipped pep rallies together. They feigned a cool indifference toward the schoolmates who teased them and shut them out. They shared secret jokes and privately made fun of those who tormented them. She could do a wicked hair-tossing, chest-thrusting imitation of . . . what was her name? Patty something. She was always ready to escape to the beach with him when the drinking and fighting at his home became unbearable. Her mother was good to him too, always offering him freshly baked cookies.

They talked about everything, the strangest of subjects. Could porcupines throw their quills? Why had their parents gotten married? Did ghosts exist? Was there a God? (He knew the answer to that one now; did she?) They spent hours exploring forest and beach and fantasized about far-away expeditions to Africa and the Amazon. Their goal was to be anywhere but Julesburg. They were simply friends, friends as fiercely loyal as soldiers in battle.

Although there was the time he'd tried to kiss her . . .

He smiled at the memory. They were on the beach, waiting for the green flash. She was taller, so he'd climbed on a rock. But he slipped when his lips were a few inches from hers, and — clunk! Their foreheads slammed together hard enough to send them both sprawling in the sand. She got up slowly, blinking and shaking her head. Then her hazel eyes focused on him. "Don't ever do that again," she muttered. And he never did.

Would she still be in Julesburg? No. She'd wanted out, as he did. Which brought up the question. Why was *he* there in Julesburg?

Logically, of course, because of his job. Yet somehow there seemed to be more to it than that.

He'd tried hard to avoid coming to Julesburg. There was an apartment fire in Seattle. He'd asked to be reassigned to it. Usually the company cooperated with such requests, but not this time. Then he'd tried to take his remaining week of vacation time. "No, not now. We're too shorthanded," he'd been told.

He could almost believe the Lord had deliberately closed all escape routes and purposely marched him back to Julesburg.

How come, Lord? More character building? Haven't I had enough of that already? Yet as he watched the sunset, he had an odd sense that he was standing at a crossroads.

Then he scoffed at that unlikely image. He was grounded in a right relationship with the Lord, an active member of a friendly church back in Portland. He had a comfortable condo with a great view of the Willamette River. Last payment made on his Blazer, bank account healthy. He was on track for promotion to regional manager of the Arson and Fraud Division when Steve Richter retired next year.

No, no crossroads. Just a straight line ahead. A sharp investigation on the assignment in Julesburg could clinch his promotion. Without arrogance or false conceit he could say he was very good at what he did, a fact a number of convicted arsonists had learned to their regret.

He wanted to see the mill, but he did not go there directly. Remembering the layout of the town, he circled several blocks until he found a hillside street above it. He stepped out of the car and leaned against the open door. In the blue shadows of evening, only a few tendrils of smoke still rose from the burned mill, but a scent that wrinkled his nose lingered.

The scene of devastation below was not a shock. He'd seen his share of fire damage, but this destruction was more complete than most. Crumpled metal framework, piles of blackened debris, fallen smokestacks. A mangled conveyer system, misshapen remains of vehicles and equipment. A chain-link fence that had encircled the perimeter of the area lay flattened and broken. Not a wall still stood. The only movement was a big yellow dog rummaging through the debris.

Even though he regretted the wasteful destruction he saw below, Ryan felt the familiar surge of excitement that always accompanied the beginning of an investigation. The blackened debris held mysteries to be solved, secrets to be uncovered. *I'll find them!*

He climbed back in the car. He'd find a motel room and dinner, and then he'd hit the investigation hard in the morning. He didn't intend to linger in Julesburg an hour longer than necessary.

He bypassed the new motel and rented a room at the old Sea Haven south of town. The window overlooked the highway and a wooded slope with glimpses of surf between the trees. He unpacked his suitcase and walked back downtown to eat. The touristy looking Singing Whale didn't appeal to him, and he bypassed it in favor of the Julesburg Café.

He ordered the ling cod. Fresh and tasty, with scalloped potatoes like his mother never used to make. He studied the for-sale seascapes scattered around the room as he lingered over coffee. One caught the power of the ocean, another captured the whimsy of a child and dog playing on the beach. The one by his booth was signed with the name Julie Armstrong.

The waitress, with coffee carafe poised over his cup, saw him admiring the paintings. "Julie's new in town. Really good, isn't she?"

"Exceptionally good."

"How about a refill?" She was middle-aged, with a friendly smile and blond hair piled in high scallops on her head. "And maybe some pie? The blueberry is terrific. I should know. I've eaten three pieces of it today." She patted a plump hip. The name tag on her blue uniform said Rosie.

Ryan returned her smile. "Sure, blueberry pie it is." When she brought it, with a big dollop of whipped cream, he asked, "Have you lived around here long?"

"Going on forty years."

"I lived here for a while, about . . . fifteen or sixteen years ago, I guess it is. I went to the seventh and eighth grades here."

"No kiddin'? Well, the place has changed some since then, hasn't it?" Her generously made-up face beamed with pride, then sobered. "Of course, we had a real catastrophe just a few nights ago. The plywood mill burned down."

Ryan wasn't ready to reveal his professional interest in the fire — he'd learned that listening to local rumors could be helpful. "That's too bad. I remember the mill. My dad pulled green chain there for a while. I wonder what started the fire?"

"Oh, there's all kinds of gossip going around about arson and accidents and such." Rosie dismissed the rumors with the lift of a hefty shoulder. "I don't put much stock in any of 'em. The mill was closed for the Fourth of July holiday when it happened."

"Must have put a lot of people out of work."

"Sure did. And it's gonna be rough around here, what with commercial fishing pretty much on the skids too." Her mouth sagged for a moment, but then she smiled a look-on-the-bright-side smile. "But there's always the tourists to keep us going, right?"

Ryan made some noncommittal murmur.

"I imagine a lot of the people you knew back in school have moved away, but some of your old friends should still be around. In fact, you're about the same age as my daughter." She paused to do a quick numbers check, then shook her head. "No, I guess not. She's younger. Jill Peabody?"

Ryan also shook his head.

"Maybe you'd know her if you saw her. Little and skinny and blond? Played flute in the band?" She laughed, and the hearty chuckle fluttered her white apron. "Well, maybe you wouldn't recognize her, after all. After three kids, she's not so little and skinny anymore. And her name is Ramsey now, since she married Clyde. Hey, maybe you knew Clyde? He's a couple years older."

Clyde Ramsey. Yeah. I remember. Kid built like a tank who liked to ram his bullet-shaped head into my skinny belly just for fun.

"Clyde got pretty well banged up in a logging accident a couple years ago. He's on disability now."

Ryan doused his first surge of animosity and drew on his compassion for the man's misfortune. "I'm sorry to hear that."

He didn't inquire about any other "old friends." In fact, if all his old classmates were right then having a reunion across the street, he wouldn't move out of his booth to see any of them. Except for one, of course.

Someone beckoned to the waitress to refill a coffee cup, and Ryan was relieved when she didn't return to present him with more names. He ate the blueberry pie and left a generous tip. But when he paid the check at the cash register, he did inquire about the only person from the past who mattered.

"You wouldn't happen to know what became of Stefanie Canfield, would you?"

"Stefanie?" Rosie glanced at the watch on her generously padded wrist. "Sure. She started an exercise place called Fit 'n' Fun a while back. She's probably teaching a class there right now. Which is where I oughta be instead of here, eating pie."

Stefanie still in Julesburg? Running a health club? Ryan couldn't believe it.

"Where is her Fit 'n' Fun?"

"In the old brewery building, just a couple blocks up from the post office. You remember it? I guess only us old-timers still call it the brewery building. You can probably catch her if you go over there right now."

Ryan left the café feeling charged up. A chance to see Stefanie again, after all those years! Why was she still in Julesburg? Had she left and returned? And how come her name was still Canfield? Surely she'd have gotten married.

Although I didn't . . .

He stopped abruptly at the corner. He had an uneasy thought: Could he ethically do this? Stefanie's grandfather had owned the company with a partner when Ryan lived in Julesburg. Her father had been the general manager. It wouldn't be appropriate for Ryan, as arson investigator for the insurance company, to renew an old friendship with her if her family was still connected with the mill.

But he quickly dismissed that concern. There was no Canfield listed as an owner. Ownership of Cougar Creek Timber Products was in entirely different hands: Hunter and Odetta Blackwell. About whom the insurance company was more than a little suspicious.

He jogged the last block to the old brewery building. A chance to see Stefanie again! He couldn't believe it. A full moon was just rising over the ridge to the east. Outlines of trees loomed dark and spiky against the silver-white globe. He remembered a time when he and Stefanie had sneaked out and waited in the wintry cold to watch an eclipse. They'd seen the earth's shadow gobble up God's "lesser light" of

74

the night, although they weren't thinking in terms of God's light back then.

He spotted the peculiar little cupola on top of the old building when he rounded the corner. The outside didn't look much different than he remembered, except for the fresh, cream-colored paint. The name "Fit 'n' Fun" was arched in metal script over the doorway. Bright light streamed from the windows. Music — 'N Sync, wasn't it? — came from within.

Inside, the reception desk was empty. Several women were puffing on weight machines. Two men climbed uphill slants on treadmills as if they planned to attack the Himalayas. Music and thumps of activity blasted from a door to another room.

A petite brunette in a black leotard left a machine where she was helping another woman with technique on leg presses. "Hi. May I help you? I'm Tina." She said with a friendly smile, "Drop-ins are welcome. You don't have to be a member or anything. It isn't that kind of health club."

"I'm looking for Stefanie Canfield."

"Right now she's working with a group of girls who want to try out for the high-school cheerleading squad." Tina pointed to the door. "I can interrupt if it's urgent?"

"No, I can wait. Okay if I watch?"

"Sure. There's a bench just inside the door, on the left. They'll be taking a break before long."

"Thanks."

Ryan paused in the doorway. He didn't know what he had expected. Some changes in Stefanie after all those years, of course. But was that slim, willowy woman with the killer legs and chiseled cheekbones really her? The hair was the same brown, but it was short and swingy rather than long and tangled. It bounced as she kicked and turned. The voice, calling instructions and chanting numbers to the girls, held a certain familiarity. But it was deeper than he remembered, more mellow, so he couldn't be certain. Then she smiled at the girls as the music changed to a different beat. *Yeah, that's Stefanie.*

He slid to the bench to watch. She didn't notice him — she was totally involved with the girls and the music and the action. Back in their junior high years, he'd seen her pretend disinterest in the enthusiastic jumping and cheering and flipping of all these lithe young girls on the cheerleading squad. But he'd also seen the hurt in her eyes when the pyramid of cheerleaders took a tumble at a game one time and some kid yelled, "Hey, you guys oughta let Stef on the squad!

Nobody'd get hurt with all that fat for everyone to fall on!"

Now there she was, leading the current crop of potential cheerleaders. And looking stronger and more fit and graceful and beautiful than any of them. *Revenge of the underdog.* He'd bet half their classmates were frumpy and dumpy, and she looked like something out of an ad for a workout machine.

He leaned back and enjoyed. The would-be cheerleaders were young and cute and bouncy, but Stefanie soared far beyond their league. *Go, Stef,* he cheered as she led a series of kicks and turns. When the music ended, the girls fell to the floor in various postures of melodramatic collapse.

"Miss Canfield, I'm not going to be able to get up off this floor for an hour," one wailed.

"Yes, you will, if you want to be in shape to be a cheerleader," Stefanie answered cheerfully. She glanced Ryan's way for the first time.

He stood up and took a step forward to let her know he was waiting for her. She slipped into a terrycloth cover-up and toweled her throat as she walked toward him. Her chest rose and fell from the exertion, but she was in no state of collapse.

"Hello." Her voice held friendly interest, not recognition. "May I —"

"Stefanie?"

"Yes?" A faint line formed between her dark eyebrows. Her eyes were still the same sweet hazel, but no rebelliousness or mischief flashed in them now. In fact, he could almost believe some shadow lurked behind the tentative friendliness on her face.

"Maybe you don't remember me," he suggested. Okay, it was a little dorky, but he couldn't resist a moment of playing the old game of bet-you-don't-know-who-this-is. He smiled and offered some hints. "It's been a long time. Junior high? Miss Garland's garlic breath? Mystery meat in the cafeteria? Yearning to be old enough to get a driver's license?"

A wary look leaped into her eyes, as if being sleek and energetic had not fully erased those unhappy days. "That was a long time ago."

He gave her a more personal clue. "Did you ever see the green flash?"

"The green flash?" She looked blank for a moment then leaned forward to peer more closely at his face. "Ryan?"

"Ryan who?" he teased.

She flung out her arms in joyful recognition. "Ryan!"

He picked her up and swung her around until they were both laughing and breathless. Such an action would have appalled both of them back then . . . he couldn't even have done it, given how scrawny he had been. Now it seemed natural.

When he finally set her down, she leaned back in his arms to look up at him. "Ryan. I can't believe it. It's really you! What are you doing here? How long can you stay?"

He hesitated. Did he want to drag in everything about the investigation and the mill? No. Right then he was only interested in renewing the friendship that had meant so much to him growing up. "I'm just here on business for a few days. But I'm surprised to find you're still in Julesburg. I figured —"

"Long story." A hint of shadow momentarily darkened her expression but then disappeared under the bloom of a glorious smile. "It's just so good to see you!"

Hey, I may not be so eager to rush out of Julesburg after all.

"This is absolutely wonderful!" She pounded her palms on his shoulders in happy emphasis. "Where are you staying?"

He didn't answer the question. Instead, he voiced what he couldn't help thinking as he looked down at her. "Stef, you look fantastic."

She stepped back but held on to his hands as she let her eyes do a full-length appraisal of him. "So do you."

He grinned. "I finally grew a little. Put on a few pounds. Got a haircut. Outgrew all those allergies that always had me wheezing and coughing —"

"Got handsome enough to make my high-school girls drool!"

Ryan glanced over at the dozen or so girls. Perhaps not drooling, but definitely curious. He laughed. "It's so good to see you again, Stef." The words seemed weak and redundant, but they were heartfelt. "Can we go for coffee when you're through here?"

She glanced at the big clock on the far wall. Some pipes from the days when the building was a brewery still formed a maze high overhead, but they were painted over now. He leaned over to speak in a conspiratorial whisper. "Do you remember the time I sneaked in here to explore, and you stood guard outside?"

"And you got your foot stuck between a couple of pipes, and I had to crawl up there and help you get it out? Oh, yes, I remember." She looked at the clock again. "I have another twenty minutes here, and then I have to shower and finish up in the office.

But if you have time to wait or come back later . . . ?"

"I'll wait."

Stefanie turned to go, but he grabbed her arm and swung her around. "Hey, you never did answer my question. Did you ever see the green flash?"

The green flash was a story they'd heard that on rare occasions, just at the last moment before the sun disappeared into the sea, a magnificent flash of eerie green color was supposed to flare across the sky. Wonderful things would happen to anyone who managed to catch a glimpse of that magical green flash, and they'd spent hours watching for it.

She shook her head. "No, I never did." She smiled, but it seemed to him that the smile held a trace of sadness. Or was it a grown-up disillusionment, a knowledge that magical green flashes didn't really change lives?

But there's something much more important that does change lives. I want to share it with you, Stef.

6

Stefanie spent twenty minutes more with the girls before she headed for the shower. Standing under needles of hot spray, she marveled at the small miracle of Ryan's presence.

They'd promised to write when his family moved away from Julesburg. *But we weren't much at correspondence, were we, Ry?* The letters had trickled to an end within six months. Now he'd come back. And if she ever needed the kind of friend he had been back then, it was now. In junior high he'd taken on Buck Anderson, even though the guy was twice his size, when Buck ridiculed her when her pants split a seam in the school cafeteria. He'd tutored her in math when she fell behind. He read Nancy Drew — Nancy Drew! — over the phone to her when she was stuck at home, contagious with measles.

Did you send him, Lord? Trust the Lord, she'd heard over and over. "And we know that in all things God works for the good of those who love him," the Bible verse said. I *wish I could believe that.* All too often her prayers had seemed to go unnoticed — wisps of smoke dissipating into an empty sky. Yet Ryan was here, just when she needed him. She didn't even have to pray for him to come.

Stefanie stepped out of the shower and grabbed for a towel. She tousled her hair with it and thought about Randy Wilson's request for a hair sample. Ben had returned and questioned her again, so now she knew what that fuss with the hair sample was about. Often when an arsonist started a fire with some flammable liquid, hair was singed. She knew her credibility with Ben was crumbling, because before she knew about singed hair, she'd stopped by Lisa Benedetti's shop and had her hair cut.

She dressed in leggings and an oversized white shirt and bent over from the waist to blow-dry her hair. Ryan was standing by the reception counter when she came out. She studied him from the doorway, remembering the small, wiry, unkempt boy he had once been. Trapped in a home with drinking, battling parents. Plagued with allergies that left him gasping for breath. Called "Wheezy" by the unfeeling kids at

Julesburg Junior High. They never saw what a great guy he was underneath. Funny and sweet, tender-hearted and courageous.

The face of his boyhood had matured, with a strong jawline, good-humored crescents around his mouth, and crinkles around his eyes. His hair was a darker, thicker brown than she remembered. And his physique! *Give me your secret, Ry. I'll make a fortune with it here at Fit 'n' Fun.*

Val and Tina, like leotard-clad vultures, had converged on Ryan, almost pinning him against the counter. Stefanie laughed. She could tell they were just dying with curiosity. Should she favor them with an introduction or just let them stew?

Ryan looked up and smiled as she approached the counter. *I'm glad for you, Ry. Glad you look like this, as if you're on top of the world.*

Stefanie decided that she was not, like some oh-woe-is-me, helpless female, going to dump her problems on Ryan. He had looked her up simply to honor an old friendship. She put a smile on her face when she joined the trio at the desk. She was still inclined to keep Val and Tina in suspense, but Val looked so close to exploding with curiosity that Stefanie relented and made proper introductions.

"I'm so pleased to meet you," Tina said with a handshake and the kind of sincerity that took the statement beyond rote politeness. Her curiosity apparently satisfied, she excused herself to wipe down the machines before closing time.

Val didn't budge. She eyed Ryan with open speculation and female approval. "An old friend from junior high, eh? Stef, you lucked out. An old boyfriend looked me up once. He had a toupee, a beer belly and three ex-wives."

"Val! He's not —"

"Not an ex-wife anywhere on the horizon," Ryan interrupted, gallantly uttering no word to deny a youthful romantic relationship with Stefanie. "And you can check out the hair for yourself."

Ryan leaned forward, presenting a full head of dark hair for Val's inspection. She was not the shrinking-violet type, so she checked out the hair with an exploration of fingers and a rough tug. If Ryan was surprised that she took him up on the offer, he didn't comment. He grinned when he lifted his head.

"Well?"

"The real stuff," Val proclaimed. "And very nice stuff, I might add." Her look roamed his lean figure in khaki Dockers, a neat sports shirt, and a tan jacket. Her nod seemed to say that the "nice stuff" included more than the hair.

Stefanie reached over and lightly slapped Val's apricot-tipped fingers. "Calm yourself," she warned with mock severity. To Ryan she added, "Never mind my panting friend here. Julesburg is a little short on eligible males, and she gets a bit overexcited when she spots a live one."

Val shook her head with spirit. "No way. I'm just checking things out for you, dear. I've learned from experience. After the Silver-Tongued Rat, I'm through with men forever."

Val always bad-mouthed her ex-husband, but Stefanie strongly suspected she was still in love with him. It was perhaps a matter of "the lady doth protest too much" about what a rat he was and how she was through with him. The ruby earrings he had given her while they were married were her most prized possession, and would she treasure the earrings if she didn't still have feelings for the gift-giver? Valerie went out with other guys occasionally, but never more than a date or two.

"Well, my duty is done here; he's a keeper, Stef. So I'll be running along. Talk to you later?" Val shot Stefanie a meaningful look that said, *I want to know everything. The sooner the better.*

Stefanie excused herself to turn off the office light. The bookkeeping could wait.

"Tina, you'll close up?"

"Sure." Tina gave her a little wave. "See you in the morning."

Stefanie scooped her jacket from a hook behind the counter. No matter the time of year, the Oregon coast at night usually required a jacket.

"So, where would you like to have coffee?" she asked Ryan when they were outside on the dirt pathway to the street. A concrete walkway was still beyond her budget.

"Actually, how about if we save coffee for another time and take a stroll on the beach instead? I hated Julesburg when I lived here, but I always loved the beach. Unless you're too tired? That was quite a workout with the girls."

She smiled. "I'm fine, and the beach it is. We'll have to walk to get down there. I left my car at the house. And yours is . . . ?"

"At the Sea Haven."

It was a beautiful evening, with a full moon soaring overhead and just a few lacy clouds flirting with the stars, giving the night sky texture. The ocean was not visible from where they were behind Lighthouse Hill, but the muffled roar of the waves was ever present. The only flaw in the night was the lingering odor of the burned mill.

"Do you notice the smell?" Stefanie asked over her shoulder. Ryan was following her on the grassy shoulder of the street. "The mill burned a few nights ago."

"The waitress at the café was telling me about it. Really too bad."

"Have you been to see the house where you used to live?"

He caught up to walk beside her. "No. That old cracker-box isn't among my fonder memories. I don't have any big desire to see it."

"Just as well. It isn't there anymore. A developer bought up that whole block, intending to build apartments. After he tore down the old houses, his financing fell through. It's gone back to blackberries and Scotch broom now."

"Does Julesburg really need some big apartment complex?" Ryan asked.

Stefanie laughed. "Probably not. Maybe that's why the financing fell through. Although Julesburg isn't such a bad place, really." They reached the main street and turned south. She tucked her hands in the pockets of her jacket. "Most of the kids we hated with such a passion grew up to be pretty decent people. They never were the evil monsters we thought they were, I guess. Just unfeeling, self-centered teenagers. Unsure of themselves and worried about their own popularity. Probably as confused as we were about their place in the world."

"Okay. If you say so. I'll take your word for it that they all turned into model citizens. I know it's better not to hold grudges."

"Although they didn't *all* wind up as model citizens," she had to admit. "Jeff Deetz is in prison for embezzlement."

"Somehow that doesn't surprise me. I remember him confiscating my lunch money a few times."

Stefanie laughed but she could understand Ryan's skepticism about their old classmates. Her own growing-up years in Julesburg had been miserable, but they couldn't compare with Ryan's two years there. The kids had teased and ostracized her, but many of their dads worked for her father and grandfather at the mill. There were limits to how far they'd carry their youthful unkindness to her. Ryan, however, had been the victim of actual physical bullying along with the teasing and ostracism. Not that he took the bullying lying down. Jeff Deetz may have gotten the confiscated lunch money, but he'd also gotten a bruise on the shin. Unfortunately, Ryan had wound up in trouble more often than his tormentors.

But Stefanie didn't want him to think too badly of the local people. "Most of them really did become solid citizens. Do you remember Patty Sumptner?"

"The overdeveloped sexpot of the seventh grade? Yeah, I remember Patty. I think she was the one who called me 'Shrimp.' I never knew who thought up the 'Wheezy' tag."

In spite of his comment, Stefanie couldn't help laughing. All the guys remembered Patty as the junior-high sexpot, much to Patty's chagrin. "I'm sure she'd tell you she's sorry about that. She teaches first grade now. The kids all love her."

"People do change, I suppose."

"And Lucy Arnish — you remember her? She married a minister, and they have a church in The Dalles now. And Buck Anderson. He drowned trying to rescue a friend when a wave swamped their fishing boat."

They reached the parking lot overlooking the beach at the south end of town. A notch in the rock wall led to wooden steps angling down the grassy slope. At the bottom, Ryan took Stefanie's hand as they climbed over the tangled driftwood washed in during the winter storms. Treacherous crevices lurked among the logs and stumps.

"And Dan Eggleson," she said when they reached the sand. "Do you remember —"

"Stef, I'm glad to hear our old tormentors grew up to be wonderful people," Ryan said, putting his hands on her shoulders. "But I'm really not all that interested in them."

"Oh, I'm sorry!" She pulled away, embarrassed. "I didn't mean to bore or upset you."

His hands tightened, not releasing her. "I don't mean it that way. I just mean that right now I want to hear about you. How you did this big makeover on yourself. Everything that's happened in the last fifteen years."

"I tend to avoid the story of my life," Stefanie admitted. "There are some rather large potholes in it."

"I want to hear about it, potholes and all."

She remembered how they'd shared almost everything those years he lived in Julesburg. He'd told her about wanting to be an FBI man when he grew up, or maybe an astronaut, and how it felt as if a monster sat on his chest when he woke at night and couldn't breathe. They'd told each other about nighttime dreams and tried to figure out what they meant. But that was so many years ago. She didn't want to burden him with her troubles. There was also nothing he could do about them.

"C'mon, let's take off our shoes."

"I think you're changing the subject," Ryan said.

"I can take off my shoes faster than you can!"

He eyed her as if she'd offered a challenge. "I'm not so sure about that. I think I could take your shoes off pretty fast."

She giggled, the first time she'd done that in a long time. She zipped out of her shoes and tucked them under driftwood washed up against the beach regulations sign. Ryan followed her lead.

The tide was out, the sand cool and damp under her feet. Waves broke in lazy curls on the beach. Somehow her hand was in his. It felt natural and comfortable there, even though their junior-high bond had never included hand-holding.

"Do you still walk the beach often?" he asked.

"Sometimes. Not often. Fit 'n' Fun isn't profitable enough that I can afford to hire as much help as I really need, so I'm busy there most of the time." *And it's been a long, long time since I've walked here in the moonlight. Much too long.*

Stefanie loved the feel of the night and the

sea. Familiar, yet mysterious. Calming, yet invigorating. Ever the same, yet always changing.

Hunter had not been a moonlit-beach walker. Maybe that was a character test she should apply if she was ever on the verge of serious involvement with a man again. *You don't like moonlight strolls on the beach? You're off my list, buddy.*

Stefanie was curious about Ryan's love life. He had denied ex-wives, but did he have some current involvement back home?

"Hey, where do you live now?"

"I have a condo in Portland. I'm away from home too much to get involved with real home ownership, but one of these days I plan to do the whole lawn-mowing, backyard-barbecuing, fix-the-roof bit. But I can't get over the fact that you're still here in Julesburg. How come?"

"Actually, I did leave. My parents thought it would be a good idea if I went to college a long way from home. They never mentioned it, but they knew my popularity status in Julesburg. I was eager to go, of course. I went to a fairly prestigious college in the Midwest for a year. But, strange as it sounds, considering how badly I wanted to get away, I got homesick for the mountains and the ocean. I decided to transfer to a Northwest college.

But then I started working in the Cougar Creek Timber Products office that summer, and I got a different perspective on life there. I still was no belle of the ball, but I finally saw that popularity wasn't so important. Life in the real world didn't revolve around whether you were invited to some dance or excluded from a party."

Ryan nodded. "Very true."

They passed a tent set up near the line of driftwood where beach and forest met. Smoke curled upward from a campfire, and a man and woman sat on a log beside it. The two laughed together when a marshmallow fell from the woman's stick into the fire.

"That looks like fun," Ryan said.

"Yeah, doesn't it? Would you believe I've never been camping?" Hunter had not been a camper.

"A few words of advice. Check the tent for leaks. Take plenty of extra socks. Don't forget the sleeping bags."

She glanced up at him. "Am I hearing the voice of experience?"

Ryan laughed. "Oh, yes. Cold, wet experience. But lots of fun." He detoured briefly to place a stranded starfish in a hollow of seawater near a big rock.

"So you worked in the mill for how long?"

"A little over three years. Then I got married." She was pleased not to feel much emotion when she added, "That lasted about five years."

Ryan didn't ask what had gone wrong, although she knew he must be curious. Too many years had passed for immediate re-entry into their old friendship.

Can we ever regain that old closeness?

His hand was holding hers again. It was a loose grip, but nice. Val was a terrific friend, loyal and dependable and fun with her wry, slightly cynical attitude toward the world. Stefanie had other friends too, at Fit 'n' Fun and church. But none were the kind of friend Ryan had once been.

Maybe that kind of friendship isn't possible once you grow up.

"So you're divorced now?" he asked.

"We've been separated over a year. The final decree came through a couple of months ago."

"Fortunate for me that you use your maiden name. I might have had difficulty locating you otherwise."

"Would you have tried?"

"I'm not sure," he admitted. "My first inclination was to finish up and get out of town as fast as possible." He lightly squeezed her hand. "I'm glad I found you before I did that."

They'd reached the creek that crossed the beach. During the winter, potent from heavy coastal rains, the creek roared straight from the bridge under the highway to the ocean. In summer its course depended on how the ocean chose to shift the sand. Just now, the water flowed a half mile down the beach before entering the ocean. A flock of seagulls making gentle night noises rested on the swell of sand between running water and sea.

"Let's see, I think I remember . . . Wandering Creek, isn't it?" Ryan asked.

"Where we kept trying to pan for gold."

"And never found anything but worthless flecks of mica." Ryan laughed. "Well, I guess this is where we turn back."

"You're afraid to get your feet wet?" Stefanie challenged. She felt unexpectedly playful, glad they were over the hump of talking about the divorce. "I'm shocked. I think you've turned into a tender-toed city-slicker."

7

"No way!"

Ryan plunged into the creek. The shallow water came only to his knees, but it was fast running and cold enough to numb his legs. Jumbled rocks covered the creek bottom. Some felt like sharp pyramids, others like slippery balls. Once only a giant sidestep kept him from crashing into the water. His arm plunged in to the elbow.

His toes felt like anesthetized stubs when he climbed up the sandy bank on the far side. Wet pantlegs clung to his legs. He turned to look back at Stefanie. She'd pulled her leggings up but not far enough to escape the water. She flung her arms out for balance as she picked her way across the rocks.

"Who's tender-toed now?" he called.

Her answer was an impudent slam of palm, and water sprayed across his chest. Yet even as she giggled, with arms spread she looked like an elegant butterfly about to take flight into the moonlight. Behind her, their footprints walked side by side across the sand.

The paired tracks awakened an unfamiliar yearning for something he couldn't quite identify. *Something you're trying to tell me, Lord?*

Ryan offered his hand to help Stefanie up the embankment. A small avalanche of sand crumbled into the creek as she scrambled for footing. He knew her feet and legs had to be as icy as his, but he didn't think she would admit it.

"There, now, wasn't that fun?" she inquired.

"Oh, delightful." He grinned. "Right up there with getting a bucket of smelt poured down the neck. Which, I recall, was another of your strange ideas of fun."

"And that was a great demonstration of your machismo just now. Not even a pause to consider how deep the water was before plunging in. Not so great a demonstration of brains, of course."

He laughed, delighted with the teasing. That had been part of their buddyhood, though no one else ever saw it. Against outsiders they had never wavered from a shoulder-to-shoulder solidarity, but with each other they had teased all the time.

"Macho is my middle name," he proclaimed. He thundered a Tarzan pound on his chest.

" 'Frozen feet' is mine," Stefanie admitted. "Let's jog to warm up."

They jogged a good half mile without talking before she slowed to a walk. "Okay, I can feel my toes again. How about you?"

"I'll survive." Impulsively he reached for her hand again. He thought for a moment she might mutter, "Don't ever do that again." Instead, she smiled and let their hands remain joined.

"Okay, I've told you all the deep, dark secrets of my life. Now it's your turn."

Stefanie had not revealed enough to him to expose any "deep, dark secrets." But beneath her flippant tone, he could sense how deeply she'd been hurt by the breakup of her marriage. With that old feeling of protectiveness, he had an unexpected urge to go pound some sense into her ex. *What's wrong with you, dude? Can't you see how terrific she is?*

Ahead of them, the highway rose to a high curve on a point jutting into the sea. Red taillights disappeared around the bend as if dropping into empty space. The tide had turned and waves were rolling farther up the beach. It was an imperceptible shift when it happened, but the spot they were standing on would be underwater within a few hours.

Sometimes changes are like that. Barely noticeable at the moment, yet eventually sweeping over you . . .

Stefanie yanked on his arm. "Why so deep in thought? Inventing a past that's more exciting than the real stuff?"

The teasing question jerked his straying thoughts out of the philosophical vein. "Would you believe I became an astronaut? Or an undercover agent for the CIA? Maybe a sword swallower at a carnival?"

Her glance measured him. "I always thought you could do or be anything you wanted." Her smile teased again. "And were weird enough to try anything from sword swallowing to planet hopping."

"Thanks for the vote of confidence . . . I think. In any case, I didn't take up any of those glamorous occupations, and I will tell all. But first I want to ask about your mother. She was always so good to me."

Stefanie's head dipped. With quiet pain in her voice, she told him about her mother's struggle with breast cancer. It had spread to the liver and then to the bone. She'd had surgery, radiation, and chemotherapy.

"But eventually she lost the battle. She died seventeen months ago."

The fact that she knew the exact number of months since her mother's death told him how hard it had hit Stefanie. He also realized the marriage breakup had come only a few months after Laurine Canfield's death. *Great guy, this ex-husband. All heart.*

He turned and took both her hands in his. "I'm so sorry, Stef. She was a wonderful person. You must miss her a lot." He hesitated, wondering if his next question was another pothole. "Your father . . . ?"

"He, my grandfather, and the partner who started Cougar Creek Timber Products were all killed in a plane crash a few months before my marriage. The private plane they had chartered to fly to a business meeting in Portland went down in the mountains. The pilot was killed too."

Which explains why the mill is under different ownership now.

Ryan could think of little to say to comfort Stefanie for her losses. He offered an arm around her shoulders. She leaned against him, and he stroked her hair in silent sympathy.

Stefanie straightened and gave herself a little shake that he suspected was mental as well as physical. "Enough of that. Now it *is* your turn."

Is this the right time to tell her? Yes.

"One single, life-changing event is more important than anything else. That's what I most want to tell you about."

He looked at her and she nodded. She'd always known when to offer playful insults and when to reach out in sympathy and support.

"You remember all those discussions we used to have? Is there life on other planets? Do aliens visit earth? Is there a God over it all?"

"I remember."

"I still don't know about visiting aliens or life on other planets. But I do know about God. He exists."

"Really." She paused for a moment. "How did all this come about?"

Stefanie resumed walking, as if she preferred not being face-to-face.

"Well, my life was messed up by the time I got out of high school. You knew my parents split up when we left Julesburg, and Ted and Angie — you remember my little brother and sister?"

She nodded. "Good kids. Angie was a real brain, I remember."

"Right. Now she's also a New York model. Ted has a wife, two kids, and a successful plumbing business in Seattle. So they're both doing great. But back then we were shuffled back and forth between our parents, sometimes together, sometimes separately. Not," he added, "because they were fighting over custody. At least not in the usual way. It was more a case of 'I've had 'em long enough. You gotta take 'em now.' Anyway, after high school I bummed around for a while and then signed up for four years in the service. After a couple of years in the States, I wound up in South Korea. At that time it wasn't as bad as some of the trouble spots around the world, but it was no picnic. There was a missionary-sponsored orphanage nearby, and I started helping out there in my free time."

She stopped again to face him. "Ryan, how wonderful! That must've been really rewarding."

"It was. But at the same time it was sad and frustrating. A lot of the kids were in such pathetic physical condition when they reached the orphanage. And the orphanage didn't have many resources to provide for them."

"That's so sad."

"I know. And I wasn't much interested in saving the orphans' little souls. I thought that was a luxury that could wait. I thought they should concentrate on the problems of food and shelter and heat, and worry about spiritual matters later. So my work was mostly on a dormitory they were trying to put up.

"Then this one little boy, Kim Ju-yung, elected himself my helper. He was about nine years old, and he knew a surprising amount of English. The missionaries thought his father was probably an American serviceman who'd taken up with a Korean girl, then abandoned her and the little boy when he went home. This kid was always right beside me, handing me nails or running to get tools, always so cheerful. Then, because he thought maybe I didn't have enough to eat, he tried to give me food out of the little he received. 'Because that's what Jesus would have done,' he said. I bought a pair of shoes for him, but he gave them to another little boy. Because that's what Jesus would have done too. He was confident that his mother would come get him someday soon, because he was praying about that every day."

"Oh, Ryan . . ."

"He started nagging me about the Jesus stuff. How I should come listen when they had Bible stories. How I ought to give my heart to Jesus. I finally let him drag me to some of his little-kid stuff. I felt pretty strange sitting there in a kiddie chair, with him whispering a translation from Korean to English for me. But I also realized I *wasn't* very happy. In spite of his situation in life, there was so much more real joy in little Kim than in me. I started reading a Bible that one of the missionaries gave me. Later, I started going to a weekly study the missionaries held in English for soldiers from the base. And one night, I went forward to accept Jesus as my Savior."

"And a little child shall lead them," Stefanie murmured.

"What?"

"And a little child shall lead them," she repeated. "From Isaiah, isn't it? And that's what happened to you. A little child led you."

"How come you know the quotation?" He was familiar enough with the words, but he wasn't certain he could have placed them in Isaiah.

She didn't answer the question. "And what became of Kim?"

"That's another miracle. I'd never have believed it would happen." *Oh, ye of little faith!* "One day his grandmother showed up, and a few weeks later she took him home to live with her. Which was pretty close to what he'd prayed for."

Stefanie's smile held relief. "That's wonderful. I was afraid you were going to tell me something terrible had happened to him." Her smile faltered, and she looked down at their bare feet. "I guess I'm a little disillusioned about . . . happy endings."

They'd reached the end of the beach. The sand gave way to a jumble of huge rocks piled like broken dominos tossed by some giant hand. A tiny creek gurgled alongside the rocks. Far above, a curve of metal guardrail reflected moonlight at the edge of the highway. He guided her to a driftwood log half buried in the sand.

He sat beside her, their shoulders touching. "Are you a Christian, Stef?" he asked. Her reaction to his statement of faith had been unenthusiastic, but her knowledge of Isaiah marked her as someone not ignorant of biblical teachings.

She squirmed her feet into the sand, covering the high instep, lifting her toes and letting the sand trickle around them. "I thought I was, for a while."

"But you don't think so now? Tell me about it, Stef." He wove his fingers with hers, then covered their joined hands with his other hand. "Tell me how you found the Lord. And what went wrong."

"Well, my mother started going to church first. She urged me to come with her. I went because my life seemed to be . . . on hold, I guess you might call it. My husband and I had a beautiful new home. I'd thrown myself into decorating and landscaping. But after two years, even I couldn't think of anything more to do with it. I was still overweight. I wanted children but didn't get pregnant. And by then, although I didn't know it at the time, he was already involved in one of his several affairs —" She broke off. "No, that's not true. Subconsciously, I'm sure I did know. But I wasn't acknowledging it to myself."

"Stef, you don't have to tell me all this," Ryan protested. He felt guilty for prying and pushing her. "I can see how painful it is for you —"

"This is all part of the answer to your question about my relationship with the Lord." She looked up at him. Tears shimmered in her eyes, but her tone was tart. "So shut up and listen, okay?"

"Okay. Shutting up now." He squished damp sand between his toes.

"So I started attending church with Mom. I became a regular whirlwind of activity. Committees, missionary work, rummage sales, bake sales. I helped put out a church cookbook and started a newsletter." She paused, head tilted. "It was a shallow in-

volvement at first, all glitter and no substance. But before long, I was actually
studying that Bible I carried for show. I connected with the Lord in prayer and opened
my heart to him."

"How did your husband feel about this?
Was that a problem between you?"

"I tried to talk to him about my emerging
beliefs. He wasn't interested, but he didn't
object to my church activities. Looking
back, I can see now that he was probably relieved that church activities kept me so involved. Too busy to notice what he was
doing."

"You were very much in love with him."

"Oh, yes. I was so astonished when he first
showed interest in me. Me, the Porky Princess!" She shook her head, as if she found it
incredible that she'd been taken in by him.
"He's an attractive man. Tall, blond, good
looking. Capable of making a woman feel
like a real princess. I fell for him like the pro-
verbial ton of bricks. Unfortunately, I didn't
recognize that for him it was more a business consolidation than love."

"And eventually you did notice what he
was doing."

"Eventually. But what I first noticed was
that in my whirlwind of church activities, I'd
started to lose weight. I was so encouraged

that I threw myself into a storm of dieting and exercising. At that time, Fit 'n' Fun didn't amount to much, just a few exercise machines. But Mom and I decided to buy it together. At the same time, my relationship with the Lord was becoming real and personal and exciting. One Sunday morning, Mom and I went forward together and accepted Jesus as our Savior. I felt as if we were standing on a mountaintop that day. With the angels singing all around us."

Ryan wanted to yell, "Stef, that's fantastic!" But he knew the downslope of that glorious mountaintop was coming, and he remained silent.

Stefanie brushed a strand of hair away from her cheek. "And then it seemed as if that commitment to the Lord was the starting signal for everything to go wrong. Almost as if God said, 'Gotcha!' and abandoned us. Less than three months later, Mom found the lump in her breast. I prayed . . . I prayed so hard when she went through surgery and chemotherapy and nausea and losing her hair. Everyone at church prayed too. They held an all-night vigil when she had a second surgery. But the prayers didn't change anything, and the pain was so bad when it got into the bone . . ." Her voice cracked.

Ryan put his arms around her. "I'm sorry, Stef. So very sorry."

With the determination he remembered, she pulled herself together. "And, as I've already told you, Mom died. Just as if all my prayers were . . . spiritual graffiti. And God just erased them."

"But isn't it a comfort knowing that she didn't die alone, but with Christ in her heart?"

"What I remember is how much she suffered. What I remember is wondering, Where are you, God, when my mother desperately needs you?"

"Your faith died when she died?"

Faint lines of a frown creased her forehead. "No, not quite. My faith was badly damaged at that point, but it wasn't totally demolished. But — you see that rock down there?"

The rising tide was creeping up the beach. Waves and moonlight washed over a terrace of dark rock, turning it into a pavilion of silver.

"That rock is wearing away. You can't see it, but bit by bit the waves are eating into it. Eroding and wearing it down. That's how it's been with my faith: eroded by the incoming waves of life. The pain of Mom's illness. The futility of prayer. My husband's betrayal. More futile prayers."

"Prayers may not be answered as quickly or in the way we'd like them to be answered, but they're not futile."

A lift of her shoulder dismissed that statement as opinion open to question. "I struggled to keep my faith going, but the more I struggled, the more problems God seemed to throw at me." Her toes dug deeper into the sand, as if she wished she could excavate her way through to some deep, dark hiding place. "I still talk to the Lord sometimes. Force of habit, I guess. But mostly it all seems like some feel-good fantasy I fell for. As phony as my ex-husband's sweet-talking line."

Ryan ached for her. There was no hole larger and more empty than the one left when someone pushes the Lord out of their life. But no matter how it looked to Stefanie now, the Lord didn't turn his back and abandon people.

"Stef, I know how black things can look, but it doesn't mean God doesn't care. He's brought you through to where you are now. You can —"

"Oh, yeah, things are great," Stefanie interrupted. She gave a short bark of humorless laughter. "Now my only problem is that I'm the chief arson suspect in the fire that destroyed the mill."

Apprehension stiffened his muscles. *Arson suspect?* "I don't understand —"

"The authorities think I burned it down."

"But why? I know your family used to own the mill. But now, with new owners, why —"

"There aren't new owners. Hunter and I still own the mill. The lawyers are trying to figure out what to do about that. The police chief thinks burning the mill was my way of getting back at Hunter and the next Mrs. Blackwell."

"Your ex-husband is *Hunter Blackwell?*"

"Yes, of course. Hadn't I mentioned his name?"

"But the papers we have say the mill is owned by a couple named Hunter and *Odetta* Blackwell."

"Odetta." Stefanie groaned. "Unfortunately, that's me. Yours truly, Odetta Stefanie Canfield Blackwell. And then, subtracting Blackwell, back to Canfield again. My grandfather wanted me named after his mother, and my folks went along. But they always called me Stefanie, and I've hated Odetta with such a passion that I hid it from everyone. Even you, I guess. But it does show up on official papers now and then."

The shock felt like an explosion going off in Ryan's head. The company was definitely suspicious of Hunter and Odetta Blackwell.

Cougar Creek Timber Products was in deep financial trouble, a notorious motive for arson. But Stefanie was Odetta . . .

"But surely the local authorities know you better than to think you'd burn the mill. You've lived here all your life."

"Ben says people don't necessarily act rationally when it comes to 'affairs of the heart,' as he put it. He thinks people do strange things and don't consider consequences when they want to get even."

Ryan could vouch for the 'doing strange things to get even' part of her statement. He'd investigated more than one fire in which revenge had been the flash point behind the arson.

"Their other thought is that since Hunter and I are arguing over the division of company ownership, I may have decided I'd rather have insurance cash than a piece of a struggling mill. It doesn't help that I washed the clothes I was wearing the night of the fire, before they had a chance to examine them for traces of gasoline or some other fire accelerant. Or that I got my hair cut before they could test to see if it had been singed by fire."

Her head jerked up, as if it had just dawned on her that something was not right. She slid sideways, opening a foot-wide space between them on the log. "I don't understand. You said you saw the name Odetta. . . . And what do you mean, the 'papers we have'?"

He searched for some way to soften the truth and found none. "The insurance company papers. I'm the arson investigator for the company that holds the insurance policy on the mill."

She jumped up and backed away from him. "That's why you're in Julesburg? To investigate the fire? To investigate me?"

"No —" He broke off. Denial was hardly accurate. The fire had all the earmarks of arson, and he *was* in Julesburg to protect company interests and probe deeper if authorities too readily came to the conclusion that the fire had been accidental. Investigating owners or other suspicious persons was a part of that.

They stared at each other across the chasm that had just opened between them. Stefanie rammed her hands in her pockets.

"You're very good at your job, aren't you?" she observed. "The company must be proud of you."

"What do you mean?"

"You looked at the situation and thought, 'Well, hey now, lookee here! My old buddy Stef is the big arson suspect. I'll just sneak in, make like an old friend, and get the goods on her before she knows what's happening.' "

"No, that is not how it was! I had no idea —"

"You came here to extract information from me, and you got it. Oh, yes, very clever. So what am I? The stepping stone to a big bonus or promotion? Nail the wife as the arsonist, save a bundle in insurance payoff, and you become the company's golden boy?"

Yes, I did come to town thinking about promotion and what this investigation could do for me. But those ambitions never involved you, Stef.

"Maybe you expected to hit the real jackpot? A handy-dandy little confession? One old friend desperately confiding in another? You can forget that happy little scenario, Ryan. It isn't going to happen. Because I didn't do it."

"I didn't come here to 'nail' anybody. I'm an investigator. And what an investigator may uncover is that a fire is an accident. An investigator's findings may rule out arson."

He started to add that, within the company, Hunter was more a suspect than Stefanie. But that was a confidential company matter, not something he was free to share. It also occurred to him that the company had not known details Stefanie had just revealed to him. The revenge factor. The ownership complications. That this new information could indeed widen the company's suspicions. But collecting inside information was not the reason he had sought her out.

"Stef, I had no idea you were still an owner of the mill when I came here. Until this very minute, I didn't know that you're a suspect any more than you knew I'm the investigator."

He reached for her, but she backed away. "You'll pardon me if I have a problem believing that. It seems just a bit too coincidental that I don't hear anything from you for fifteen years. Then, when our old friendship could be useful to you, I suddenly get the long-lost-buddy treatment."

"Stef, did I ever lie to you?"

"No, I don't think so," she conceded. Her chin lifted and jutted a fraction of an inch, a gesture of stubbornness he remembered well. "But that was years ago. People change. Some for the better, some for the worse."

No question about which category she put him in.

"In any case," she added, "you're the investigator, and I'm the suspect. Which I think brings this conversation to an end."

He watched her stride away, her back rigid, her head high.

The waves of the incoming tide were washing their paired footprints away.

8

Stefanie strode down the beach. She no longer saw the curl of incoming waves or heard the rush of pebbles caught in retreating waves. Her only aim was to get away as quickly as possible.

Was he following her on the beach? It was the only way back to town, at least as far as the creek. But perhaps he had decided to sit on the log for a while.

She wanted to look back to check his whereabouts. It took all her willpower to keep her gaze aimed straight ahead. After a hundred yards she broke into a jog. The running was more difficult than it had been earlier. With the tide coming in, she had to move up the beach to avoid the incoming waves. The softer, dry sand dragged at her feet, but she kept going, not stopping until a stitch of pain cramped her side. She leaned forward, head down, hands on her thighs, while she caught her breath.

"You okay?"

Stefanie swiveled her head to peer at Ryan

through the upside-down curtain of her hair. He was breathing hard but apparently not suffering the minor disability that had halted her. Behind him, their footprints tangled like the steps of a complicated dance.

"I'm —" she paused for breath between the gritted words, "fine."

"Stef, I'm telling you the truth. When the company sent me here, I had no idea you had any connection with the mill now. I didn't look you up with some sneaky plan to trick you into giving me confidential information or a confession. I just wanted to see you again."

She waited until she could breathe without the pain knifing under her ribs. Then she pushed her hair back and straightened her shoulders. "Since you're staying at the Sea Haven, you can follow the trail along the creek up to the highway. It's a shorter route back to the motel than hiking all the way into town on the beach."

"I'm not going to leave you alone here on the beach at night! Bad things happen even in places like Julesburg." Before she could argue that she'd be fine and didn't need his protection, he added, "Besides, I have to go back the beach route to get my shoes."

She couldn't think of any rebuttal to that logic, so she turned and plunged down the sandy bank into the creek. The rocks on the bottom were just as sharp and slick as before, but she sloshed across them without pausing. Ryan splashed out of the water just a few steps behind her.

"I don't think our status as investigator and investigatee, if that's a word, should prevent us from carrying on a polite conversation about other subjects," he said. "You could tell me about your friend Valerie and her 'silver-tongued rat.' "

Stefanie hesitated, then shrugged. Maintaining a total silence was petty and childish. Perhaps even suspicious. But she vowed not to give him any more personal information.

"Silver-Tongued Rat is what Val calls her ex-husband. I've never met him, but from what she says, he's a good looking charmer. Sophisticated, the kind who always knows the right wine to order. Intelligent. Exciting. Then he had an affair and left her for the other woman."

She knew Ryan had to see the similarity to her relationship with Hunter, but he didn't comment on that. "This was here in Julesburg?"

"No, over in Eugene." She hesitated, wondering whether there was any incriminating information in the topic of Val. "Val came here when Volkman Laser Systems moved from Eugene to Julesburg. It's a small company but big in something called laser diode technology. They're involved in everything from laser sights for firearms to bar-code scanners."

"Wasn't Julesburg an odd choice of location for a company like that?"

"Not really. They brought most of their people with them, although they've hired some locals for nontechnical positions. Val is head of the personnel department. The company moved here when the city council set aside land for an industrial park and included some big tax breaks. Although I think the council was astonished when a company actually moved in."

Stefanie had purposely slanted the conversation into an impersonal area, and she added nothing to encourage further conversation. It was several minutes before Ryan tried again.

"It looked as if you have a good variety of machines at Fit 'n' Fun. I work out at a health club near the condo when I'm home."

His physique showed it, but Stefanie made no comment.

Ryan tried again. "You could tell me more about how our former classmates turned into such model citizens."

Stefanie gave him a desultory rundown. At the beach sign, she grabbed her shoes from under the driftwood and headed for a nearby log.

On her way over to the log, she stepped on something that felt like a flaming torch rammed into her foot. Never one to screech, she gave only a small gasp of pain before dropping to the sand and cradling the foot with both hands.

Ryan crashed through the driftwood between them and knelt beside her. "What's wrong? What happened?"

"I stepped on something."

She turned her foot upward. A broken shard of glass glittered with the movement of her foot. Ryan carefully extracted it. Blood, ink-dark in the moonlight, ran from the gash. Stefanie fumed in frustration even as she bit her lip against the pain. *Of all the worst possible times to have such a dumb thing happen!* She dug in her pockets for a tissue and found nothing but a packet of oyster crackers.

Ryan whipped out a clean white handkerchief. His hands were gentle and competent as he started to wrap it around her foot, but she jerked away. She wanted to tell him to take his handkerchief and go, but she needed something to stop the flow of blood.

She grabbed the white square. "I can do that."

"Okay, fine. And then you can sit right there — don't try to move — while I go get my car."

Stefanie knew from past experience that argument with Ryan was useless. So instead, she ignored him and tightened the wrap around her foot. *After you're gone, I'll put on my shoes and walk home. I'm not going to owe you any favors.*

Ryan looked at her for a moment, then grabbed her shoes.

"What are you doing?" Stefanie yelped.

"Taking your shoes."

She grabbed for the shoes, but he dodged out of her reach. She didn't ask why he was taking them; she figured he knew what she intended as soon as he was out of sight.

"You can't just run off with my shoes!"

"Can't I?"

Poised on two good feet atop a log several feet away, he obviously could take the shoes.

"Is there a doctor in Julesburg now?" he asked.

"I'm not dragging Dr. Halmoose out of bed for a little scratch on my foot."

"We'll see about that when I get back with the car."

He took the wooden steps two at a time.

The parking-lot lights momentarily silhouetted his figure before he disappeared beyond the rock wall. She waited a moment and then got to her feet. Shoes or no shoes, she was not going to sit like some stranded fish. She scrambled over the log and started across the driftwood at the bottom of the wooden steps.

And stopped. Each connection of her foot with anything solid felt like a rerun of the original jab of broken glass.

By the time she half-crawled to the bottom step, she was forced to reconsider her plan to walk home.

Ryan ran along the dirt path that connected the end of the town's sidewalk with the Sea Haven motel. From the phone in his room all he got at the doctor's office was a recording. "Our office hours are 9:00 to 5:00, Monday through Friday. If this is an emergency, please call the ambulance for transport to the Coos Bay hospital. The number is —" He slammed the phone down, grabbed a motel towel, and ran out to the Blazer.

He thought Stefanie had gone when he reached the top of the steps. She wasn't in the sand where he'd left her. He wasn't surprised. *Stefanie Canfield, when I get hold of you* . . . He spotted her hidden in the shadows on the bottom step. He loped down to her.

"Very impressive," she muttered. "You've just earned your hero-to-the-rescue badge."

In spite of the tart remark, she gave a grunt of pain when she stood up. He didn't try to help, knowing how she'd react. *I'm the enemy now, aren't I? With good reason, I guess.*

"I called the doctor. All I got was an answering machine. But if you know where he lives, I'll go pound on his door till he answers."

"I have some first-aid supplies at home. I can manage."

"You probably should have a tetanus shot."

Stefanie didn't respond. He could almost hear her teeth grit as she mounted the first step.

"I can carry you to the car —"

"Ryan, I do not want to be carried anywhere."

He held out the towel he'd brought from the motel. She padded the injured foot with it, and he put an arm around her for support. She stiffened, but apparently the pain was severe enough, because she let him help her make a slow ascent up the stairs.

Halfway, she paused to rest the foot.

"It really would be easier if I carried you," Ryan said.

No answer. Another step.

Impatience with both the slow pace and her stubbornness finally got to Ryan. He shifted his grip and swooped her up in his arms. He half expected her to hit him on the head and shoulders. Instead, she stiffened, laying across his arms like a slab of driftwood.

"You aren't making this any easier," he said. In spite of her rigid stiffness, she felt warm and feminine in his arms.

"I didn't request this particular display of gallantry."

He'd left the passenger door of the Blazer open. He deposited her inside and buckled the seat belt around her. After turning the Blazer around in the parking lot, he realized he didn't know where she lived.

"Same place I lived when we were kids," she responded in answer to his question. "My parents' old house."

"I thought you said you and Hunter had a new house?"

"I moved out when we separated. Hunter somehow put the house under company ownership, so it's tangled in that dispute. His fiancée moved in several —" Stefanie's jaw clamped shut.

"Stef, I'm not trying to —"

"I have just one question for you as the arson investigator, Ryan. Don't you think that if I were really an arsonist bent on revenge, I'd have gone after the house they're living in together, maybe even directly after them, rather than torching the mill?"

That was indeed more logical. But revenge, as he knew from past investigations, didn't necessarily operate on logic. And maybe she really was after a big chunk of insurance money.

Get off it. This is Stefanie, not some wild-eyed crazy person.

He remembered the way to the house on a hillside overlooking town. It hadn't changed much in the past fifteen years. Quaintly Victorian, the house had gingerbread trim and a peaked tower on one side. Steep steps led up from the street to the railed front porch. A new detached garage stood at the rear of the house, and a four-door Toyota occupied the driveway.

"If you'll pull up behind my car, I can go in the back way. There aren't as many steps."

She had the door of the Blazer open before he could get around to the passenger's side, but the long step to the concrete driveway forced her to accept his assistance.

127

"Thank you for bringing me home. I can make it by myself from here."

If you think I'm going to dump you and take off, think again. Ryan put his arm around her shoulders and helped her to the back door. "Where's your house key?"

"I can handle everything from here."

"Stef, I'm not leaving until I see you safely inside and the foot taken care of. If you don't want to cooperate with a key, I think a little shove will take care of this door."

"The key's on a nail under the bottom step."

Once inside, she directed him to the bathroom, where he found disinfectant, gauze, and a tube of antibiotic salve. He filled a plastic washbasin with warm water and added a few drops of disinfectant.

Stefanie was sitting on a chair beside the kitchen table when he returned. They didn't talk as he washed the foot, disinfected it, and applied salve. He made a pad of gauze, then wrapped more gauze around the foot to hold the pad in place. For the first time, he noticed the Band-Aids on her knuckles.

He nodded toward the hand. "What happened there?"

"Ben thinks I hurt my hand while I was

torching the mill." She offered no alternate explanation, and he decided to drop the subject.

"The wound bled quite a bit. That's good. God's method of self-cleansing a wound."

Stefanie wiggled her toes, and the bandage held. "I appreciate your bringing me home and bandaging my foot. Part of your job description?"

"I had some first-aid training while I was a fireman in Seattle for a year."

"Where you also learned about arson?"

"I took a thirteen-week course in arson investigation while I was there. And I've had considerable experience since then." Stefanie made no comment, so he added, "I can come by in the morning and take you to the doctor for a tetanus shot."

"I can make it on my own. I believe you have an arson investigation scheduled."

You're right. He doubted the company VIPs would be pleased if they knew of his personal association with a mill owner. He brushed that thought aside. "You may not be able to drive —"

"The car is an automatic. It takes only one foot on the pedals."

"Well, at least I can help you upstairs —"

"*Go,* Ryan. Now. Before I pick up this

pan of bloody wash water and throw it at you."

But when Ryan's hand was on the doorknob, she stopped him with a question.

"Ryan, do you really think I did it?"

"I make it a point not to form an opinion before an investigation is complete."

"But you are suspicious of me."

He wanted to yell *No, I'm not suspicious of you! How could I be suspicious of you?* Stefanie, sneaking into the closed mill, spreading some flammable liquid, gleefully torching it? Impossible. If he had to make a choice, Hunter was a far more likely suspect.

Yet it almost appeared as if the arson — if it was arson — had been timed carefully not to endanger lives. It was the kind of concern someone caring and decent might show even when driven to violent action.

No. Not Stefanie. Violence and destruction were not in her makeup. And burning the mill would take not only a desire for revenge, but nerve and guts.

But she'd always been a daredevil. She'd climbed high into the maze of pipes at the brewery to help free his foot. He remembered a time they'd both come close to sliding over a cliff when they foolishly chose to explore beyond the warning sign on the seaward side of Lighthouse Hill. Another time, they'd stood together in surging surf to free a seagull tangled in fishing line.

As an adult she had even more strength and agility. And endurance. He'd seen that when she gave the potential cheerleaders a workout. Sneaking into the mill wasn't beyond her physical capabilities, and she knew the mill's layout well. And, from what she'd said about operating Fit 'n' Fun, she could use a piece of insurance money.

She smiled humorlessly at his long hesitation. "Never mind."

Ryan turned around to go. When he got in the Blazer, he saw her shoes. He took them to the house and opened the door without knocking.

"Your shoes," he said, setting them just inside the door.

"Thank you."

"Taking a couple of Tylenol might help the pain."

"I'll do that."

"Stef, I know you don't want any advice from me —"

"Ben Mosely has already advised me I'd better find a good criminal lawyer."

"I'm not talking about the mill or the fire or — I'm just asking you not to give up on God. Under the circumstances, I don't blame you for closing the door on me. But please don't close it on God."

For a moment she seemed to waver. She rubbed her palm on her leggings.

"Don't stop talking to him, even if you think he isn't listening, Stef. Sometimes it may not seem like it, but he is listening. And caring. Stick with him, Stef, please?"

Stefanie's eyes filled with tears, but she fought them back. "I'm afraid it's a little late for 'sticking.' We've already come unstuck."

4

Stefanie felt gritty and in need of a shower, but she didn't want to get her bandage wet. She took the Tylenol Ryan had advised and settled for a sponge bath.

She climbed into bed exhausted, but she couldn't sleep. Seeing Ryan again had been wonderful. He'd acted like the same loyal buddy who'd been the closest friend she ever had. But there were intriguing differences now that they were adults: the light in his blue eyes when he looked at her, the warmth of his smile, the strength of his hand around hers. She even found a certain appeal in the way he overrode her objections and carried her up the stairs.

Would he have been as glad to see her if she'd still been overweight, hiding behind a wild mop of hair? She wanted to believe he'd have cut their reunion to five minutes of "hey, it's good to see you." Then she could scorn him, classify him as shallow and superficial.

But I don't really believe that, do I? He'd

looked into her eyes, not measured her size or weight when he swung her until they were both breathless. Ryan was still Ryan.

Except now Ryan was a Christian.

And an arson investigator.

Discouraged and depressed, and foot still throbbing, Stefanie was just about to turn out the lamp when the phone on the bedstand rang. She didn't want to answer the phone if it was Ryan, but a call that late at night could mean an emergency. Stefanie picked up the receiver.

"Hello?"

"Are you alone?" The voice was low, conspiratorial.

Stefanie leaned back against the pillow. "Of course I'm alone, you snoop."

"Oh." Val sounded disappointed. "I thought you might have an overnight guest."

"Val Halstead, surely you know me better than that by now!"

"Yeah, I suppose I do." Val gave an exaggerated sigh. "I wouldn't have called if I really thought you had company, would I? But you'd have a lot more fun in life, you know, if you weren't so straightlaced."

"I don't see you sharing your bedroom with overnight guests," Stefanie pointed out.

"I might, if my past could whip up a guy like your gorgeous friend Ryan." Val paused.

"Who also, unlike most gorgeous males, strikes me as a pretty nice guy."

"Appearances can be deceiving."

"He's not a nice guy?"

Stefanie shrugged. "Ryan's here to investigate the fire at the mill. He's the insurance company's arson investigator. Which means he's here to investigate me."

"Yuck. Very sticky situation."

"It makes for no situation between Ryan and me." Stefanie said, punching her pillow with her fist.

"I wouldn't say that." Val's tone turned reflective. "In fact, this could be a very fortunate turn of events."

"Since when have you started digging silver linings out of dark clouds?"

"Think about it," Val argued. "You and Ryan are old friends. You have a history. Plus, he's attracted to you. Very much attracted, unless my radar has suddenly gone haywire. Don't you think he'll go out of his way to prove you're not the arsonist?"

"No, I do not. He's like Ben Mosely. Duty comes before friendship. Ryan isn't going to change his investigation or give me some special treatment just because I'm an old buddy."

"He might if you were *extra* friendly," Val said.

"I'll pretend I didn't hear that!"

"Okay, okay. Don't get up on your sanctimonious high horse," Val grumbled. "I thought you'd given up on the churchy stuff."

"Even if I have given up on it, Ryan always had high principles, and now he's also a very strong Christian."

Val sighed, as if that information sealed Stefanie's fate. "Then I guess all I can say is that I'll be a faithful visitor to your jail cell. But don't expect me to bake you a cake with a file in it. You know what a lousy cook I am."

Stefanie jumped on Val's comment about visiting her jail cell, even though she knew it was facetious. "You sound as if the fact that I'm innocent is irrelevant. That I'll wind up in jail anyway."

"Well, of course it matters. But I'm a realist, sweetie." Val's voice sobered. "I didn't get a chance to tell you earlier, but one of our local gendarmes questioned me today. Officer Wilson, I believe it was."

"He questioned you about me?"

"Unfortunately I couldn't give you an alibi for the time period before we met for the fireworks. Which is what he seemed most interested in. But I told him in no uncertain terms that you couldn't possibly have anything to do with the fire. I also gave you a character reference that should qualify you for sainthood."

"Thanks," Stefanie said faintly.

"But I don't think anything I said accomplished much. The rumor going 'round is that they're almost sure it's arson, with you and Hunter as the logical suspects. Me, I'd toss Liposuction Queen into the pot."

"Trisha? Why would she want to burn down the mill?"

"Insurance money. Pay you off and get you out of her bottle-bleached hair. And maybe, with the mill gone, persuade Hunter to leave Julesburg. I doubt Trisha Duvall wants to spend the rest of her life stuck in what I'm sure she considers a backward outpost of civilization."

"I'd never considered that," Stefanie admitted. She'd assumed Trisha was so infatuated with Hunter that she'd take him any way she could get him. "But it's rather flimsy. I can't quite picture Trisha getting all smelly and dirty hauling gasoline into the mill to burn it down, can you?"

But could Hunter be worrying that Trisha might not stick with him if Julesburg remained part of the package? Was that yet another motive for him to destroy the mill?

"Well, in any case, when they do decide it

was definitely arson," Val added, "you don't think your clever ex is going to let them pin it on him, do you?"

10

Ryan found the temporary offices of Cougar Creek Timber Products on a side street across from the police station. A dozen men milled around the open door, probably workers looking to collect pay or get jobs cleaning up the burn site. He sympathized with how desperately some of them probably needed work, but cleanup couldn't begin until both he and the law authorities had completed their investigations.

He pushed through the crowd to the door. Inside, a middle-aged, dark-haired woman occupied the front desk. She was talking on a phone scrunched against her shoulder, typing on a computer keyboard and snagging an occasional sip of black coffee. A hallway leading off to the rear revealed several doors, all closed. Was Hunter Blackwell back there somewhere?

Ryan squelched an unprofessional surge of antagonism toward a man he'd never met. He was less successful with the curiosity he felt toward Stefanie's ex. *No doubt about it. I want a look at the guy.*

Ryan extracted a business card from his wallet and set it on the desk. When the receptionist got off the phone, she glanced at the card then framed it with her fingertips.

"You're from the insurance company?" she asked. The card said that was exactly who he was, so he assumed she was stalling while she decided whether he should be treated as friend or foe.

"Yes. I'd like to speak with Mr. Blackwell, please."

"Someone from the state fire marshall's office was here yesterday. And the federal Bureau of Alcohol, Tobacco, and Firearms has called." She sounded mildly exasperated, as if she thought enough was enough.

"I'm with the insurance company's Arson and Fraud Division, and we'll be conducting our own investigation. A claims adjuster from the company will also be arriving."

The words "arson" and "fraud" apparently gave her a jolt. With a turn toward neutral diplomacy, she said, "I'm sorry, but Mr. Blackwell hasn't come in yet. But I'm sure he's eager to meet with you."

"Well, when he arrives, please tell him I'm at the mill starting my investigation. And that I'll need blueprints for the building and figures on plywood inventory."

As Ryan watched the woman make a note of his message in big, loopy script, he wondered if she was the "next Mrs. Blackwell" Stefanie had mentioned. Her makeup was a bit heavy but well done, her brown hair smartly styled. But she was a bit too mature and matronly to be temptress material. Nor did she appear as interested in insurance as he assumed the next Mrs. Blackwell would be.

Which showed, Ryan had to admit, that he'd already established an unfair prejudice toward Stefanie's ex and his fianceé. Just because the man was an adulterer and the woman a husband-stealer didn't mean either were arsonists. After all, the mill was fully insured, but it wasn't overinsured. Coverage had not recently been increased. Several insurance claims had been filed in the past five years, but the amounts were not excessive, and all had appeared legitimate. Those facts were points in Hunter's favor, because arsonists tended to be overtly greedy.

Once outside, Ryan eyed the police station across the street. In most cases, he'd contact the local police for whatever facts they knew before starting his own investigation. But he hesitated, one foot in the

Blazer, one on the ground. There were good arguments for not following his customary routine. Small-town police departments often weren't all that knowledgeable about arson. Sometimes they misinterpreted evidence about the fire and possible suspects. Personal connections or histories could color their judgment.

He slid into the vehicle and slammed the door. He'd start this investigation from neutral ground. Keep his mind uncluttered by local prejudices. Then he'd see what the police had to say.

He also slammed the door on any thought that he might not be as solidly planted on neutral ground as he wanted to believe, that he might be letting concern for Stefanie influence his actions.

I'm a professional; my past or present relationship with Stefanie won't affect the job I'm doing here.

Ryan parked by a "Keep Out" sign nailed to a trio of sawhorses barricading the street by the burned mill. A long line of yellow plastic tape with the words "Fire Line — Do Not Cross" printed in black stretched in both directions from the blockade. A guard stood at a far corner. *Okay, I see everybody is doing their job so far. Good.*

He opened the back of the Blazer and dug out khaki coveralls. He slipped them over his clothes, then changed into heavy boots. Fire debris was notorious for treacherous booby traps. His first burn site investigation had given him a bad puncture wound on the foot, and another time a burned floor had collapsed under him, plunging him a dozen feet into a hidden meth lab.

He opened one of the rear doors of the Blazer, exposing the tools of his trade. A shovel and rake, measuring tape and latex gloves. His cameras, of course. And microscopes, various containers to hold materials for laboratory examination, wood-moisture meter, ohmmeter. He often found especially useful a small handheld instrument called "The Sniffer," which detected combustible vapors. In the catchall tool box were the hacksaw, knife, chisel, pliers, magnet, screwdrivers, and a dozen other items he'd found useful over the years.

A state police car was parked just beyond where the guard stood. Beside it was another vehicle with an insignia he couldn't make out. Several people were at work in the blackened debris, but it wasn't overrun with investigators.

He started toward the flattened chain-link fence, then changed his mind and returned to the Blazer. He drove to the steep street from which he'd looked down on the burn site last evening and parked at the weedy edge of the gravel. He leaned on the open door to survey the scene.

Accident? Or arson? He walked out to a rocky promontory for a better view.

Arsonists were notorious for thinking they could set a fire so hot and powerful that all trace of its origin would be destroyed. That seldom happened. Usually ignorance or carelessness supplied clues, like the time when Ryan used hidden footprints to lead police to an arsonist.

But Ryan knew there had to be cases when arsonists got away with it, when their crimes were mistakenly written off as accidents.

Not this time. Not if I have anything to say about it.

And if his investigation led back to Stefanie? He set that thought aside and concentrated on studying the burn site below.

As he knew from both training and experience, the way to investigate any fire was to work from the area of least damage to the area of greatest damage. Not easy to do at the mill, with such wholesale destruction. At first there didn't appear to be areas of greater or lesser damage; it was all devastation.

But as he studied the burned mill in a visual grid pattern, using binoculars for more detailed inspection, his experienced eye picked out small differences. Pipes more twisted and melted in some places, a bit of fallen but unburned wall in another. There were at least three, possibly four separate areas in the central part of the building that exhibited signs of more intense heat. A front section, with lumps that may have been metal desks, was totally destroyed. That had probably been the office. He'd need the blueprints to identify the other areas. The area near a rear loading dock showed somewhat less damage. Misshapen lumps in the yard were identifiable as vehicles and various pieces of equipment.

An area of intense destruction usually indicated a fire's point of origin. So what he was seeing, although it was certainly not conclusive evidence, indicated multiple points of origin. Accidental fires tended to start in one place, not several, so the multiple points of origin were an indication of arson. Someone had moved through the mill, starting fires as he or she went. That implied an arsonist familiar with the layout of the mill.

Ryan got his camera from the back seat and carefully photographed the area. He used a wide-angle lens first, then a zoom to target specific spots. He videotaped the same territory, keeping careful records of everything in a spiral notebook. *Mutt, you just got photographed,* he noted as he observed the yellow dog he'd seen yesterday wandering around again.

He returned to the mill, slipped on latex gloves, and methodically started his hands-on inspection. He hadn't seen any signs to suggest the fire had started at an outside wall and burned inward, but he wanted to make certain. He circled the perimeter first, stopping along the way to show the guard his identification. The yellow dog showed up to accompany him. It was a skinny but friendly mutt with amber eyes. The dog's plume of tail stirred ashes as he wandered through the debris, adding more layers of grime to his rough coat.

The tour around the outside edge of the mill reinforced Ryan's original observations. The damage was definitely lighter there. It was a little like a campfire leaving unburned bits in a ring around the central fire. This burn had definitely originated inside the structure and moved toward the outside. Next, Ryan went to what he thought had been the office and got down to the nitty-gritty of examining individual bits of material. The melted-down lumps he'd spotted earlier were metal desks, as he'd thought. There were also differently shaped lumps that he identified as metal file cabinets. He took more photos and made notes and sketches in his spiral notebook. The other investigators were working in a different area, and he didn't cross paths with them.

He dug beneath the surface layer of debris in several places. The exposure intensified the acrid scent, and fluttering ashes settled on his hair and skin. The dog stayed with him, sticking his inquisitive nose into pockets and holes. Occasionally the animal dug industriously, ashes billowing in a dark cloud around both of them. After a few such exploratory digs, the dog's yellow coat was almost black, and Ryan was spitting grit.

"Go on, dog. Dig somewhere else. Didn't you read the 'Keep-Out' signs?" Ryan waved his arms at the skinny animal, but the dog's amber eyes looked at him so reproachfully that he muttered an apology. "Okay, I'm sorry. Stay. The police can run you off if they don't like you helping with the investigation, okay?"

Ryan crushed and sifted ashes with his fingertips, using both his nose and "The Sniffer" to detect telltale signs of an accelerant. Within minutes, he was almost certain that gasoline, that old-fashioned standby of arsonists, had been used at the mill. "Not someone experienced in the finer points of modern arson," he observed to the dog. Sophisticated and creative arsonists could choose from a whole spectrum of newer, high-tech accelerants more difficult to detect than gasoline. "Although there was that one woman who did it with a half dozen bottles of vodka. She destroyed the computer room where she thought her husband spent too much time. How's that for being clever as well as vindictive? She got rid of both his computer *and* his vodka." The dog acknowledged this commentary with a dignified tilt of head.

Ryan took samples for laboratory analysis, photographing everything before sealing each sample in a separate metal can. He numbered each can and recorded in his notebook where it had come from in the mill. The measuring tape helped him find exact locations. "If you really wanted to help," he grumbled to the dog, "you could hold the other end of the tape."

He found broken glass from the office windows, noting that it was covered with a fine black soot, which indicated a fast, hot fire. A smoldering, accidental fire would have left the glass smoke-stained rather than sooty.

Neither exterior or interior walls remained to show the cone shape that indicated where a fire had started and flared upward against a wall. A wooden floor or carpeting might also have revealed a burn pattern, but the main floor of the utilitarian office was concrete, and concrete gave up little information. The dog dug up what looked like the misshapen remains of the office's coffeemaker. He presented it to Ryan. "Good dog," Ryan said.

Ryan had left the office area and moved deeper into the mill when a tan-and-brown pickup arrived. A tall, blond man came toward him, plunging through the tangled debris with a macho disregard for smudging his neatly creased pants.

"Harrison? My receptionist told me you were here." The man's tone was friendly, and he smiled and stuck out a hand. "I'm Hunter Blackwell."

Ryan rubbed his own blackened hand on his coveralls and shook hands with Stefanie's ex. Hunter's handshake was strong and confident. He didn't seem troubled that some of the soot on Ryan's hand came off on his own. He apparently did not appreciate the dog sniffing around him, however. He pushed the wide yellow head away with his knuckles.

"I'm afraid I can't provide any blueprints

of the building to help you. As you can see, the fire completely destroyed the office. And everything else." Hunter waved his hand in a half-circle over the burned-out mill. "Not that we had any actual blueprints anyway. It was an old building, originally built by my grandfather and his partner in the fifties, then enlarged and modernized at various times over the years."

Hunter's grandfather was one of the original partners? Ryan realized what Stefanie had meant when she said Hunter had married her as a "business consolidation."

He also, reluctantly, could see what Stefanie had seen in Hunter. A good-looking face, lean and rugged physique, crisp blond hair, blue eyes women probably gave some fanciful name to. Sea blue? Sapphire? A movie-star smile, manner affable but self-confident.

But he also knew what Hunter had done. Cheated on Stefanie. Abandoned her for another woman. Tampered with the mill ownership.

"Is something wrong?" Hunter asked.

Ryan realized his fists had clenched while he studied the man. He flexed the fingers, forcing them to relax. *You're doing it again, Ryan. Don't lose your professional neutrality.*

"Perhaps you could just draw a rough

sketch of the mill's layout for me." He opened the spiral notebook to a fresh page and handed it and a ballpoint pen to Hunter.

Ryan wasn't an expert on plywood mills, but he'd done some quick research before coming to Julesburg. He could give nods of recognition as Hunter sketched the areas where logs were peeled to make veneer, the dryers, the hot presses, the patching and sanding operations, the storage and office areas.

"This is where we believe the accident started." Hunter pointed with the pen to the area identified on the sketch as where the sanders were operated. He looked up and lifted his arm to translate that into a location within the burned mill itself. "We've had electrical problems off and on there for several weeks."

"My understanding is that the mill was shut down when the fire broke out."

"That's true. But it was apparently an electrical short, something unrelated to whether or not the sanders were actually operating at the time."

"I may need to talk to whoever maintained your electrical system."

"That'd be our millwright, Mac McKenzie. The receptionist can give you his

151

phone number. The big problem was that the fire got a huge head start before anyone noticed it. It happened on the Fourth, you know, and everyone was off watching the pageant and fireworks."

And what better time for a fire to start if you preferred no one know about it for a while. Ryan didn't voice that thought, though, because in his experience, silence was unnerving. Suspects tended to hang themselves the longer they talked. And he was willing to let Hunter talk all he wanted.

"Our local police force isn't convinced the fire was an accident," Hunter continued. "They're suspicious some arsonist, maybe someone who'd worked here, tossed something flammable over everything and lit it. But I can't believe that. We've always had excellent relations with our employees here at Cougar Creek Timber Products." Hunter frowned, as if the possibility of a disgruntled employee retaliating for some supposed wrong disturbed him. He followed the frown with a disarming smile. "Of course, because the company has experienced some financial difficulties and setbacks due to poor market conditions and shortage of logs, the other rumor going around is that I or my ex-wife snuck in here and torched the mill ourselves in the hope that the insurance company would throw buckets of money at us."

The information was delivered with a rueful, I-may-as-well-tell-you honesty. Ryan rewarded that with the expected smile. "So why don't you show me exactly where you think the fire started?"

"Sure. Be glad to."

Hunter led the way, detouring debris and clambering over chunks of distorted metal and collapsed metal beams. The dog followed, as if it were some duty he'd assigned himself. Ryan gave the dog a pat on the head.

"It was a real shock, seeing this place go up in flames." A slight breeze ruffled Hunter's blond hair as he tossed the words back over his shoulder. "I started work here on the green chain years ago, working summers while I was in college. My grandfather was still alive then. So it was kind of like watching the old homestead burn. It would have broken my grandfather's heart if he was alive to see it."

Spoken as if he, of course, would have crawled through hot embers on his knees before doing anything to break the beloved grandfather's heart.

Back off, Harrison. Keep an open mind.

"You've been managing the mill since . . . ?"

153

Hunter paused at a twisted beam to answer the question. "My grandfather, his partner, and my wife's father, who was manager of the mill at the time, were all killed in a plane crash. I took over after that."

That corroborated what Stefanie had said. "But you didn't grow up here?" That question really wasn't relevant. He'd remember if they'd been classmates at good ol' Julesburg Junior High. But he allowed himself the liberty of asking anyway.

"My mother grew up here. She hated it and couldn't get away fast enough. But I came to visit Gramps some summers even before I started working at the mill, and liked it. Of course, it helped that he said right from the start that if I could, as he put it, 'grab hold' of the mill, then his half of it would be mine someday." Hunter smiled. "Old Gramps was a great guy, tough as nails, and hard to keep up with even when he was in his seventies."

Hunter spoke with what appeared to be a genuine affection for his grandfather. But Ryan couldn't quite accept being taken into Hunter's confidence at face value. He suspected an ulterior motive. Hunter wanted to provide negative information he thought Ryan might uncover elsewhere, because offering it himself would dilute its power.

Would Hunter also subtly try to plant a suggestion that Stefanie may have been involved in the fire?

Ryan waited, giving Hunter the opportunity. But Stefanie's ex remained silent so Ryan picked up the conversation.

"I understand there was no watchman on duty the night of the fire." That fact had been in the original police and fire department reports he'd asked to be faxed to his office.

"That's right. In the past we haven't needed a watchman because we were running three shifts, seven days a week. But with the current log shortage, we cut back to two shifts, five days a week. Pete Dooley has been standing watch on graveyard shift, plus weekends and holidays. But I thought it would be a shame if he couldn't take in the fireworks with his grandkids, so I told him to take the night off. Not a wise move, obviously, as things turned out."

"Did Dooley ask for the time off?"

"No. I offered it. The Fourth of July celebration is a big deal here in Julesburg. That's where I was, too, when the fire started."

Was there the slightest hesitation before Hunter admitted the request for time off hadn't come from Pete Dooley himself? But

155

that wasn't necessarily an incriminating act, even if it left the property unprotected. It could've been a totally nice-guy gesture on Hunter's part.

Ryan remembered seeing on the property description for the policy that there had been a sprinkler system for fire control in the mill. He nudged his toe against a tangle of mangled pipe that may have been a part of that system.

"How about the sprinkler system? Was it on?"

"So far as I know, it was. It should have been. But the controls are near the sanding area, which as you can see, was totally destroyed. So they could also have been destroyed early on, which would have deactivated the system. The controls for the sprinkling system on the log deck are located elsewhere. As you probably noticed, the logs didn't burn. So I think that indicates the controls for the sprinkler system within the building itself probably burned out before the sprinklers could do any good."

Or they could have been shut off. "I understand some controls work on a negative basis. That is, if something happens to the controls, the sprinklers automatically come on." He made the question mild, nonaccusing.

"I'm afraid our system wasn't that modern," Hunter said. He moved on. Black streaked his pants now, and his shoes were covered with ash. When he stopped again, he brushed more ashes from his socks before saying, "This is where the plywood received a final sanding and where we were having electrical problems."

It was a likely point of origin. A twisted, oblong shape was all that remained of a large metal box that had held a complicated array of electrical gear, but it was still possible to see that the door had been in an open position.

"Was that control box door usually left open?"

"No, but it may have been left that way accidentally when everyone was hurrying to get things shut down for the holiday. Looks like the electrical short may have been right there in the box, doesn't it?"

The control box was indeed destroyed, but Ryan was almost certain the heat was from an outside source, not from an electrical problem within the box. He'd check it later, after Hunter was gone. He pointed to another area where the debris was deeper, tangled with mangled ductwork and collapsed venting. "That's where the veneer dryers were located?"

"Right. Minor fires aren't uncommon in the dryers. Probably a week doesn't go by but what we have a small one. The dryers operate at a very high temperature, about four hundred degrees. That dries the veneer down to about 5 percent moisture content. It also produces the characteristic plume of harmless steam that people who don't know anything about making plywood always seem to think is some terrible pollutant contaminating the environment." Hunter gave a mildly exasperated shake of the head.

Ryan couldn't help thinking that Hunter was trying to confuse him with a barrage of irrelevant information. He responded, "But the dryers were shut down, of course, because the mill was closed for the holiday."

"Correct. But it's possible a fire could have started there and smoldered for a time before really taking off. So I guess, basically, it's just up to you experts to figure out what happened here." Hunter smiled, then glanced at his watch. "I hate to run, but I have a mountain of work back at the office. Oh, by the way, you asked about inventory figures, and we do have them. Fortunately, I'd taken the computer printouts home with me over the holiday to check them against the orders on hand. I'll get them to you."

Well, now, isn't it convenient for insurance-

claim purposes that the inventory figures are so readily available? "I'd appreciate that."

"So, unless you need me for something further . . . ?"

"Nothing now. I'll contact the office again if something comes up. I appreciate your help and information. You are aware that it may be necessary to move some of the heavy debris to find out what's underneath?"

"The other investigators haven't said anything about moving anything."

"I'll discuss it with them," Ryan replied.

"I can have the debris moved, of course, if it's really necessary. But all our equipment is burned, so I'd have to bring in outside equipment, which could take time. I was hoping to get this all settled as quickly as possible." Hunter paused, then smiled. "But I want to cooperate in every way possible, of course. I'll get the equipment if it's really needed."

"Is the company planning to rebuild the mill?"

"We haven't decided yet. It depends on various factors."

An answer worthy of a politician. Ryan nodded as if he understood. "Thanks again for your cooperation. We'll be in touch. As you probably know, a claims adjuster from the company will also be in to see you."

"Any time."

Hunter lifted his hand in a little farewell gesture of departure. Ryan's gaze followed him as he picked his way through the blackened debris toward the pickup. The yellow dog that had been lying at Ryan's feet stood up to watch.

"Well, Mutt, what d'you think?" Ryan asked. "Nice guy, salt of the earth, honest as the day is long, et cetera? No? I'm with you. I wouldn't trust Mr. Hunter Blackwell any farther than I could throw Lighthouse Hill."

Yet how would he see Hunter if the man wasn't Stefanie's ex? On the surface, Hunter was friendly and congenial. Helpful, open with information, personable. Even likable. But Ryan saw a guy giving confidences too deliberately. Trying too hard to be ingratiating and disarming. Too pushy with his accident theory.

Was what he felt a professional distrust, a gut-deep instinct that had served him well in other arson cases, or something entirely different? Maybe it was righteous anger on Stefanie's behalf, a continuation of the old your-battles-are-my-battles loyalty they'd given each other as kids. Or was it something considerably less noble? Something as simple as an ugly little jealousy of the man who had been Stefanie's husband, a man she'd loved and shared her life with?

A totally unacceptable emotion, he decided with a grimace of distaste. He needed to focus on the investigation. "C'mon, Mutt, let's do it."

He worked steadily, stopping only once to walk back to the Blazer for gulps of water from the canteen he always carried. The dog lapped eagerly at the old Taco Bell cup he filled for him once, then again. At noon, on a longer break for clam chowder at the Julesburg Café, he thought about calling Stefanie. Had she gone to the doctor for that tetanus shot?

Instead, he decided to drive to her house; he didn't think she would be working with that injured foot of hers. Maybe she'd find slamming the door in his face harder to do than hanging up on him if he called.

Her car wasn't in the driveway, however, and there was no answer when he prodded the doorbell persistently. He drove by Fit 'n' Fun, but he didn't see her car there either. Finally, not knowing where else to look, he returned to the burn site shortly after 1:00.

The mill was buzzing with activity. A car marked Julesburg Police, an additional state-police car, and two vehicles with the county sheriff's insignia were parked near the site, and radio squawks blared from all of them. There was also an unmarked blue van and a small crowd of onlookers. Then, as he offered the mutt a handful of crackers left over from his lunch, Ryan saw what was going on. A sniffer dog had been brought in to work the burn site. The dog was a black-and-white animal of nondescript appearance, but it looked as if it knew what it was doing. Nose down, tail waving. All business. It sat down suddenly, as such dogs are trained to do, identifying an area where it smelled traces of accelerant. The handler stepped up to give the animal a small reward. One officer photographed the area where the scent of accelerant was found, and another took a sample of the debris, placing it in a metal can and labeling it.

Ryan stroked the broad head of the dog beside him as they watched together. "There, you see how it's done? You could have been the big star like your canine friend over there if you'd sniffed up something flammable. But all you did was dig up an old coffeemaker."

The dog, as if unimpressed with the other animal's accomplishments, stuck a cold nose into Ryan's palm.

The elite sniffer dog was off on a new search. Ryan started in the dog's direction and was immediately intercepted by a deputy sheriff. He presented his identification and was let through, but the officer unceremoniously shooed Ryan's furry yellow companion off the premises.

Ryan and the entourage of officers followed along behind the trained dog as it efficiently targeted three more areas where accelerant had been used. The two officers busily took more samples for lab analysis.

At about 5:00, the handler loaded the dog into the van, and within minutes, officers, vehicles, and onlookers were gone. Only the guard and the debris remained. Ryan wandered around a little longer, revisiting spots the sniffer dog had identified. His own canine buddy returned to accompany him.

"That dog is probably going home to a cashmere-lined bed and filet mignon, and what do you have?" Ryan had earlier assumed the animal belonged to someone in the neighborhood, but now he suspected it was a stray. When he felt underneath the rough yellow coat, he realized the dog's ribs climbed its sides like a bony ladder. "To quote a wise man, 'Life ain't fair,' is it?"

Ryan was momentarily undecided as to how much further to carry his own investigation at the burn site. The fire was arson, no doubt about it. Lab tests would identify what accelerant had been used, but Ryan was already reasonably certain it was gasoline.

His energies were probably best directed toward identifying the arsonist. Someone husky and strong enough to carry the several cans of gasoline it would have taken to start big fires in four separate locations. Or someone not so big and strong, perhaps even a woman, efficiently using a maneuverable hand cart.

"Hey, Mutt, don't waste your energy," Ryan called to the dog as it was energetically digging in the area where the dryers had been located, a flying spray of ashes and debris shooting out behind him. "I might even be persuaded to buy you some dinner."

The dog kept digging until only the tip of his tail showed.

"Okay, Mutt, that's enough. The cops will get you for disturbing evidence at a crime scene." Ryan clambered over debris and gave the dog's tail a yank.

The dog reluctantly backed out of the hole it had created. He shook, showering Ryan's dirty coveralls with a fresh coat of ash. Ryan peered into the hole to see what had interested the dog. His stomach roiled.

The elite sniffer dog had done what it was trained to do: sniff out accelerants. But this untrained mutt had sniffed out something far more disturbing.

11

Stefanie flexed her foot when she woke. *Could be worse.* But by the time she'd made coffee and toasted a bagel, she knew it was definitely too ouchy for anything bouncy and energetic at Fit 'n' Fun. She called Tina's cousin, who already worked part time for her, and asked her to come in for the day.

Stefanie had left the bloody handkerchief and towel soaking in cold water overnight. Now, adding bleach to the water, she ran a load through the washer. The results were satisfactorily snowy. She dried and folded the handkerchief and towel neatly. *Now what do I do with them?*

Nurse Ganzer in Dr. Halmoose's office gave her a tetanus shot. After that, she drove on to the Laurel Cove Nursing Center in Dutton Bay, where she conducted the easy exercise class from a chair. Gracie had made progress with her efforts to touch her toes. "Don't push yourself too hard," Stefanie cautioned, having visions of the sweet little lady freezing herself into a permanent U-shaped position. At lunch in the dining room, Gracie talked about her girlhood during the Great Depression, and others joined in. They told of eating only oatmeal for days on end and wearing dresses made out of chicken-feed sacks. The tales were fascinating enough to keep Stefanie's mind off arson, Ryan, and her foot.

Afterward, she dropped the handkerchief and towel off with the desk clerk at the Sea Haven, then spent a couple of hours catching up on office work at Fit 'n' Fun. Dinner that evening was leftover spaghetti from the freezer and a slightly limp salad. She managed an awkward bath in the old-fashioned clawfoot tub, her bandaged foot draped over the rounded lip of the tub to keep it out of the water. Several times during her bath, she heard sirens wailing on the north side of town. The sirens sounded as if they were coming from the mill, but she hadn't seen anything left there to burn. Once, she peered out a front window, but summer fog against the glass cut off visibility at the end of the driveway.

At about 9:00, Val phoned. "Hey, what's going on at the mill?"

"I have no idea. Is something going on?"

"Didn't you hear the sirens? I was picking

up a burrito at the Calico Pantry, and Mrs. Maxwell said something was happening over there. So, you know nosy ol' me, I checked it out. They have huge floodlights set up, and a bulldozer is shoving stuff around. Looks like a war zone. And there are enough cops to stop an invasion of the bodysnatchers. I tried to talk to one of them, but he blew me off."

More law enforcement officers? A bulldozer? That morning, on the way to the nursing home, she'd surreptitiously driven to the rocky promontory looking down on the mill. Only Ryan and a couple of other people were poking around. No activity like Val was reporting.

"Maybe Ryan or Hunter or the authorities decided the investigation would go faster if they put in longer hours," Stefanie suggested.

"I think they're looking for something specific. And maybe they've found something."

"What could there be to find?"

"I don't know. But *you* have a right to know what they're doing. After all, you're still part owner of the mill. Maybe you should go see what's going on."

Curiosity strongly tempted Stefanie to do exactly that. Why were the police so interested now? Why the sudden urgency with the investigation?

But she felt a distinct uneasiness about dashing over to the mill. Would such action be interpreted as an inordinate display of interest on the part of a suspect? The kind of interest someone fearful of incriminating evidence might exhibit? Or perhaps they'd see it as the arsonist drawn back to the scene of the crime.

With a pretense of disinterest, she said to Val, "I'm sure someone will tell me tomorrow if there's anything I should know."

"If it were my mill, you couldn't keep me away with a dozen bulldozers," Val declared.

In spite of her apprehension, Stefanie laughed. *Probably true. Val is a bit of a bulldozer herself.*

Stefanie wasn't laughing, however, when she saw the mill on the 11:00 news. Floodlights lit the debris. Red-and-blue police lights revolved in the fog. Heavy equipment roared in the background. Stefanie had missed the beginning of the segment, but a woman reporter holding a microphone was saying, "— badly burned body has just been removed from the Cougar Creek Timber Products plywood mill here in Julesburg.

The body was discovered late this afternoon by insurance company investigator Ryan Harrison, who was on the site investigating the fire that destroyed the mill earlier this week. Heavy equipment had to be brought in to free the body, which was trapped under a jumble of metal beams — Oh, Mr. Harrison, could we have a word with you?"

The video camera caught Ryan in dirty coveralls. His dark hair fell in disarray, and ashes smudged and streaked his face. He turned away waving the reporter off. The reporter expertly switched targets and captured a deputy sheriff. The officer said that a stray dog digging in the debris had led Ryan to the body, which was as yet unidentified. The officer was careful not to make conjectures about the fire or the body, but he did point out that indications were that gasoline had been heavily spread around the mill to start the fire.

The news switched to a truck accident north of Coos Bay, and Stefanie flicked the power button on the remote control. She lay back against the pillows of her bed.

A body. Lying there in the debris all that time. Who could it be? An innocent mill worker, accidentally trapped? No; a local worker would surely have been missed. A transient, seeking shelter in the mill for the night, perhaps starting a fire to keep warm? The foggy night of the Fourth had been chilly. No, not with gasoline probably involved in several areas.

What had come through the officer's cautious phrasing was that the body was probably the arsonist himself, trapped in a fire of his own making.

What a horrible way to die!

It wasn't until Stefanie turned off the lamp that another thought occurred to her. Distaste, even a small stab of guilt for thinking such a thought, made her shiver. But seeing the benefit was unavoidable.

Discovery of the body lets me off the hook.

It was true. The man's death proved that she hadn't torched the mill. It also proved Hunter hadn't done it, and she felt another jab of guilt, because she'd been almost certain he was guilty.

More information surfaced over the next few days. Stefanie heard it the same way everyone else in town did, by radio, TV, and word of mouth. All of the half dozen vehicles destroyed in the fire had been assumed to be company vehicles, but one pickup parked next to the building turned out to have a different ownership. Enough of the car remained for identification through Department of Motor Vehicle records as belonging to a man named Greg Haggerston. The burned man had fallen with his wallet under him, and charred scraps of identification in the wallet further identified the body. A foreman at the mill said Haggerston had been employed there for several months. After numerous absences and reprimands, he'd been fired about a month before for drinking on the job. He'd been living in Dutton Bay but had vacated his apartment two days before the fire. The conjecture was that he'd tried to destroy the mill as revenge for being fired but was accidentally trapped and killed in the blaze.

The morning after Haggerston's pickup and body were identified, Police Chief Ben Mosely showed up at Fit 'n' Fun. He came to the door of Stefanie's office, his officer's hat in his big hands.

"I came to apologize, Miss Stefanie. I should have known you couldn't have anything to do with burning down the mill." The apology was straightforward, devoid of excuses, and offered with both sincerity and dignity. Ben was a proud man, but a man willing to admit when he was wrong. "I'm sorry for any trouble my suspicions caused you."

"You were just doing your job."

"We can thank that insurance investigator for doing his job. He not only found the body, he was the one who discovered that one of the burned pickups wasn't a company vehicle. We missed that."

Is Ryan still in Julesburg? Stefanie was reluctant to ask the question of Ben directly, so she approached the subject from an oblique angle. "This means the investigation into the fire is complete now?"

"Reports from the state crime lab confirm that gasoline was used in several places as an accelerant to start the fire. There's no doubt in my mind but what the body is Greg Haggerston's, and that he set the fire. According to all accounts, Haggerston was hot tempered and mean. He was also a heavy drinker and had a police record in California. Everyone figures he set the fire for revenge."

"And that *does* end the investigation?"

"Not completely. Dental records will be used to make further positive identification of the body. And then there's the autopsy, of course, to make sure he actually died in the fire, that he wasn't already dead from some other cause when it started."

Stefanie touched her throat, shocked.

"But this is routine stuff," Ben assured her. "Like I said, there's no doubt in my mind that it's Haggerston's body. Also no doubt that he died in the fire while he was setting it. But we have to be thorough about these things."

"Yes, of course. I feel sorry for the man, in spite of what he did."

"Yeah, it was a terrible way to go." Ben rotated the hat in his hands. "I hope there's no hard feelings, Miss Stefanie."

Stefanie circled her desk and gave him a big hug. "No hard feelings. Julesburg is fortunate to have you on the job."

"Twila says you're still pretty scarce around church."

"I cut my foot on the beach the other evening." Stefanie held out the foot. The bandage was down to a Band-Aid now, so nothing showed outside her Reeboks. Yet even if a bandage had been visible, a cut foot was no explanation for her long absence from church. They both knew it, but Ben nodded.

"You take care now," he said.

Stefanie returned to her bookwork with a feeling of relief and gratification that Ben had confirmed her innocence. Would Ryan see fit to make a similar apology?

But Stefanie heard nothing from Ryan. She assumed he'd left town until she came home from Fit 'n' Fun two afternoons later and found his Blazer parked in her driveway. She parked her own car on the street in front of the house so she wouldn't block his exit.

He was leaning against the rear of the Blazer, legs crossed at the ankles. He folded his arms as he watched her march up the sloped driveway.

"The foot doesn't seem to be bothering you much now."

"It's fine."

"Thanks for returning my handkerchief and the motel's towel."

"You're welcome."

"You heard about the discovery of the body at the mill?"

"Yes, of course. And the conclusion that the man had a grudge against the company because he'd been fired a month earlier." She didn't care that her voice held an edge of triumph.

But if she expected any apology from Ryan, she was mistaken. He straightened and put his hands in the rear pockets of his jeans. "From what I've learned, the man brought at least seven or eight five-gallon cans of gasoline to the mill in his pickup. He parked close to the loading dock and carried them inside. He spread the gasoline around the office and several other areas and got all but the last fire started successfully. On that one, he miscalculated and was caught in the blaze. Actually given all the gasoline he was sloshing around, I'm surprised he didn't incinerate himself when he lit the first match. Not a smart way to start a fire."

Stefanie shivered. "There's supposed to be an autopsy . . . ?"

"Yeah. It's been done. Haggerston died in the fire, not by some other cause. And the body was definitely Haggerston's. It was too badly burned for fingerprint identification, but dental records have made it positive. I located a dentist in Dutton Bay who'd done a root canal on a molar for him a couple months ago."

"How did he get a pickup loaded with cans of gasoline inside the chain-link fence around the mill?"

"We found a key to a padlock on the body. The foreman says Haggerston wouldn't have had any difficulty stealing or copying a key, because one hung right by the loading dock. Security at the mill was not exactly tight."

"I don't think there's ever been any need for tight security." Stefanie hesitated, picturing the scene of destruction again. When the wind was just right, it still stirred up an acrid scent. "It must have been an . . . ugly experience discovering the body."

Ryan nodded, not elaborating. He just stood there, leaning against the Blazer, a slight frown on his face. Given the important part he'd played in the successful conclusion of the investigation of the fire, he did not seem as pleased or satisfied as Stefanie would have expected. Was there something more that troubled him about the case? Or was he simply concerned that the insurance company would now have to make a big payoff?

"You'll be leaving Julesburg now, I suppose?"

"Yeah. I'm driving back to Portland tonight."

"Long drive."

"Actually I stopped by to ask a favor of you."

"A *favor?*"

He moved his shoulders in a shrug of embarrassment. "I realize that our relationship isn't exactly at a favor-asking level, but I don't know what else to do."

He walked to the other side of the Blazer, opened the passenger's-side door, and a big yellow dog jumped out. Stefanie recognized the animal from TV and newspaper photos as the stray that had led Ryan to the body.

She backed away shaking her head. "Oh, no —"

"All I'm asking is if you'll take care of him

for a few days. Maybe a week, until I can make other arrangements."

"Ryan, I have no place to keep a dog. I'm away from home at Fit 'n' Fun all day and most evenings."

"He wouldn't be any bother. He's really a great dog and very well behaved. I couldn't take him into the motel, so he's been sleeping in the Blazer. A perfect gentleman. He could sleep in your garage. Your backyard is fenced, so he could stay there during the day." He hesitated and then, with the old Ryan honesty, added reluctantly, "Although he does like to dig. So you kind of have to watch him around flowers and stuff."

He peered over the fence at her backyard. She couldn't produce a strong argument about protecting her lovely flower beds from dog-digging damage. It would have taken a flower with the ego of a megalomaniac to mingle with the untended weeds in her backyard.

"If he's such an exceptional creature, why aren't you taking him home with you?"

"The condo doesn't allow pets. I suppose I could put him in a kennel, but I don't think he's used to being caged up."

"I wonder what breed he is."

"Purebred BSM, I think."

"BSM?"

"Big Shaggy Mutt."

The dog swooshed his tail on the concrete driveway in affable agreement. *He does have a certain ragamuffin charm. But also enough shedding, shaggy yellow dog hair to cover every inch of carpet and piece of upholstered furniture in the house.*

"What's his name?"

"I just call him 'Mutt.' "

"You can't call a dog 'Mutt,' " Stefanie protested. She covered the dog's ears. "It's disrespectful. You'll give him some kind of complex."

"If you'll keep him for a few days, you can name him anything you want. He comes with a bed, a leash, a couple of dishes, and a sack of dog food."

"That's not much in the way of bribery."

"He also comes with a lot of doggy charisma."

The dog stuck a cold nose in her hand. Reluctantly, she found herself stroking the wide head. "He isn't as dirty as he looked on TV."

"I gave him a bath in Wandering Creek. Actually, by the time I was done, we'd both had a bath."

Stefanie had to make an effort not to smile as she rubbed a shaggy ear. She also reminded herself that taking care of a dog

178

was an impossible idea. He would have to be fed, watered, and walked. He might need another bath.

But if it was for no more than a few days . . .

"You'd definitely come back and get him in a week? This isn't just some trick to dump him on me?"

"I'll be back. Cross my heart and hope to eat a rattlesnake tail."

Stefanie couldn't help smiling now. It was their old pledge from long ago, wildly silly but reserved for solemn occasions, like the time they'd pledged never to reveal that they were the culprits who'd hidden a stink bomb in Patty Sumptner's locker. She hadn't thought about that old vow in years.

Maybe it was the memory of that pledge. Maybe it was because some part of her wanted to see Ryan again. Or maybe it was just the shaggy haired mutt himself.

"Okay, I'll keep him for a few days. But if you don't show up in a week, you'll find us both camped on your condo doorstep."

"Is that a promise?" Ryan leaned over and planted a kiss on her cheek. "Thanks, Stef. I really appreciate this."

"Why do I feel as if I've just been conned?" she murmured. *And why does the spot you just kissed feel like it's been warmed by a bit of that mythical green flash's magic?*

Ryan carried the dog supplies to the back porch. He knelt to give the dog a rough-house petting, accepted a sloppy slurp on the cheek, then headed for the Blazer. The dog started to follow, but Ryan pointed to the ground in front of Stefanie.

"No. Stay," he commanded. The dog's amber gaze followed Ryan, but the dog obediently plopped down at Stefanie's feet. To Stefanie, Ryan added, "I'll see you in a week or so." Then to the dog, "You, too."

Ryan was doing his best to hide it, but Stefanie could see that parting with the dog affected him. *Same guy who got teary when he helped me bury my pet guinea pig.*

"I'll take really good care of him," she called after Ryan.

"I know you will."

"Ryan?"

He stopped with one foot in the Blazer.

"This ends it, doesn't it?"

"The investigation?"

"Finding the man's body and proof he had a grudge against the company and spread gasoline in the mill, that settles everything, doesn't it? It's all over now?"

"I think that's the official determination that will be made within a few days."

"And you, is your case also closed?"

"If you're asking if the company will pay off on the insurance claim now, I don't know. That isn't my decision. I met with the claims adjuster a couple of times while he was here, and he's working on it." Ryan looked at his watch. "Well, I better get moving. I'll see you in a few days."

Stefanie watched Ryan drive away, then turned to the dog. "He didn't really answer my question, did he?"

12

Ryan preferred the scenic drive up the coast, but he took the faster route, cutting through the coast mountains to Eugene and then heading up I-5 to Portland. The scenery was still beautiful, but he barely noticed the forested slopes and lush farmland. He'd told Stefanie the truth. He didn't know how the claims adjuster and main office would handle the case. They wouldn't be in any big hurry to settle, but then what insurance company would be? He knew the company would have questions for him. Was his conclusion the same as that of the various official agencies?

He concurred with the identification of the body. Haggerston had started the fire, and gasoline was definitely the accelerant. Revenge against the company provided powerful motive.

Ryan had spent the previous three days investigating Haggerston. Immediately after being fired from his job at the mill, Haggerston had been vocal with bar acquaintances about his unfair treatment. He'd also hinted that Cougar Creek Timber Products would be sorry they'd tangled with him. In an unrelated matter, several months earlier a neighbor in Haggerston's apartment complex had suspected him of slashing a neighbor's tires after a dispute over parking spaces. He'd been arrested once for a brawl in a tavern and several times for drinking and driving. His record in California included burglary and assault.

Ryan had located four different stations where Haggerston had filled five-gallon cans with gasoline. Buying the gas at several locations had kept any one station from getting curious about a large purchase. But some attendants remembered the narrow, sour face from the driver's license photo Ryan showed; some remembered the pickup.

Haggerston had vacated his apartment in Dutton Bay two days before the fire, ten days before the month's rent was up. He'd dropped the key off with the landlord and said he was heading immediately for North Carolina. "Got family there," he'd confided. "My cousin says he can get me a good job in the mine. Better'n anything around here."

Such thoughtfulness about the key was at odds with Haggerston's surly character, and so was the chatty conversation. Both

Ryan and the law enforcement people to whom he'd given the information saw this as Haggerston's attempt to establish an alibi just in case he was suspected of the arson.

Motive, vindictiveness of character, and planning were all neatly confirmed, and the authorities wrapped it up there. Ryan hadn't found any neon sign pointing in any other direction.

So why am I still suspicious?

Maybe Haggerston hadn't acted totally on his own initiative. Maybe someone had hired him to burn the mill.

But why think that? What was the logic in it?

The timing of the fire. Mill closed for the holiday. Watchman dismissed. Safety sprinklers shut off. Key conveniently available.

An arsonist couldn't have asked for a more convenient setup.

And Hunter Blackwell had more to gain than lose from the fire. Hunter Blackwell with the flimsy theory about an electrical accident and an airtight schedule.

But what about Stefanie? She also had a lot to gain from the fire. The additional weight of a revenge motive hung on her.

Ryan pounded a fist on the steering wheel. *No. Not Stefanie.* He couldn't believe she'd hired Haggerston, even though his investigator mind lined her up right beside Hunter. Stefanie could not have arranged those arson-friendly conditions at the mill. And would the kind of person who fell for a shaggy haired mutt be the kind of person who could hire an arsonist?

Flawed logic. But I'll bet the dog is right now happily flaked out on Stefanie's living room floor.

Ryan was partly right. The dog was indeed flaked out, but it was on a cushion in the window seat of Stefanie's bedroom. She'd put him in the backyard after Ryan left and later fed and walked him. She'd made certain there were no drafts around his bed in the garage.

He'd stayed there for an hour, uncomplaining. She was the one who couldn't stand it any longer. With unmistakable joy, the dog accepted Stefanie's invitation to join her in the house. There he sniffed and inspected everything, leaving a calling card of yellow doggy hair on everything.

He also provided more company than she'd had in months. Within minutes, she found herself carrying on one-sided conversations with him.

"Tomorrow we should buy you some

canned dog food, don't you think? This dry stuff could get boring." And, "Okay, what'll we watch on TV? Sitcom? Nature show? Here's a great one about cats you might like."

Although the conversations weren't necessarily one-sided, she'd decided. "What do you think?" she asked. "Is Ryan really coming back? Or are you my permanent roommate?" The dog tilted his head with a quizzical look that seemed to say, "He gave the rattlesnake-tail pledge, didn't he?"

"Okay, that he did. Sorry for doubting your big hero."

She gave the dog a little curtsy of apology. He responded with an agreeable slap of tail, leaving the inevitable memento of dog hair on the bedroom carpet.

"What you need is a good brushing."

Stefanie pawed through drawers until she found a brush that had seen better days. The dog took to grooming as if he'd spent his life in the best salons. He stood motionless while Stefanie worked the brush through knots and tangles.

"I heard about this woman who saved her dog's hair, spun it into yarn, and knitted herself a sweater," Stefanie told him as she collected a handful of long strands from the brush. She scooted around to tackle his other side. "The sweater did have a tendency to slip off her shoulders and chase cats, but I'm sure that was a minor inconvenience."

Doggy yawn.

"Not into shaggy dog humor, huh? Okay, to change the subject, I've been giving your name some thought." She couldn't brush through a tangled knot on his underside and got up to locate scissors. "I'm considering Digger, since that's how you became a celebrity. But I'm not sure I want to be reminded of that particular talent. What do you think? Digger?"

No response. She snipped at the knot, careful to avoid skin. "Something strong and manly, then? Hercules? Or grander. Napoleon, perhaps? Too ancient? Yeah, you're right. How about modern glamour? Movie star stuff. What's the name of that guy all the girls are swooning over now? Brad, Bret?"

She tried it out. "Here, Brad. C'mon, Bret." She shook her head. No way.

She finished the brushing, and the dog returned to his window seat.

"Of course, you probably have a name already," Stefanie said. "I apologize for not using it. But I don't know what it is, so you'll just have to live with a new one, okay?

Women do it all the time, you know, when they get married."

The dog was still unnamed by morning. Stefanie put him in the backyard with a dish of water and a promise to check on him at lunch. At Fit 'n' Fun she led a beginners' and then an advanced aerobics class, helped the girl with Down Syndrome exercise on a weight machine, fruitlessly tried to repair a leak in the women's shower room, and finally went to the office to call a plumber.

When she entered her office, she stumbled over a yellow lump spread like a rumpled rug on her floor. The lump looked up and swooshed his tail to welcome her.

"Tina!" Stefanie yelled. "How did this dog get in here!"

Tina came to the office door and peered at the dog. "I have no idea. I've never seen him before. He must have sneaked in when someone opened the outside door. Want me to shoo him out?"

"No. He's kind of . . . mine, I guess. I thought I had him locked in the backyard." She remembered Ryan's mention of the dog's tendency to dig. Apparently he had tracking as well as digging talents. "Oh, you're a real detective, aren't you? Just what I need. A shaggy Sherlock Holmes following me around."

★ ★ ★

Ryan called that night. Stefanie had just stepped out of the shower and was toweling her hair dry.

"I thought I should check on the mutt."

"His name is Sherlock," Stefanie corrected.

"Okay."

"Because he's a detective."

"Okay."

"I put him in the backyard, just like you said. He dug his way out and tracked me down at Fit 'n' Fun."

"Sounds like an excellent private eye."

"Have you found a home for him yet?"

"I've called a couple of people, but so far everyone is full-up on big, shaggy dogs. I'll keep looking. But it may be a little longer than a week before I can get down there again."

"I suppose I can take care of him for a few extra days."

"I'll be staying for about a week when I get there." The tone of his voice swung upward at the end, as if it were more question than statement.

"You have more investigation to do on the arson?"

"I've asked for the week of vacation time I still have coming. I'm planning to spend it in Julesburg. I thought maybe we could have that cup of coffee we never got. Maybe watch for the green flash?"

She started to ask if that meant the case was closed, then decided to skip it. There had been no activity at the mill. The guard was gone. She decided she could accept Ryan's claim of vacation at face value. "We might set out a crab pot," she offered.

"Hike the Wandering Creek trail?"

"Roast marshmallows over a campfire on the beach."

"Maybe we could even hold hands again?"

She smiled. "Maybe we could."

Val was there when Ryan called on Saturday evening. Stefanie had prepared an experimental low-fat tofu-and-steamed-vegetables dish that made them feel virtuous if not necessarily well fed. They had topped off the meal with popcorn, supplemented with an antacid tablet for Val. *Pride and Prejudice* was playing on the VCR in the living room.

Stefanie punched the stop button on the remote control and picked up the ringing phone. Val politely removed herself to the kitchen to refill her coffee cup. By the time she returned to the sofa, her tactfulness had lost to curiosity. "Was that The Hunk?"

"What makes you think that?"

"Because your face got this glow when you picked up the phone. As if you just found out you'd chosen the right numbers in the lottery."

"I don't play the lottery."

"Irrelevant change of subject."

Stefanie didn't argue. "He's coming to Julesburg again in a week or two. He's going to spend his vacation here."

Val did an exaggerated double take. "Wow!"

"What wow?" Stefanie scoffed. "Lots of people spend their vacations here. The tourist industry is big business in Julesburg. He also says that the insurance company has given their okay for cleanup to start at the mill."

"Great! That must mean they've decided to pay off. Maybe you and Hunter can get things settled now. I think this deserves a celebration! Let's go to champagne brunch at the Singing Whale tomorrow. They have that marvelous sparkling cider if you don't want champagne. And those fantastic little seafood quiches."

"Actually, I was thinking I might go to church tomorrow."

"Aha. The Hunk is getting to you in more ways than one."

Could be. "You could come to church with me, and then we could go to brunch."

Much to Stefanie's surprise, Val gave a shrug and agreed. "I suppose it wouldn't kill me to be preached at once or twice a year."

They arranged to meet in the church parking lot at five minutes to eleven the next morning.

After Val left, Stefanie got out her Bible and "wandered around" in Psalms for a while. It felt good, like entering a house long unvisited and strolling through the familiar rooms.

Just after 9:00 the next morning, Val called and canceled on both church and brunch.

"Stomach thing." She sounded as if she was grimacing.

"My cooking last night?"

"No, no, dear girl, not your cooking. Don't always be so quick to blame yourself. You know my stomach. You, of course, could probably eat a gravel-and-nail casserole and do just fine. But I can get an upset stomach on a lettuce leaf."

"It's probably the Silver-Tongued Rat's fault."

"Could be. Although I don't suppose I

can blame him for everything. I was never up for any Wife of the Year awards."

"I could bring over something soothing. Jell-O, chicken soup?"

"I suppose you could pray for me while you're in church."

The statement was made facetiously, yet Stefanie suspected that Val was halfway serious. "I'll do that, and I'll check on you later today."

Stefanie felt awkward at church after such a long absence, but everyone greeted her warmly. The regular pastor was on vacation, but a visiting speaker gave a good message on "The Engine or the Caboose?" The theme was that worship should be the engine driving the train of people's lives, not the caboose dragging along behind. *Worship in my life has definitely been in caboose status lately, hasn't it, Lord?* Hugs followed the service, with an especially generous one from Twila Mosely.

"I've been praying for you," Twila said.

"Don't stop now." Stefanie touched Twila's veined hand and received a reassuring squeeze in return. "Is the teen group meeting now?"

Twila shook her head. "Not since last spring, I'm afraid. But it would be wonderful if we could get it going again." The questioning lift of her graying eyebrows was hopeful.

"Yes, wouldn't it," Stefanie murmured.

Stefanie felt restless on the drive home. She'd been looking forward to brunch with Val at the Singing Whale. *Hey, there's no reason I can't go alone.* The morning fog, so prevalent on the coast in summer, hadn't lifted yet, but patches of blue showed it was beginning to break up. She felt a lift of spirits. She decided she'd take Sherlock for a run on the beach that afternoon.

She parked at the Singing Whale, and a fragrant whiff of the restaurant's popular cinnamon rolls reminded her she'd skipped breakfast. The moment she stepped inside, however, she realized coming there was a mistake. The booths and tables were full. Several couples stood in line at the "Please wait to be seated" sign. But the crowd was not unexpected; the Singing Whale's Sunday brunch was one of Julesburg's weekly highlights. The mistake was the couple sitting in the glassed-in alcove jutting from the main dining room. Stefanie drew a steadying breath and thought of what Val might say.

Look at them. The King and his Liposuction Queen holding court on their royal thrones. If she undoes any more buttons, she's going to catch pneumonia.

But Trisha truly was spectacular in a jade-green silk jumpsuit. The wide belt emphasized her slim figure, and a turned-up collar above the carefully undone buttons set off her honey-blond hair like a delicate frame. Hunter's charcoal suit displayed his own Nordic good looks. Together they made a spectacular couple.

Stefanie's first impulse was to stampede out the door. Too late. Trisha had spotted her. Stefanie lifted her chin and stepped into the line of waiting couples. She wouldn't let her single status make her uncomfortable. *I want a cinnamon roll. And seafood quiche.* The hostess beckoned to her a moment later.

"Hi, Lily," Stefanie said. Lily, before her hostessing days, had occasionally done housework for Stefanie's mother. She was petite but buxom in a blue crepe dress with a handkerchief hemline.

"Good to see you, Stef." Lily gave her arm a small, affectionate squeeze. "Would you like that tiny table in the back?" She sounded apologetic as she motioned toward the minuscule table. It was located between the doors to the kitchen and the lounge, barely large enough for one. "At least you wouldn't have to wait."

Neither the size nor the undesirable location mattered to Stefanie at that moment, because from the table she would not be able to see Hunter and Trisha. "Looks fine to me. I'm just here for a quick trip through the brunch buffet."

Stefanie draped her jacket over the chair at the table. Lily brought a tulip-shaped glass of sparkling cider and a plate for the buffet. "The crab puffs are especially good today, and we're about to run out," Lily confided. "Grab a handful."

Stefanie picked up her plate, steeled herself, and stepped around the corner. A quick glance in the direction of Hunter and Trisha's table was unexpectedly rewarding. Vacant! Empty champagne glasses sat on the table. They'd gone.

She was annoyed that Hunter and Trisha's presence or absence mattered. It shouldn't, she knew, but that didn't alter the relief she felt. She carried her plate toward the buffet in the center of the room, then stopped short.

No, Hunter and Trisha had not gone. They were in line at the buffet. Stefanie suppressed an urge to slip back to her tiny table. *They are not doing anything to me. And I will not do this to myself.*

She stepped into the line opposite from

Hunter and Trisha. Too late she saw she'd made another mistake. She should have gotten into the line behind Hunter and Trisha. Her line, defying the usual laws of line movement, was pushing forward rapidly. In moments she was directly opposite the couple. She couldn't see Trisha's face because of the stained-glass sneeze guard between them, but she watched Trisha's slim hand take a spoonful of fruit salad and skip over the cinnamon rolls.

Stefanie slapped items onto her own plate. Mixed salad, vegetables, rolls, scalloped potatoes, quiche, fish, ham, applesauce. She tried to push ahead faster, but she and the slim figure in the jade jumpsuit moved down the opposite sides of the buffet as if they were in lockstep.

There was no avoiding it. They were going to meet at the end of the counter. Stefanie braced herself as if the headlights of a car careened toward her.

13

"Hello, Stefanie." Trisha smiled her glossy, superior smile. Behind her, Hunter made a quick turn toward their table. His gaze skated over Stefanie as if she were a grease spot on the floor.

This isn't so bad. I can handle this. Better to be a grease spot than wife of a cheater, right?

"Hi, Trisha."

Trisha's gaze dropped to Stefanie's plate, and Stefanie realized that in her nervousness she'd piled on enough food for three people. Trisha's own plate held only fruit salad and a few raw vegetables. *So Trisha isn't one of those miracle women who can eat anything and stay slim, after all.* Stefanie smiled. And the smile knocked a hairline crack into Trisha's plastic composure.

"What a surprise to see you here," Trisha said.

"Yes, isn't it?" Stefanie started to turn away, then stopped short. Within the frame of the jade collar, resting on Trisha's flawless skin —

"Where did you get that cameo?" Stefanie gasped.

Trisha's hand flew to her throat. The silhouette was delicately carved in pale-green jade and surrounded by an oval of old-fashioned gold filigree. It hung from a thin gold chain around her throat. "Hunter gave it —" Trisha glanced at Hunter, then narrowed her eyes at Stefanie. "My jewelry is none of your concern."

"That's my mother's cameo! I couldn't find it when I moved out of the house!"

This time Stefanie saw venom in the look Trisha shot Hunter. "Don't be ridiculous. This came from an antique shop in Portland." She smoothed the pendant possessively, but something in Stefanie's astonished face apparently jarred her again. In an about-face, her silk-clad shoulder moved in a dismissive shrug. "It's just cheap costume jewelry. I only wore it because it matched my jumpsuit."

"That is my mother's cameo," Stefanie repeated. "My mother gave it to me on my sixteenth birthday, and her mother gave it to her on her sixteenth birthday."

Stefanie remembered her mother lovingly fastening the gold chain around her neck. She remembered how the green jade had looked cool but radiated a wonderful warmth against her skin. She'd felt a tender heartlink with the women who had come before her.

Stefanie had treasured the necklace then and treasured it even more after her mother had died. She'd searched and searched for it when she was moving out of the house. She'd continued to keep an eye out for it, hoping it might turn up in some unlikely box or drawer.

Now it hung around Trisha's throat.

Unmindful of the full plate in her hands, Stefanie took a step forward. A crab puff skipped to the floor. "I want my cameo back. I want it *now*."

Trisha took a step backward. Her green eyes widened in alarm. "Stefanie, you're making a ridiculous scene."

Stefanie knew her voice had risen when she demanded the necklace. People were staring. She didn't care.

Briefly, Stefanie's gaze shot to Hunter. He was watching the confrontation as if he'd never seen either woman before. His aloof attitude made Stefanie's hands shake. He knew the truth about the cameo. He knew how much she treasured it.

"I want the necklace," Stefanie repeated. She heard the growled threat in her voice as if it were someone else speaking.

"And what else do you want?" Trisha demanded. Her voice turned shrill. "My engagement ring? Well, you're not getting it either!" She lifted her left hand and shook the ring in Stefanie's face. Stefanie looked past it and saw only the treasured cameo nestled against Trisha's skin.

She wasn't certain if she lunged for the necklace . . . if Trisha lifted her plate in self-defense and Stefanie's plate clashed with it . . . or if she did do what Trisha suddenly shrieked.

"She threw her plate at me! She *threw* it!"

Stefanie saw the scene through the veil of claustrophobia that had descended around her. Plates on the floor, salads and sauces on Trisha's face, in her hair, and cascading down the front of her jumpsuit. People staring. A harsh voice croaked.

"The necklace is mine, and I am going to get it, Trisha. I am going to get my necklace!"

The claustrophobia clutched her. Her head felt light, detached, but her body was too heavy to move. Her tongue clung to the roof of her mouth. It felt thick and foreign, and she struggled to speak before the ability vanished. "You stole my husband, Trisha. You stole my house. You got away with that. But you are not going to get away with stealing my mother's necklace!"

She was sitting on a hard chair. Above, the sky was blue and cloudless. Sunshine warmed the damp spots blotching the front of her dress. A bit of lettuce clung to the heel of her shoe. She wiggled her fingers. Lily's arm clasped her shoulders.

"You okay, sweetie?" Lily asked anxiously. She brushed at a damp spot on the dress. "I tried to clean you up a bit. I thought the fresh air out here in back of the restaurant might help."

"How long have I been here?"

Lily glanced at the watch on her freckled arm. "Oh, maybe twenty minutes. You ran out the front door — don't you remember, hon?"

"Everything is kind of . . . blurry." She looked up into Lily's concerned eyes. She tried to smile. "Did I do anything really awful?"

"I'm not sure what happened. I heard this big commotion, and I ran out of the kitchen just in time to see you shove that woman —"

"Shove her?" Stefanie repeated. "I *shoved* her?"

"Oh, you gave her a good one all right. Someone grabbed her to keep her from hitting the floor. Then a couple of people got hold of you. I guess they thought you were going to attack her or something."

"Attack?" *I don't attack. Or do I?*

"But you broke away and ran for the door. All the time that woman kept screaming bloody murder. And she's good at it! You should have heard the fit she threw here one time when she snagged her fancy dress on a chair. A spoiled-brat temper tantrum if I ever saw one. Anyway, I went out the door after you. You were trying to get in your car, but the door was locked." She patted Stefanie's arm. "It's a good thing your purse and keys were still in the dining room, because you were in no condition to drive."

"I'm sorry. I guess I lost my temper. And then everything gets . . . blurry."

"Blurry" didn't begin to cover what had happened. The time between when she'd stared at the spilled food and right then wasn't blurry; it was gone, vanished in one of those frightening episodes of lost minutes. And during that time, she'd shoved Trisha, perhaps even tried to attack her.

Lord, forgive me! "Have I said anything while I've been sitting here?"

"No, you've just seemed kind of dazed." Lily picked off the bit of lettuce clinging to Stefanie's heel. "Who wouldn't be, after such an unpleasant scene? That Hunter, he should have his head examined."

"I —" Stefanie tried to swallow, but her mouth felt clogged with cotton. "I'll go find my purse and keys —"

"They're right here." Lily pulled the purse out from under the chair. "Sweetie, I'm sorry, but I'm going to have to get back to work?" The uplift at the end of the statement added an anxious question: Are you going to be okay now?

"I'm fine," Stefanie assured her. "And I'll pay for any damage I caused."

"Don't worry about it." With a bit of fire in her eyes Lily added, "If there's anything to pay, we'll send the bill to your ex. As I see it, it was all his fault anyway."

Lily went back inside the restaurant. Stefanie sat in the chair a few minutes longer to let the lingering disorientation dissipate then drove home with extreme caution. Sherlock raced down from the back porch to meet her when she got out of the car. She'd filled his escape hole with rocks and put him in the backyard before church. She didn't care that he'd dug a new exit. She was too grateful for the enthusiasm of his one-dog welcoming committee. She knelt and threw her arms around him and buried her face in his shaggy coat.

"Can you believe it? I threw a plate of food at her. I shoved her! I might have done even more if someone hadn't stopped me."

Sherlock offered no criticism, just comforting licks.

Stefanie changed into jeans and an old cotton blouse. Sherlock watched as she stood at the open door of the refrigerator. *I should eat something. Skipping meals is not the way to weight control. Or a balanced mind.* She fingered a carton of yogurt. But at that moment, the thought of putting food into her stomach merely created a churn of rebellion. She settled for tossing Sherlock a bite of leftover ham. He caught it in midair. Then she saw milk and eggs and decided to make a custard for Val. Stefanie's mother had been a strong believer in the healing powers of old-fashioned custard. Stefanie also felt a need to do something in the good-deed category to balance out her incredible actions at the restaurant.

An hour and a half later, Pyrex dish of custard in hand, Stefanie rang the doorbell of Val's condo.

Val cowered a step backward when she opened the door. She flung a hand to her face and peered through spread fingers. "Don't throw it, please!"

Stefanie balanced the dish against her hip. Val's melodrama made her laugh in spite of her astonishment. "I can't believe it. I know Julesburg is a gossip mill, but it's only been a couple of hours. Who told you?"

Val, in pink shorts, a gray sweatshirt, and bare feet, motioned Stefanie inside. Scarlet polish on her toenails emphasized the smooth sheen of her bottle-tanned legs. "I drove down to the store to get something for my stomach." Val gestured to a package of Rolaids and a bottle of Mylanta on the kitchen counter. "The big topic of conversation was this knock-down, drag-out battle you and Trisha had right in the middle of the Singing Whale. I'm sorry I missed it. I'd have led a cheering section for you."

Stefanie set the dish of custard on the counter beside the Rolaids. "It was not a knock-down-drag-out battle," she protested.

"No?" Val got bowls from the cupboard and started dishing up the custard. Her enthusiasm suggested her stomach felt better. "I heard you slugged her like you were trying out for the Golden Gloves."

"I did not! Although I'm not exactly proud of what did happen."

They stood on opposite sides of the counter separating the kitchen and the

206

dining room, and Stefanie related a less flamboyant version of the events while they ate custard.

"But I can't actually remember everything," she admitted. "I had one of those . . . odd episodes. And during it, I guess I did give Trisha a rather hard shove."

"Was it self-defense? Did she shove you first?"

"I don't think so. I started it."

Val shook her head in disagreement. "No. Trisha started it when she stole your necklace. To say nothing of when she stole your husband. The woman is a menace to the institution of marriage." She hesitated, then added in a harsher tone, "She's an evil person, Stef. Beautiful on the outside, but all ugly and evil inside."

Stefanie looked up from her dish of custard. She'd always appreciated Val's loyalty although Val's condemnation of Trisha sometimes seemed a bit out of proportion. The escalation from caustic flippancy to a dark intensity of hatred startled her.

"I suppose I should call her and apologize," Stefanie said, glancing at Val's phone. "I don't suppose they make an appropriate card to cover a food assault."

Val ignored Stefanie's attempt at lightness. "No way should you ever apologize to

Trisha." She slapped her palm on the counter. "That . . . *woman* deserves whatever she got and a whole lot worse. If I'd been there, I'd have jumped right in the middle of her while she was down and danced a flamenco on her husband-stealing bones. And then clawed her eyes out. After all she's done to you!"

In spite of how shaken she was by what had happened at the Singing Whale, Stefanie couldn't help laughing. "Do you even know how to flamenco?"

Val returned the smile and waved her spoon. "No. But I'd give it a good try. And Trisha would know she'd been stomped on."

The laughter caught in Stefanie's throat. "It was a terrible thing for me to do. I'd just come from church . . ." She grabbed a tissue from the box on the counter. She swiped at her nose, surprised at the closeness of tears. "Not a Christian thing to do."

"It isn't as bad as what she did to you."

"That isn't the way being a Christian works. You don't pay back evil for evil."

"I thought you were soured on the Christian stuff."

Stefanie twirled her spoon in the creamy custard. "I don't know what I am," she admitted. An unrelated thought occurred to her. "Maybe Trisha will file a complaint for assault against me. She can probably sue me."

"Sue her right back for stealing your husband! I read about a woman winning a case like that not long ago. Of course, the only problem with suing is that you might not get money. They might just award you custody of Hunter. And that would hardly be winning."

Stefanie set her dish and spoon in the kitchen sink. Val's dolphin-shaped clock showed almost 4:00.

"I'd better get home. I promised Sherlock a run on the beach. Want to come?"

"No, but thanks anyway, hon. Something has come up."

"Oh?" Stefanie tilted her head to study her friend. "That has the sound of male involvement."

"Actually, Damon called."

"Damon?"

"My ex."

"Oh. I guess I've never heard you call him anything but the Silver-Tongued Rat."

"You're going to think I'm a complete idiot or a wimp or something, but when he called this morning and asked if I'd meet him over in Dutton Bay for dinner this evening, I said okay. I know it doesn't make much sense, the way I've always bad-mouthed him . . ." Val smiled with a hint of self-conscious embarrassment.

"I've always suspected you still had a soft place in your heart for him."

"The soft place may be in my head," Val admitted. "But you're right. Something is still there. We'll see how today goes."

"For the best, I hope."

Val followed Stefanie to the door. "What are you going to do now about the cameo necklace?"

It was a question Stefanie had not yet considered. "I don't think there's anything I can do." Yelling that she was going to get the necklace back, that Trisha wasn't going to get away with stealing her mother's cameo, had been a hollow threat. She had no way to carry it out.

"Too bad you didn't just yank it off Trisha's greedy little neck and run with it. She certainly has no right to it."

True. Trisha had no right to the necklace. *But what did my ugly scene accomplish? I look like a crazed ex-wife. I feel foolish and ashamed. And Trisha still has the cameo.*

Stefanie took an ecstatic Sherlock for a run on the beach. He found fascinating scraps of driftwood, bit at incoming waves, and dug holes like some mad pirate searching for buried treasure. Stefanie found a tiny treasure of her own, a lovely red carnelian agate that glowed in her palm. By the time they returned home, the unpleasantness of the day had dimmed. She even had appetite enough to fix a bacon and tomato sandwich.

Ryan called while she was eating. Stefanie started to tell him about her confrontation with Trisha, then backed away from the embarrassing confession. She told him about the beach run with Sherlock instead. The almost-nightly phone conversations had eased the tension between them, but she was still aware of their investigator/suspect status. She also was not completely convinced that Ryan's return to Julesburg was solely for vacation reasons.

Yet that night, it wasn't the arson or Ryan's suspicions that kept her from sleeping. It was Trisha and the necklace and her own inability to do anything about the situation. Possession, as the old saying went, was nine-tenths of the law, and Trisha had possession of the cameo.

Stefanie threw the bedcovers back and joined Sherlock at the window seat. *I have no way to prove the necklace is really mine. No purchase receipt. No one to identify and verify that this is the cameo my mother gave to me.*

Her hand paused as she stroked Sherlock's shaggy back. There was one way she could get it back . . .

No. Impossible. Unthinkable. Possibly even illegal.

14

No, surely not illegal. The cameo was hers. Because of Hunter's sly manipulations with the house ownership — which she suspected may have backfired on him — she was part owner of the house until the legal problems with the company ownership were settled. Her idea of how to reclaim what belonged to her was a bit irregular. Her lawyer would surely frown on it. But it wouldn't be breaking the law, would it?

Yet she couldn't quite picture herself skulking in the shadows, peering around corners, climbing through windows. What if she got caught? Even if it wasn't illegal, even if she had the moral high ground, getting caught would eclipse the scene at the Singing Whale in embarrassment and humiliation. Hunter and Trisha, and no doubt their lawyers as well, would have a field day with it.

And getting caught was a very real danger. She had keys to the house, but the locks were undoubtedly different. She'd have to find another way to get inside. What if she made a mistake and crawled through a window . . . and into their laps?

It's a totally preposterous scheme. Right up there with Val's idea of dancing a flamenco on Trisha's "husband-stealing bones."

There was another way to get the cameo back, although it was slower and more frustrating. The cameo belonged to her; she shouldn't have to bargain or beg for it. But the other way was surely a more sensible and acceptable plan than leaping into a harebrained cat-burglar scheme.

She called the Hagstrom & Standish legal offices in Coos Bay first thing Monday morning. Her attorney, Miles Hagstrom, called back that afternoon. The call came in the middle of one of her aerobic classes. She dashed to the office.

"Thanks for returning my call, Mr. Hagstrom."

"I was planning to call you anyway. We need to schedule another conference with Mr. Blackwell and his attorney concerning the mill fire and the situation with the insurance company.

"Awkward as joining forces with Mr. Blackwell may be," Miles Hagstrom continued in his formal manner, "it's important that we present a united front to the insurance company."

"I can come to a meeting almost any time. But first . . ."

She explained about her mother's cameo necklace and how Trisha was claiming it as her own. She also offered details on the messy confrontation at the Singing Whale.

His reaction was on the disapproving edge of neutral. "That doesn't sound like you, Stefanie."

"It isn't like me. I've never done anything like that before in my life. I'm shocked and I'm ashamed and I'm sorry." She paused. "But what I'm wondering is if the necklace could be included with the settlement on mill ownership."

"It's a rather odd request, but we can try." She could almost see him frowning and giving his gold-rimmed glasses a tweak with his forefinger.

"I'm willing to make concessions to get the necklace."

"Concessions?" The attorney sounded taken aback. "What sort of concessions?"

"Whatever concessions it takes," she said. "I think it's time to move on."

"I see." The reserve in the attorney's voice did not surprise Stefanie. Miles Hagstrom was not a man of concessions. But she heard an unexpected note of understanding when he added, "In the long run, I believe that could prove the wisest course of action."

"I want to do it as quickly as possible."

"Nothing, I'm afraid, happens quickly in the legal arena. But I'll lay this on the table with Mr. Blackwell's attorney immediately. What is the necklace worth?"

"For me, it's a priceless treasure. As for actual monetary value, I have no idea. It's jade surrounded by gold filigree, and it's old, and that's all I know. I never had it appraised."

"Very well. My secretary will call you as soon as we hear anything from Mr. Blackwell's attorney. May I suggest offering to sign off on the house first? Then, if they balk, we'll up the offer. By the way has Miss Duvall pressed assault charges against you?"

"Not yet. But I suppose she may."

"Let me know if she does." The note of protectiveness in the attorney's voice surprised her. "I don't handle cases like that, but I can refer you to someone tough who does."

Val phoned Monday evening to report on dinner with the Silver-Tongued Rat. She was calling him Damon now.

"We had a wonderful time, Stef. I'd almost forgotten how funny and sweet and endearing he can be."

Stefanie hesitated. She knew nothing about Val's ex-husband other than what Val had told her. He'd always sounded like a first-class rat, but she had to grant that an ex-wife's comments could be colored by a bit of prejudice. Perhaps Damon was a wonderful guy who'd learned his lesson.

"Did you talk about . . . the problem that separated you?"

"Not really. That's behind us. I think we both decided it would be better, in the words of some wise old sage, to let sleeping dogs lie. I know how sorry he is, without hearing some big apologetic speech."

I think I'd have preferred to hear a "big apologetic speech." "I hope it all works out for the best for you."

"Thanks for being such an understanding friend. I appreciate your not jumping on a soapbox to give me advice. I wouldn't listen to it anyway."

But is staying off that soapbox really what I should be doing? Perhaps I should be jumping on that soapbox and pleading and screaming at the top of my lungs. "I don't want to see you get hurt again, Val."

"I won't. This time it's going to work."

Miles Hagstrom's secretary called Wednesday morning while Stefanie was working in the office at Fit 'n' Fun. "Would you hold for Mr. Hagstrom, please."

Stefanie skipped the preliminaries when the lawyer came on the line. "What about my cameo necklace?"

"Mr. Blackwell's attorney tells us that Mr. Blackwell says the necklace belonged to *his* mother. That you did wear it during your marriage to him, but it was never actually a gift to you. He also said it now belongs to his fianceé, Miss Duvall."

Astonishment momentarily blocked Stefanie's fury at the blatant lies. "He won't give it up even if I sign over the house?"

"At the moment, that appears to be the situation. Actually . . . this is pure speculation, of course . . . I believe a resistance on Miss Duvall's part may be the problem."

"Surely Trisha would rather have the house than the necklace!"

"The house is mortgaged to the hilt. That might enter into her reasoning. Or she may simply feel that if she hangs tough, she can have it all. I also feel there is a possibility of some conflict between Mr. Blackwell and Miss Duvall."

Stefanie recalled Trisha's venomous glance at Hunter in the Singing Whale. Had he tried to make himself into a sentimental hero by presenting her with a necklace that had supposedly belonged to his mother? Had Trisha suddenly realized he'd lied to her?

That might make Trisha more stubborn about the cameo — Trisha liked snatching someone else's treasures, whether the prize was husband, house, or necklace. If only she'd just yanked the necklace off Trisha's neck and run with it!

"We do have a meeting scheduled with Mr. Blackwell and his attorney, but it's not until next Thursday at 2:00. We'll meet in the temporary offices of Cougar Creek Timber Products on Manzanita Street."

That was over a week away. "Why the delay?"

"After the altercation in the restaurant, Mr. Blackwell's fianceé claims to be suffering from a debilitating 'nervous strain.' She is presently in seclusion."

"I don't believe we're obligated to include her in the meeting!"

"True. But Mr. Blackwell has also just left town. I presume he's joining Miss Duvall somewhere, although his attorney did not specify that."

Hunter and Trisha both out of town?

"I think you and I should also meet for a private discussion before the meeting with Mr. Blackwell and his attorney. Would next

Tuesday, here in my office at 10:00, be convenient for you?"

"Yes, that will be fine. Thank you." Stefanie hung up the phone. But her thoughts were not on the meeting. They were elsewhere, and her hands felt slick with nervous perspiration.

Because the idea was back. Back and crackling with supercharged energy.

15

It was still just as preposterous and outrageous an idea as ever. But with Hunter and Trisha being out of town, there wasn't as much danger of getting caught.

Stefanie was curious about where they were. The exclusive resort up at Salishan? Mt. Hood? Perhaps they'd gone to San Francisco. Wherever they were, Hunter was no doubt charging it up as company expense. The accountant had only recently discovered that was how Hunter handled a good many personal expenditures.

Irrelevant. What's important is that the house will be empty for a few days.

Of course, Trisha could have taken the necklace with her, but the old-fashioned cameo wasn't Trisha's style. Especially not if her "seclusion" was being enjoyed at some ritzy resort.

A final argument clinched Stefanie's decision. If she looked, and the cameo wasn't there, what would she have lost? Nothing.

It was worth the gamble.

★ ★ ★

Stefanie cautiously straightened a leg to relieve the spreading numbness. *What time is it?* She felt as if she'd been crouched behind the wet bushes half the night. Rainwater from an earlier drizzle spilled from the slick rhododendron leaves and spattered her already damp black leggings. Nervous perspiration trickled down her ribs. The soggy stocking cap itched against her neck.

Faint light filtered through the drapes covering the wall of glass in the living room. Was someone inside the house? No, she didn't think so. By then, late Friday evening, Hunter and Trisha were surely enjoying a romantic reunion well away from Julesburg. She'd seen no shadow of movement against the drapes. No other lights had gone on or off. Her straining ears caught no murmur of TV.

The light in the living room was probably set by timer to come on when darkness fell. But she couldn't be certain of that. Maybe they had a housekeeper in residence. Stefanie ran her thumb over the sharp-toothed edge of one of the three keys in her pocket.

Below, the lights of the town glimmered through the damp mist. They faintly lit the redwood gazebo she'd designed and the

222

graceful Japanese maple she'd nurtured. Even the hanging planters she'd chosen still hung from the deck. Yet she felt no twinge of nostalgia, no sense of loss, no regrets. She fingered the keys again. The only thing that interested her in the house was her mother's cameo necklace.

And I'm not going to find it lurking out here in the bushes.

She grabbed her flashlight and stood up. The tall bushes showered her head and shoulders with cold spray. She crept along the narrow space between the rhododendrons and the thick tangle of natural growth edging up to the property line. A blackberry tendril snagged her cheek. She felt a wetness of blood when she put her hand to her face. She brushed it away.

She quickened her pace. No neighbors could spot her there. The closest house on that side was almost a quarter mile of thick foliage away. The only danger of discovery came from inside.

The shortest route to the master bedroom was through the sliding-glass doors opening from the deck to the living room, then up the curved staircase. One of her keys was to the sliding doors, if it still fit. But if the house wasn't empty, she was most likely to run into someone that way.

If she went around to the driveway side of the house, the motion-sensitive outdoor lights would catch her in their quick snap to attention. If the house wasn't empty, someone would come to check.

Then what? Then she would pull the stocking cap low on her face and run.

She edged around the corner of the house and eyed the pale expanse of concrete in the circular drive. The first motion-sensitive light didn't catch her; she slid behind its area of surveillance. The next one trapped her. She stood frozen in its arc. For a moment she saw herself as she must look standing there: a statue in an amateur burglar outfit. Visible as a black cat on a white sofa.

Nothing happened. No door opened, no more lights came on, no scream erupted.

Stefanie crept swiftly to the single door beside the triple-car garage attached to the house. She bit her tongue as she slipped the key into the lock. It worked! No need for jumping to risky Plan B involving a window.

Doorknob in hand, the moment of elation plummeted. Hunter had been talking about installing a sophisticated security alarm system even before she moved out. Had he done it? Would bells ring or whistles shrill? Or would she not even know an alarm had gone off until someone showed up to arrest her?

It's still half my house. My house, my cameo. I can't be arrested for entering my own house to claim something that belongs to me . . . can I?

But she knew Miles Hagstrom wouldn't approve of her behavior. Neither would Ryan. Nor would the Lord.

But none of them are getting my cameo back for me.

Stefanie cracked the door open. She let what felt like a small eternity pass before deciding there was no alarm system. The door clicked softly as she closed it behind her. Darkness instantly enveloped her, and the all-too-familiar claustrophobia circled like a hungry vulture. A light-headed emptiness swallowed all sense of direction. Up? Down? She felt herself tilting, floating. In a panic she pounded the button on the flashlight.

The light melted the darkness. Her claustrophobia receded. She gave herself a few moments longer, then cautiously flicked the flashlight beam around the garage. It revealed only one of Cougar Creek Timber Products' brown-and-tan pickups. Both Hunter's Porsche and Trisha's Mercedes were gone.

Which, of course, did not necessarily

prove the house was empty. There could still be a housekeeper.

Carefully, a fraction of an inch at a time, Stefanie turned the knob on the door opening into the mud room.

Gloves! How could I not have thought to wear gloves? She remembered Randy Wilson inking her fingerprints. She scrubbed at the knob with the edge of her jacket. She'd have to go back and wipe off the outside knob, but she decided to do that on her way out.

She rubbed her damp palms against her leggings. A trace of her presence probably wouldn't matter. It was unlikely Ben Mosely would dust for fingerprints. And Trisha had to know the cameo had belonged to Stefanie's mother. Once Trisha realized it was gone, she'd probably ignore the loss. She might even think she'd simply misplaced the necklace. That thought soothed the roar along Stefanie's nerves to a hum.

Stefanie moved cautiously through the kitchen and dining room. The house had a different scent than what she remembered. Not a food scent, but something faintly perfumy. Incense? Too heavy for her taste. The dining room table and chairs were unchanged. She peered into the living room. New furniture there, but empty.

Stefanie tiptoed up the curved stairway.

She paused at the top and listened. Nothing but the hammer of her own heartbeat. She headed down the carpeted hallway to the master bedroom. She kept the flashlight aimed low and paused at the open doorway. Searching with only the beam of the flashlight would be difficult. Did she dare to turn on the bedroom light? Would someone in town look up and notice? Probably not, and her search would go faster with good visibility. Her hand found the familiar switch just inside the door. Lamplight flooded the room.

Trisha had completely redone the bedroom. Burgundy silk canopied a huge new bed, and the walls were a lighter shade of velvet-flocked wallpaper. Tall crystal lamps with cream silk shades flanked the bed, and smaller matching lamps lit the dressing table. The dark eye of an enormous TV stared from a corner.

Stefanie jumped when she saw several slim, dark figures poised across the room. She swallowed a nervous titter as she realized the Catwoman figures were her, reflected in the triple-sectioned mirror of the dressing table.

On the oversized dressing table, the mannequin of a hand with fingers elegantly spread held a dozen necklaces. Stefanie inspected the draped necklaces, but the cameo was not among them. A mirrored tray held an assortment of bottles and jars. Trisha favored Eternity and White Diamonds perfume. Stefanie jumped when a face stared up at her from the tray; then she realized it was her own reflection. Her skin was pale, her eyes enormous.

She shoved the padded bench aside and started opening drawers. She wanted to get it over with; she hadn't realized she'd feel like such an intruder in what had once been her own bedroom.

She found a velvet-covered jewelry box and swiftly rifled through the contents. Bracelets, earrings, a pin in the shape of a ruby-eyed cat. It was mostly just costume jewelry, but a pair of emerald earrings looked genuine. No jade cameo, though.

She searched through more drawers of the dressing table, then through two chests of drawers that stood against the far wall. Stefanie felt a guilty distaste pawing through everything, but she did it anyway.

The adjoining bathroom boasted a beauty boutique of lotions and creams and hair-care products. No jewelry. She moved on to the walk-in closet. Several small cartons stacked on the shelves. A possibility?

She was digging through a box when an

unexpected noise turned her as immobile as that elegant hand on the dressing table. A car out on the road or turning into the driveway? She strained to hear, but rows of clothes muffled the sound.

She grabbed the flashlight at her feet. Had Hunter asked Ben Mosely to drive by and check on the house while he and Trisha were away? Had Hunter and Trisha come back early? Stefanie strained to catch any sound, but all she heard was the clamor of her own heartbeat.

Lord, this is the most foolish thing I've ever done, isn't it? I'm sorry . . . please, just help me get out of here! She slapped the lid back on the box and threw it on the closet shelf. She was almost to the bedroom door when she heard the unmistakable rumble of a garage door rolling up. Hunter had often complained that they'd made a mistake putting the master bedroom over the garage.

Stefanie tried to think what to do. She couldn't get down the stairs and out a door before whoever was in the garage entered the house. But maybe she could make it down the hall to another bedroom and hide there.

No, she had a better idea. The drapes hid a sliding-glass door to a small balcony. It was a risky drop from the balcony to the

229

main deck below, but she'd rather chance a broken limb than be caught in the bedroom.

She ran toward the wall of burgundy drapes, then darted back to flick the light switch. Without the giveaway light on, whoever was in the garage would never suspect someone had been in the bedroom.

Then she groaned. The light in the closet still shone like a beacon. She had no time to rush across the bedroom and turn it off. She pawed the drapes, searching for the opening to the sliding-glass door. Muffled noises rose from below now, and Stefanie could hear a door opening and closing.

She cracked the flashlight against the glass, bumped her knee, and heard fabric rip as her foot tangled in the drapes.

No footsteps sounded on the lush carpet, but light suddenly flared around her. Her heart plummeted. *I'm caught.*

She waited, rigid. No sound. No voice. Nothing.

Then she heard a click.

She couldn't place the sound, yet it was not totally unfamiliar. The switch of a lamp? A coin dropped on the nightstand? She waited for the click to come again. Her muscles cramped, her breathing stopped. The drapes closed in around her, tightening, suffocating. Stefanie fought the panic. *It's happening. One of those episodes —*

"Come out from behind the drapes. With your hands up."

Stefanie recognized the voice. She fumbled to free herself from the tangle of drapes. She'd simply turn, march past a dumbfounded Trisha, let herself out of the house, and cope with the consequences later.

"Come out now. Or I'll shoot."

Stefanie realized then what the click was. Her grandfather had thought everyone should know how to shoot, and he'd taken her out in the woods to target practice a few times. That click was the cocking of a pistol.

Stefanie knew she couldn't just walk out now. She carefully freed herself from the entangling fabric, raised her hands over her head, and turned to face Trisha.

Trisha held the gun with both hands stretched out in front of her. Her legs were spread, as if she'd had target-shooting training. "You! I thought —" The barrel momentarily tilted downward as she stared in astonishment at Stefanie. She yanked it back into position.

"What are you doing here?" she demanded.

"I came to get my mother's cameo necklace."

Trisha barked a shrill laugh. "You're burglarizing the house for that piece of junk? That's priceless. By the time Hunter's lawyer gets through with you on this!"

Stefanie edged toward the dressing table. She wanted to get out of the line of fire; the hole in the metal barrel looked like a bottomless eye. Huge. Deadly. Even if Trisha didn't intend to shoot, her finger might slip on the trigger.

"I'm not burglarizing. I didn't break in. I have a key, and the house belongs to the company, so it's still half mine." Stefanie's hands were still over her head, flashlight dangling. She was in no position to antagonize a woman with her finger on a trigger, but she added, "And the cameo is all mine."

Trisha didn't appear impressed by her arguments. She seemed calmer, and Stefanie could see that she was thinking.

"Put the flashlight down. Stand over there." Trisha motioned with the gun to a spot in the center of the room. "Keep your hands up."

Stefanie moved like an actress taking her assigned spot on a movie set. Without breaking eye contact with Trisha, she set the flashlight at her feet and raised her hands again.

"I didn't see a car," Trisha said. "How did you get here?"

"I walked."

"Alone?"

"Yes."

"Does anyone know you're here?"

The calculated question made Stefanie shiver. "Would you mind putting that gun away now?"

"No, I don't think so." Trisha's pleasant tone seemed more menacing than threats. "And keep your hands up," she added when Stefanie started to lower them.

"Are you going to call the police?"

"I'm considering it."

For the first time, Stefanie noticed what Trisha was wearing: dressy white pants, heels, a pale lilac jacket over a white blouse. A cascade of delicate gold chains circled her throat. Stefanie also noted a faint flush on Trisha's cheeks, something more than artfully applied blush. Nerves? One drink too many?

"Where's Hunter?" Stefanie asked.

Trisha's eyes seemed to say *none of your business!* but she shrugged instead of speaking. Maybe she didn't even know where Hunter was. Trisha hadn't dashed off to spend her "seclusion" away from Julesburg, after all.

"Look, I'm sorry about this," Stefanie said. "It was a big mistake on my part. I apologize. I had no right —"

"That's true. You had no right at all to invade my bedroom. But I believe it is a fact of law that a person does have a right to defend herself in her home." Trisha adjusted her double-handed grip on the gun by a fraction of an inch.

"I just want my mother's cameo. I don't have a gun. I'm not threatening you!"

"Aren't you? I believe there are any number of people who can testify that in the Singing Whale you definitely threatened me with physical violence."

"I spilled some food! I gave you a little shove —"

"You warned that I wasn't going to get away with 'stealing' what you claimed was your mother's cameo." Trisha tilted her head reflectively. Her manicured finger on the trigger looked dangerously competent. "Now you've broken into my home. How do I know that you don't have a weapon and intend to attack me again?"

"I can't believe this! Are you threatening to shoot me?"

Trisha shrugged. "I'm tired of you and your lawyer harassing us at every turn." An angry fire burned in her blue eyes. "I'm tired of gritting my teeth and waiting while you greedily play Hunter like a hooked fish! I've warned Hunter —"

"Hunter's the one who's been greedy. He's the one who's delayed settlement because he wants to grab everything! And you stole him, remember?"

Even as she said the words, Stefanie knew arguing with Trisha was pointless. Surely Trisha wouldn't shoot her. She was a husband stealer not a murderer.

But the fire in Trisha's eyes seemed to chill to something colder. Her delicate lips compressed in a frown of concentration, as if she were working some complex mathematical problem in her head. *Computing the number of minutes left in my life? Calculating whether she can get rid of me once and for all . . . and get away with murder?*

Stefanie knew if she waited, a bullet might answer those questions for her. She took a step backward and kicked the flashlight upward in Trisha's direction. It hit Trisha's arm just as she pulled the trigger. The thunderclap of the gun joined the crash of shattering glass as the bullet smashed the triple-sectioned mirror.

Stefanie ran. She tried to dodge around Trisha, but Trisha stepped forward, blocking her way. Stefanie crashed into her, and

Trisha tumbled backward. They went down together, Stefanie sprawled on top. "Get off me!" Trisha shrieked. She rammed her head forward, and Stefanie's mind reeled as her jaw connected with Trisha's forehead. She shook her head, trying to clear her mind. The gun was still in Trisha's hand . . . wobbling, but frantically trying to focus on Stefanie.

Stefanie clamped a hand around Trisha's wrist and forced it back against the carpet. "Let . . . go . . . of . . . the . . . gun!" she said through gritted teeth. Trisha answered with a savage slash of fingernails that barely missed Stefanie's eye. An unexpected twist of Trisha's lithe body sprawled Stefanie sideways and broke her hold on the wrist. Trisha sat up, still clutching the gun, and whipped the barrel toward Stefanie. Stefanie slammed her forearm down on Trisha's arm. The gun flew across the room and ricocheted to land in the doorway shattering a crystal lamp in its path. Stefanie scrambled to her feet. She fled along the hallway, sliding and stumbling down the stairs.

At the bottom of the curved staircase she stopped. She held out her hand and stared. *I have the gun!* Some subconscious guardian of self-preservation had made her scoop up the gun when she dashed out of the bedroom.

It fit her hand neatly. Her finger slipped around the trigger; it was a small gun in spite of the fact that the hole of the barrel had looked like a cannon when she stared into it. Compact but deadly. The metal felt warm in her hand —

She gave a small cry of revulsion and dropped it.

I've got to get out of here!

But if she left the gun lying there on the floor, Trisha might grab it and come after her. She bent to retrieve the gun and looked up just in time to see Trisha careening down the stairs at her, the jagged remains of the crystal lamp raised like a lance over her head.

16

The phone rang four times, and then the answering machine picked up. Ryan left his message after the beep.

"Hi, Stef. It's me, Ryan. I'm not going to be able to start my vacation this weekend after all. There's been an apartment fire in Spokane, and I have to fly over to investigate it. I should be back early next week. Take care of yourselves, and I'll be down as soon as I can. Tell Sherlock I miss him, okay? And — I miss you too, Stef."

He hung up the phone, surprised at how true his last statement was. He'd thought of Stefanie occasionally over the years . . . especially those first months after leaving Julesburg. But the memories were fleeting, nostalgic rather than yearning. Their reunion had been brief, and a tension and wariness lingered between them. He couldn't totally dislodge the thought that she could have hired the arsonist.

But visions of her jumped into his mind at improbable times of night or day. Stefanie laughing. Stefanie barefoot on the beach. The graceful swing of her body and the playful dance of her hazel eyes. The way her face had lit up when she recognized him. He wanted to protect her from the hurts of life. He wanted to help her renew her relationship with the Lord.

He'd wondered why God had marched him off to Julesburg. It was the last place he'd wanted to go. But he was eager as a kid yearning after a carnival ride to return there. He couldn't stop thinking about a pairing of moonlit footprints on the beach . . .

He glanced at his watch. So where was she at 10:30 on a Friday evening? Fit 'n' Fun didn't stay open that late. Perhaps she and Val were doing something together. Or maybe she was out on a date.

Do I have any right to hope she isn't?

Stefanie unlocked the back door and collapsed on the kitchen floor. Sherlock immediately plopped down beside her. She buried her face in his shaggy fur.

"Sherlock, you won't believe what a mess I've made of things!"

Her legs felt boneless, her nerves shredded. She saw the evening like a series of underlit video shots strung together.

Dripping shrubs . . . wet limbs whipping her face . . . Trisha crashing down the stairs . . . black cave of garage . . . blinding glare of car lights . . . Trisha's flushed face . . . open tunnel of the gun barrel targeted on her . . .

No, that wasn't how it went. She frowned as she tried to organize the progression. The garage came before Trisha aimed the gun. And car headlights? Where were they? But even the disjointed visual memories were not what most disturbed her.

It was the tingle in her hand, almost as if the gun had left some indelible imprint. A small weapon but heavy for its size. Not cold steel but warm metal. An acrid scent lingered. Gunpowder. She remembered it from long ago, shooting with her grandfather.

She shivered, feeling as if she had just stepped out of a nightmare. She discarded her jogging shoes in the laundry room. She'd worn the black pair, and they were covered with mud. Her hand hurt. She looked at it and saw that a fingernail had been torn to the quick.

When she got upstairs, she stared at herself in the mirror. Pine needles tangled in her hair. Ragged scratches on her cheek, from blackberry thorns or Trisha's slashing fingernails. Her stocking cap was gone.

Maybe she lost it when she was running home. Or maybe Trisha had it as a trophy to present to Hunter's lawyers.

Stefanie slumped down beside Sherlock again. "You should have bit me on the ankle and never let me do such a crazy thing." Sherlock slurped her cheek. She sighed and rested her head on his back. "I don't have anyone to blame but myself, do I? I jumped in and did it all by myself."

She took a hot shower and scrubbed her hands, trying to wash away the feel of the gun. Her knuckles were healed, but she needed a new Band-Aid on the torn fingernail.

Stefanie woke frequently in the night, floating in and out of disjointed scenes that hovered somewhere between memory and nightmare. But by the light of morning she felt less disoriented. She opened her bedroom window and looked out on a clear, sunny day. Sherlock planted his front feet on the window seat to look out and share the view with her. The sea sparkled in a dance of diamonds. The scent of the mill was gone, and the morning smelled fresh-washed, with just a hint of sun-warmed pine. A seagull floated by her window.

This is a day the Lord has made.

"It helps put last night in perspective,

doesn't it?" she asked Sherlock. There would certainly be consequences for the previous night's behavior. But she didn't feel abandoned by the Lord.

I blew it, didn't I, Lord? Here I am, talking to you now, and I should have had a long conversation with you before I got myself into this mess. I'm sorry, Lord. Can you forgive me for doing such an outrageous thing? And thank you, thank you so much for protecting me, for bringing me home safely, even though I didn't deserve your help. Awkwardly, like a runaway child returning home, she added, *I want to get back to where I once was with you, Lord. Back when I felt as if I were standing on a mountaintop with the angels singing.*

She felt composed after taking her situation to the Lord. She knew that God's forgiveness didn't necessarily cancel out worldly punishment for stupid mistakes. Trisha and Hunter, whatever lovers' quarrel they might be involved in at the moment, could unite to make good use of her foolish actions. But no matter what happened, she knew one thing: She was through battling. Not even her mother's treasured cameo was worth last night's shrieking, clawing, alley-cat fight.

Stefanie headed early to Fit 'n' Fun to tackle the bookwork and bill-paying. She saved Sherlock the trouble of digging his way out of the backyard and let him come with her. He spent his time greeting new arrivals or curled under her desk.

She tensed the first time the phone rang. She was resigned to the fact that something unpleasant was going to happen because of her entry into the house. And she wasn't looking forward to finding out what it was. But the call wasn't what she feared, just a man from the laundry service saying their towel delivery would be late that day.

Then Tina tore through the front door and into Stefanie's office. "What do you think about —" She stopped short when she saw Stefanie calmly sipping coffee and eating a banana. "You haven't heard, have you?"

"Heard what?"

"It was on the car radio just now. Trisha Duvall was murdered last night."

Stefanie rose from her swivel chair. "Murdered? How . . . who?"

"They aren't saying much, except that it was a gunshot wound. Hunter got home late last night and found her body in the living room."

"I can't believe it . . ." The garbled pictures from last night fluttered in Stefanie's head. She dropped the half-eaten banana on the desk. Her stomach knotted. How long after she left the house had it happened? How close had she come to crossing paths with the murderer? She must have been the last person to see Trisha alive.

No, not the last. The killer had been the last.

Had Stefanie left the door open? Had someone taken advantage of that to rob the house — and kill Trisha when she confronted him? Was Trisha's murder partly her fault?

Or was the murderer someone closer? Someone who didn't need an open door to enter. Someone who knew Trisha.

Hunter.

No, not Hunter. Hunter had abandoned Stefanie for Trisha. He loved Trisha. He planned to marry her. Surely he wouldn't kill her. Stefanie had suspected him of arson, and that was unwarranted. This suspicion was even more unwarranted.

"Are you okay?" Tina asked. She leaned across the desk and pushed a dazed Stefanie into the swivel chair.

"It's just so . . . shocking."

"You never think things like this will happen to someone you know." Tina hesitated and then said, "Somewhere I read that in mystery novels the butler did it, but in real life it's more likely to be the husband."

Stefanie swallowed. She looked up and their eyes met. "He wasn't actually her husband yet. Why would he want to kill her?"

Tina hesitated again. She was never one to pounce on someone's flaws. "Maybe she was seeing some other guy on the side."

Stefanie thought about how nicely Trisha had been dressed. Betrayal would send Hunter into a rage — but could it be a murderous rage?

He was so different from the man she thought she had married. She'd seen Hunter as ambitious, but not deceptive or ruthless. He'd concealed his self-centered streak well. He'd once been attentive and considerate, but the real Hunter Blackwell had emerged in his sleight-of-hand dealings with the mill ownership. His adultery. His lies about the cameo.

"Have you heard something about Trisha seeing someone else?" Stefanie asked bluntly.

"There's been gossip about her and one of the owners of Volkman Laser Systems. Or maybe it's the owner's son — Oh, dear, I shouldn't be speaking ill of the dead, should I?" Tina muttered. "Or of Hunter, either. He's probably devastated."

Tina hurried off to change clothes for the workday. Stefanie sat at her desk. Her first instinct was to call Ryan, but dragging him into the situation didn't really make sense. It had nothing to do with the arson. And besides, she had no way to contact him. She'd checked her answering machine just before leaving the house and found a message that he was flying to Spokane on a fire investigation.

What I should do is go to the police.

But the prospect of admitting to Ben that she'd sneaked into the house to rummage through Trisha's things in search of the cameo filled Stefanie with squeamish dread. She wondered if telling Ben would do any good. After all, she didn't see or hear anything; she didn't know anything.

But they would find her fingerprints on everything. She'd have to explain that. And she was morally obligated to tell the truth.

As it turned out, she didn't have to decide whether or not to go to the police. They came to her. With handcuffs.

17

Stefanie was leaning over a treadmill to adjust the dial. "There, that'll slow the speed so you can keep up," she told plump Ellie Buckmaster who was puffing as she clutched the rails.

"Thanks. I felt like I was trying to outrun my grandson."

Stefanie didn't even see the three officers, Ben Mosely plus two uniformed men from the county sheriff's office, until they surrounded the treadmill. Her hands on the treadmill dial became slippery with instant beads of perspiration.

There's nothing to be afraid of. I didn't do anything. She shouldn't have gone to the house, true. But she hadn't actually broken in, hadn't taken anything, not even what belonged to her.

She wiped a damp palm across her leotard and forced her hands to clasp each other in counterfeit calm. *I must not look nervous. Well, who wouldn't be nervous, with three armed officers closing in as if I'm headed for the*

"Did you want to see me about something?" She felt a quiver start deep in a leg muscle, but she kept her voice under control. "I — I'm really quite busy here." She tried to motion around the room, but her arm wouldn't lift.

Fit 'n' Fun had been buzzing with a nice energy, but now every machine had come to a stop. The only sound was the rustle of people shuffling and craning to see what was happening. Sherlock was sitting squarely between her feet. His usually floppy ears now stood erect with suspicion.

"Okay, I can explain about being at Hunter's house last night. I was intending to come in and talk to you about it later." She ignored the officers flanking her like attack dogs and spoke directly to Ben. "You probably heard about the run-in Trisha and I had at the Singing Whale? It was over a cameo necklace that had belonged to my mother —"

"You probably shouldn't say any more until you get an attorney, Miss Stefanie." Ben spoke with kindly compassion, but his eyes were as watchful as those of the other two men. He nodded toward one of the deputies. "Officer Bradley has a warrant."

Stefanie clutched the heavy ruff around

Sherlock's neck and fought a reeling light-headedness, the familiar feeling of claustrophobia. Sherlock strained his head around and licked her hand. The anxious slurp steadied her.

"A warrant for burglary?"

Ben suddenly glared at the other two officers. "Can't we do this in private?" Without waiting for an answer, he put an arm around Stefanie's shoulders and guided her from the workout room to her office. Stefanie knew that Ben didn't have to come with the deputies; Hunter's house was just outside the city limits, out of Ben's jurisdiction. But he'd come out of concern for her.

"You okay, Miss Stefanie?"

She nodded. Sherlock was locked against her legs again. His weight on her foot was oddly comforting. Officer Bradley eyed the dog with a certain wariness, but he stepped forward briskly. "You are under arrest, Mrs. Blackwell, for the murder of Trisha Duvall."

I'm not Mrs. Blackwell now! This can't be happening!

Officer Bradley pulled Stefanie's hands behind her and clicked handcuffs around her wrists as smoothly as snapping a leash on a dog's collar. She tested the cuffs, stretching the connecting links between the metal bands. They made her feel not only helpless but strangely isolated, as if those small circles of metal had instantly shut her off from the normal world.

"It's standard procedure, Miss Stefanie," Ben said as the other officer began an impersonal recitation of her Miranda rights. The words about her right to remain silent and have an attorney only half reached her.

They think I murdered Trisha.

"We also have warrants to search your house and car," Officer Bradley said.

"There's a key to the back door under the bottom step. The car's in the garage."

The deputies looked surprised at her reply, and Stefanie was suddenly angry with herself. *Why am I helping them?*

She looked to Ben. "Ben, you know I didn't do this! You know I didn't kill her!"

Yet for all the regret and compassion in Ben's eyes, she wasn't sure he believed her. "It's time to go now," he said. "Officers Bradley and McClendon will use their patrol car to transport you to the county jail. I won't be going along."

"Stef, what do you want me to do here?" Tina called frantically as the trio of officers herded Stefanie to the door.

Stefanie stopped at the open door. "I — I should be back before long. As soon as I get this . . . this mix-up straightened out. So

250

just do whatever you can to keep things running here. And . . . take care of Sherlock, please?"

I'll be back before long. Do I believe that?
No.

The last thing Stefanie saw before Ben closed the door to Fit 'n' Fun was Sherlock struggling and whining to come with her, and Tina clutching his collar with both hands to hold him back.

The highway to the county seat wound inland along the river that entered the ocean at Dutton Bay. Usually Stefanie enjoyed the drive. Branches canopied the narrow road and cattle grazed in green pastures. Forested slopes climbed steeply from the valley. On this trip she was aware only of the hard metal cuffs clamped around her wrists and the diamond-patterned grid of the metal barrier separating her from the officers in the front seat.

At the county jail she was searched and booked, photographed and fingerprinted. There was a bit of confusion about her name.

"I use Canfield, my maiden name, now," she insisted when they tried to book her under the name Blackwell. "Stefanie Canfield."

Then they took her to an interrogation

room for questioning. She remembered Ben's warning and asked to have her attorney present before she answered any questions.

But her call to Miles Hagstrom was not helpful; he and his law-firm partner were out of town for the weekend. Officer Bradley told her she could be assigned an attorney, but she declined the offer. After a brief conference outside her hearing, she was led to a cell.

The jail had two cells reserved for female prisoners. One cell held two women; Stefanie was put in the other one.

The two women were chatty and tried to talk to her through the bars separating the cells. "Hey, what're you in for?" the carrot-haired one asked. "This place is the pits."

"You don't look good, honey," the older, middle-aged one said. "If you're sick, they've gotta get you medical attention."

"But you have to scream, or they don't pay any attention," the other one advised.

Stefanie just sat on the hard bed and looked around the cell. Concrete walls on two sides. Metal bars on the other two. Lock on the door. Less floor space than Trisha's walk-in closet. She fought an urge to wrap her arms around her waist and rock back and forth like a frightened child, but then surrendered to the urge. She waited for the feeling of claustrophobia to plunge her into memory-less minutes. She shuddered. If ever there was a place ripe for claustrophobia, that jail cell was it.

Yet it didn't happen. What she felt was . . . forsaken. Lost. Isolated.

Abandoned.

Lord, where are you?

Ryan didn't finish investigation on the apartment fire in Spokane until Wednesday. He had uncovered the fact that what had originally looked like arson was actually an accidental grease fire. A tenant, fearful of consequences, had tried to conceal that fact.

Ryan had twice tried to call Stefanie from his motel. Both times he'd heard only her recorded voice. He'd left his name and number but heard nothing from her. Would she think calling her at Fit 'n' Fun too intrusive or pushy? Why hadn't she called him back? Getting their relationship on the right track was important to him. He didn't want to derail it with impatience or wrong moves.

He flew back to Portland Wednesday afternoon. He drove straight to the office from the airport. He'd finish up his report, tie up some loose ends, and be ready to start his vacation first thing in the morning.

But he changed his mind even before he had the computer booted up. No waiting until morning; he'd drive to Julesburg that day, just as soon as he finished his work. The thought of seeing Stefanie again energized him, and he zipped through the report.

He walked down the hall and tossed the report on Steve Richter's desk. "And now my vacation week is on, right? If not, even if every arsonist in the Northwest has been working overtime, I'm claiming sick leave." He added a melodramatic cough and clutched at his chest.

Steve laughed. "Okay, you're on vacation as of right now. No need to collapse right here in my office. You must have something big planned."

"Secret." Ryan wasn't telling anyone he was going back to Julesburg, especially his boss. Steve would undoubtedly think of a few arson details Ryan should investigate if he knew where Ryan was headed.

"Okay. Have fun then. Hey, there's been an odd development down in Julesburg. You probably didn't hear about it over in Spokane —"

"You mean about the arson at the plywood mill?"

"There's no reason to think this has anything to do with the fire, but it does seem strange, one following right on the heels of the other."

"So what's happened?"

Steve shuffled through the paper jungle on his desk and extracted a file. "I cut out a couple of newspaper articles about it. The owner's girlfriend was murdered a few days ago."

"Trisha Duvall was murdered?"

Steve lifted an eyebrow. "Yeah. Shot to death in the house where she was living with him. Did you meet her while you were down there or something?"

"No. But I heard about her. When did it happen?"

"Sometime last Friday night, as I recall." Steve opened the file. "Hmmm. Wonder what I did with those clippings?"

I called Stef at 10:30 on Friday night. She wasn't at home. . . .

"Do they know yet who did it?"

"Yeah, looks like they do. They have the ex-wife in custody."

Ryan drove hard, but he arrived at the jail too late for visiting hours. He rented a motel room just a few blocks away rather than go on to Julesburg. He spent the night running a mental marathon on an emotional tread-mill of anger, frustration, and fear.

How could they possibly think Stefanie had committed murder? What kind of in-competent lawyer hadn't gotten her out on bail yet? Was Hunter Blackwell behind it, railroading Stefanie to save himself? Was it possible Hunter could somehow *succeed?*

Ryan was at the jail at 9:00 the next morning, the earliest hour visitors were al-lowed. His investigations and testimony had sent arsonists to prison, but he'd never actu-ally been in a jail before. He'd expected a private room to talk to Stefanie, but an of-ficer led him to a cubicle with a single seat, a glass wall, and a telephone. Another officer brought Stefanie to the other side of the glass.

She was in jail garb, an orange jumpsuit that was too large for her. Her hair was combed, but she wore no makeup. Her hazel eyes looked huge and bottomless, with puffs of blue shadows beneath. A scabbed line of scratches ran from cheekbone to jaw. His fists clenched.

She motioned for him to pick up the phone. She picked up the one on her side of the glass barrier. She managed a smile. "It's good to see you. Thanks for coming. How . . . ?"

"Stef, I'm so sorry. I didn't know anything about this, or I'd have been here the minute it happened. I've been trying to call you, but — how long have you been here?"

"Trisha was murdered Friday night. They arrested me on Saturday. Quick, efficient police work, the newspapers are calling it. Everyone's applauding."

He didn't tell her he'd tried to reach her on Friday evening. Maybe she had been in the shower or just hadn't felt like talking to anyone.

"But why you? How can they think you did it?"

"They have what the newspaper calls a 'mountain of evidence.' It probably wouldn't take a jury more than ten minutes to convict me."

"I don't understand. What kind of evidence do they have?"

"Witnesses who heard me threaten Trisha at the Singing Whale. My fingerprints in the house. A stocking cap with several strands of my hair on it. My watch with a broken band in the living room where they found her body. My lawyer got all that from the police reports. They're also doing some DNA tests." She touched the scratches on her cheek.

The list of incriminating evidence felt like

a fist rammed in his midsection. *Stefanie threatened Trisha? Went to her house?*

"I don't care what kind of evidence they have," he said fiercely. "Stef, you tell me you didn't do it, and I'll believe you."

Her gaze faltered and dipped. Her words came through the phone in barely a whisper.

"I — I'm afraid I can't do that."

18

"Stef, I don't understand. That doesn't make sense! You must know —"

"I can't talk about it now." She motioned to the glass barrier and the phone in her hand.

"Well, what about bail so you can get out of here?"

"Apparently I'm a menace to society if I'm on the loose. They set bail at a million dollars."

The huge figure was another ram of the fist, but he could manage it. Usually 10 percent of the figure was sufficient for bail. Ryan had a fair amount of cash in a money-market account, and he could raise more with the condo. *And Lord, I need your help too.*

"Have you had visitors?"

"Val and Tina have been here. And Pastor Gordon and Twila Mosely from the church. Tina has Sherlock."

"I'll go pick him up."

"She doesn't mind keeping him. Her kids think he's great."

"I want him."

She nodded. "The police had a warrant to search my house, but that should be finished by now. You and Sherlock are welcome to stay in the guest room, if you'd like. If you're still planning to vacation in Julesburg, that is."

Vacation. The word sounded alien, almost obscene under the circumstances, but he nodded, touched by her consideration. Did allowing him to enter her home mean she trusted him? He hoped so. She looked so fragile, so vulnerable in the too-large jumpsuit. *You haven't had much reason to trust me so far, have you, Stef?*

"I want to talk to your lawyer."

"His name is Arthur Zablonski. His office is in Coos Bay."

"Okay. I'll see him and be back later. But first, will you pray with me, Stef?"

"Pray. I prayed the morning after I went to Hunter's house last Friday night."

He tried to conceal his shock. She'd been there the night of the murder?

"I thanked God for getting me out of the house safely. I was afraid Trisha was going to kill me. I told the Lord I was sorry and that I wanted to get back to where I was with him at the beginning."

"That's wonderful, Stef!"

"I knew there would be consequences for

what I'd done in going to the house. It was an incredibly stupid thing to do. But this —" The knuckles on her fist clutching the phone paled to bony white. "I'm accused of murder, Ry. Murder."

And their state had the death penalty *Don't think about that now.* "God can see us through the worst storms of our lives, Stef —"

"I suppose he can. But will he?"

He desperately wanted to reach out and comfort her, but a glass wall stood between them.

The look Stefanie gave him seemed hopeless, devoid even of pain.

"And maybe he has no reason to see me through. Maybe I did it. Maybe I killed Trisha."

No, I can't believe that.

Ryan prayed when he got in his car. *Lord, show me what to do to help her! I don't think she did this, even if she isn't certain herself. And you know, even if I don't, what that's about. I pray you'll guide me. She feels so lost and alone. I pray you'll somehow bring good out of evil and restore her faith in you.*

He drove to Coos Bay to see Stefanie's attorney. The well-groomed young receptionist said politely that Mr. Zablonski had no immediate time available to see someone without an appointment. She opened a green calendar book with a polished fingernail. "But if you'd like to come in tomorrow morning, at —"

A door behind the reception area opened, and an older couple stepped into the hallway. Behind them Ryan could see a stout, distinguished-looking man in a gray suit. He didn't wait to hear tomorrow's time but charged around the reception desk. The woman jumped up from her swivel chair in alarm.

"Sir, you can't go in there!"

But the attorney waved off his receptionist, appearing to be considerably calmer than she was. "You seem in a hurry to see me, Mr. . . . ?"

"Harrison. Ryan Harrison. I'm here about Stefanie Canfield."

"I can see you are . . . disturbed, Mr. Harrison." The attorney inspected Ryan with shrewd blue eyes. "But I can't discuss confidential matters about a client without her specific authorization. Unless perhaps you come bringing helpful information?"

"I don't want to discuss anything confidential. I just want to get her out of there! I'm not sure how long it will take, but I can raise the money for her bail."

The attorney invited him inside the office and closed the door. "You're willing to put up the money to get her released?" He sounded interested. "And you are . . . ?"

"I'm an old friend of Stefanie's. I just found out about all this a short time ago."

"Actually," Mr. Zablonski replied, "your financial help may not be needed. I've asked for a reduction in bail, and I'm hoping the judge will go along with it. I believe Stefanie's house can then be offered as sufficient security. The hearing is this afternoon at the county courthouse. It's scheduled for 3:00, and we'll know then. If they won't accept my request about the bail, then we can discuss your offer of financial assistance."

"I'll be there."

Ryan drove down to Julesburg and Fit 'n' Fun next. Sherlock greeted Ryan with a wild display of wagging and squirming and bumping against Ryan's legs. Ryan kneeled beside the dog and mauled his head and ears in the rough way Sherlock liked. "We're going to get her out of there," he promised.

From there Ryan drove directly to the Julesburg police department. Ben Mosely recognized him from the arson investigation. His greeting started friendly, but his eyes narrowed when Ryan claimed he needed information about Stefanie's case because it could be connected with the arson investigation. He'd figured that would be the most effective strategy to get information from Ben.

I guess I was wrong.

"This isn't actually our case." Ben leaned against the opposite side of the counter in the small police station. His beefy frame outweighed Ryan by a good sixty pounds. "Hunter Blackwell discovered Trisha Duvall's body sometime around 2:45 A.M. last Saturday. All police calls are routed to the county sheriff's office at that time of night. The house is also just outside the city limits."

"So you don't know any details of the case?"

"Oh, I know details. But I don't see that they're any business of some nosy insurance company."

Ryan hadn't realized Ben would have a protective attitude toward Stefanie. Could he backtrack and straighten it out?

"Listen, I should have told you the truth to begin with," he admitted. "The insurance company doesn't even know I'm here." He filled Ben in on the details of his old friendship with Stefanie. The only thing he left out was that, for him at least, the relationship was rapidly expanding beyond friendship. "I want to help her any way I can."

"I see."

Ryan suddenly remembered a name Stefanie had mentioned. "Your wife visited Stefanie in jail?"

Ben nodded. "The whole church is praying for her. I've tossed out a few prayers myself." He reddened, as if the admission embarrassed him.

"She needs all our prayers."

Ben Mosely looked him over again and nodded. He must've decided he could trust Ryan, because he told Ryan about the run-in between Stefanie and Trisha at the Singing Whale, the evidence of the fingerprints, the stocking cap, and Stefanie's watch with a broken band. "And an eyewitness saw her running down the street away from the house about the time of the murder."

"Has time of death been established?"

"Probably between 10:00 and 12:00 at night."

"What about the weapon?"

"It hasn't been found yet. They've been searching for the gun along the route between the Blackwell house and Stefanie's place, but it's overgrown with enough brush and blackberry vines to hide a dinosaur."

"I understand her house has been searched. What were they looking for?"

"Well, the gun, of course. Also a jade cameo necklace. That was what Stefanie and Trisha had argued about at the Singing Whale. Plus Trisha's diamond engagement ring, which is also missing."

"And they found . . . ?"

"Shoes that match footprints near the Blackwell house."

Ryan drummed his fingers on the counter. "Doesn't the missing engagement ring suggest a burglary that escalated into murder, rather than some personal conflict between Stefanie and Trisha?"

"I'd like to think so. But according to witnesses their confrontation at the Singing Whale included something about the engagement ring." Ben rolled a paper lying on the counter and tapped his hand lightly with it. "I'm sticking my neck out telling you all this, and I wouldn't be doing it unless I wanted to help her as much as you do. Stefanie didn't have it easy as a kid. Her parents were wonderful people. Salt of the earth. But kids can be mean as a bunch of pit bulls."

I remember.

"But Stefanie turned into a wonderful young woman. It just doesn't seem like she could —"

"She didn't."

Ben shook his head. Troubled lines creased his weathered forehead. "I want to believe that. But with all the evidence against her . . ."

"Evidence is like statistics. Either can be twisted to prove anything."

Ben nodded. But with heaviness in his voice, he added, "I interviewed Stefanie the day after the fire at the mill. She didn't have anything to do with that, of course. But one of the things she said then was that if she wanted to get even, it was Hunter or Trisha she'd go after, not the mill."

Ryan felt his stomach sink. "Did you tell the sheriff's office she'd said that?"

Ryan knew the answer even before Ben nodded. Ben was a man who radiated law-and-order responsibility. He'd have considered it his duty to report anything he knew about the case.

"Are they continuing to investigate and look for other suspects?"

"I wouldn't say their minds are closed to the possibility of a different perpetrator, but they're reasonably certain they have their killer. Which means they're probably concentrating on finding evidence to convict."

Ryan nodded.

"She admits she was in the house that night," Ben continued. "She thought Hunter and Trisha Duvall were out of town, so she went there to search for the necklace."

"That explains her fingerprints."

Ben nodded. "It might also explain the stocking cap and watch. But the rest of her story, about Trisha walking in and pulling a gun on her, threatening to kill her . . . it just seems . . . far-fetched."

"So does a big argument between them at the Singing Whale."

"But the bedroom sure enough looked like some kind of battle scene."

"You saw it?"

"The crime was close enough to my jurisdiction that I wasn't going to ignore it," Ben said. "I'm keeping my finger on this. The mirror was broken. The drapes ripped. A lamp smashed. It was a royal mess. But Trisha was actually killed in the living room."

"What does Stefanie say about all of it?"

"I haven't actually seen a transcript from when she was questioned —"

"Was her attorney present?" Ryan interrupted.

"Yep. She was smart enough to refuse to talk until he got there. But from what I've heard, her story about that night is kind of disjointed. It seems she's had some peculiar memory problems." Ben sounded as if he was trying not to be skeptical about that point. "Legally, a person is innocent until proven guilty. But with so much evidence against her, it's going to take something extraordinarily powerful to raise reasonable doubt in this case."

"She didn't do it," Ryan repeated.

But his palms oozed dampness when he walked back to the Blazer. He wanted to believe that Stefanie didn't do it. But if she herself couldn't remember . . .

Lord, keep my faith in her strong! Don't let me doubt her even when she's lost faith in herself. And you.

He parked by the Julesburg Café to grab a sandwich for lunch, but then decided to go to the Singing Whale instead. There he found a hostess laden with an armload of menus, and he asked her if she had witnessed the confrontation between Stefanie and Trisha.

The hostess looked at him with suspicion. "Yes, I did see it. But I've already told Ben and those officers from the sheriff's office everything I know. I don't have anything to add." She made a point of looking at her watch. "And I'm busy. It's lunch hour."

The restaurant didn't look all that busy, and it was past the lunch hour, but Ryan didn't argue. "I'm not from the sheriff's office. I'm an investigator looking into this for Stefanie. But more than that, I'm an old friend trying to help her." The hostess was middle-aged; she had the look of a long-time Julesburg resident. On sudden impulse, he added, "I lived here when I was a kid and Laurine Canfield was still alive. She baked the best peanut butter cookies I've ever eaten. And I don't think Stef is guilty of anything."

Maybe it was his declaration of belief in Stefanie's innocence that softened her unfriendly attitude. Or maybe it was his mention of the peanut butter cookies. She slid into his booth after he finished a ham and cheese on sourdough and held a hand across the table to him. "I'm Lily Slaker. I used to work for Laurine."

The report she gave him about the confrontation in the restaurant was slanted in Stefanie's favor, but she sounded bewildered when she wound down to the end of her story.

"Stef couldn't remember what she'd done. I sat out back with her, and she said things were 'blurry.' But I could tell. She actually didn't know what had happened."

"Couldn't remember any of it?"

"She remembered the cameo necklace Trisha was wearing. It used to belong to Stefanie's mother. She remembered telling Trisha that Trisha wasn't going to get away with stealing the necklace, that she was going to get it back. But she couldn't remember shoving her. Shoving her . . . pretty hard," Lily admitted.

The peculiar memory thing again.

Lily added, "I don't suppose the woman deserved shooting, but she sure deserved something after all she'd done." She raised her eyebrows as if asking if Ryan knew what Trisha had done. Ryan nodded. "And then on top of all that, to take Stefanie's mother's necklace. Maybe what happened there at the house was an accident?"

Ryan knew that Lily wanted to protect and defend Stefanie any way she could. But he also could see that she thought Stefanie had killed Trisha.

Ryan thanked her. He picked up his check for the sandwich that now felt like a slab of two-by-four in his stomach and tucked a tip under the cup.

★ ★ ★

Ryan pulled into the parking lot across from the courthouse at twenty five minutes past three. A jackknifed truck had blocked the highway for a good forty-five minutes. He ran toward the main door to find someone to direct him to the hearing room, but two figures emerged as he passed a side door. He stopped short.

For a moment they just stared. Then they surged across the sidewalk toward each other. He wrapped his arms around her fiercely, and his lips against her hair offered murmurs of comfort. She felt so vulnerable in his arms . . . and so wonderfully sweet and desirable.

"Mr. Harrison." Arthur Zablonski's eyes met Ryan's over Stefanie's shoulder. Ryan didn't ask how the hearing had gone. The fact that Stefanie was in his arms said it all.

Stefanie turned to shake hands with the attorney. Ryan kept his arm wrapped around her shoulders.

"Thank you for arranging bail for me."

"I'm sorry it took so long to get it reduced to a reasonable figure."

"What now?" Ryan asked.

Zablonski didn't mince words. "The district attorney is rushing the case to the grand jury next week. At this point, with all

272

the evidence she has available to present, it's almost certain the grand jury will issue an indictment for murder. The D.A. will then schedule a trial date as early as possible. She'll bulldoze it ahead of some others if she can. She's taken flak for being too soft on some of the women she's prosecuted, and on this case she's going all out to prove she's tough. She wants a fast, smooth conviction well before the fall elections."

Great. How much more bad news is Stefanie going to have to take?

"Stefanie, right now what you need is to relax and unwind for a few days. I'll be in touch, and we'll look at our options then." Arthur Zablonski's parting nod was directed at both of them.

Ryan appreciated Arthur Zablonski's sensitivity to Stefanie's need to unwind after the ordeal of imprisonment. He appreciated that the attorney didn't offer empty assurances about delaying the trial for months.

But what is Zablonski holding back?

19

Ryan delivered Stefanie to the house. Sherlock had ridden all the way to Julesburg at her feet, and he jumped out with her.

"Would you mind if I keep him here for a few days?" Stefanie asked. "After being in jail, I feel the need of some nonjudgmental company. Company not clothed in orange jail garb. Or black judge's robes."

"What about me? I'm available." Ryan ticked off his assets. "Highly congenial company. And in addition to not wearing black or orange, I don't shed or dig holes." He wanted so much to lift her spirits, even if he had to be silly to do it. Her skin looked pale, as if she'd been in the sunless jail far longer than a few days.

She managed a smile. "That's hard to resist, but I do need to take a shower and collect myself. Maybe you could come back later?"

"How about if I pick up something for dinner and bring it here?" Ryan offered.

"That should make me feel right at home.

I'm accustomed to free room and board these days, you know." Her smile wobbled, but the crack about free room and board showed she hadn't lost her spirit.

Impulsively, Ryan leaned over and kissed her on the cheek, then climbed into the Blazer.

The house wasn't a disaster area, but Stefanie saw evidence everywhere of a thorough search by the authorities. The kitchen cabinets were in disarray, dishes piled on the counter. The cushions on the sofa were overturned. Even the freezer looked as if someone had pawed through the contents. In the bathroom, the medicine chest was open, and an aspirin bottle, a tube of ointment, and plastic containers of prescription medications were scattered across the counter. Towels spilled off the shelves of the linen closet.

Stefanie dumped jasmine-scented bubble bath in the water until bubbles frothed over the edge of the tub. She thought about the unexpected kiss as she soaked. *Don't read anything into it, Stef. Ryan is simply a great guy with a Christian concern about an old friend.*

After soaking in the tub, she washed her hair under the shower spray. It squeaked after she rinsed it twice as long as she usually did. She sniffed a damp strand, satisfied she had washed out the smell of the jail.

As Stefanie toweled her hair dry, she could think of only one thing. Bubbles and hot water could cleanse her skin. They could wash away the scent and grime of jail. But they could never wash away the fear and dread that haunted her heart and soul. Fear that went even beyond the trial and her possible conviction.

Maybe I fired that gun. Maybe I really did kill Trisha.

She shivered in spite of the heat of the steam-laden room and leaned her head against the tub enclosure. *Perhaps I should get it over with and simply plead guilty.*

No. I can't believe I'm a murderer until they prove it.

Oh, Lord . . .

She rescinded the beginning of the plea and spoke to herself instead. *You're on your own. Don't count on the Lord. He's never rushed to your aid before, has he?*

She grabbed another towel and dried until her skin felt as if it had been scoured with sand. Arthur Zablonski had said she should relax and unwind. Yes, she'd do that. She would relax and unwind and remember. Remember every second, every detail about that night.

She called Val while she was still wrapped in a towel. Val picked up in the middle of her answering machine's spiel.

"This is your local jailbird calling," Stefanie said, forcing a singsong breeziness into her voice.

"Oh, Stef, you're out? I was planning to come visit you this evening — Sweetie, this is wonderful! I'm so relieved. I knew they'd realize sooner or later they had the wrong person. Let's celebrate!"

"They didn't realize anything, unfortunately. My attorney just got the bail reduced."

"If the authorities had any sense, they'd get off your back and stick Hunter in there," Val sputtered. "Anyone with the brains of a peanut could see he did it."

"What about the missing engagement ring? Hunter wouldn't have any reason to take that." They'd talked about various details during Val's visits to the jail, dissecting fine points and floating theories and taking turns playing devil's advocate. The missing ring had puzzled both of them. "Doesn't that make it look as if some burglar just grabbed the most valuable item he saw?"

"I've been thinking about the ring. I wouldn't have guessed Hunter had the imagination to be into symbolism, but think about it, Stef. What better way to symbolize how he felt about her betrayal than by removing the engagement ring from her finger? It says that even in death he wanted to be totally disconnected from her."

"We don't know she betrayed him."

"There are rumors. And you know the old saying about smoke and fire."

Stefanie shivered at the appalling vision of Hunter twisting the ring off Trisha's dead finger. She let her towel drop and reached for a robe. "I'd think simply killing her said enough."

"So you do think he did it too."

Yes, that's exactly what I would think, if I could be sure I didn't do it myself. "But he has a good alibi. He claims he was in Eugene. I imagine he has proof to back that up."

"Alibi, schmalibi," Val scoffed. "The guy's an arsonist and a murderer. Plus an adulterer, of course. Don't you think it's just a little too convenient that Hunter always has these marvelous alibis to cover any crisis? Like maybe he diagrammed them out ahead of time?"

Yes, very convenient.

"Okay, look, maybe it isn't cause for total celebration, but you are out of jail. That's worth at least a semi-celebration. I'll bring pizza and Pepsi, and we'll toast your freedom."

"Ryan is coming in a few minutes —"

"Well, well, well. Riding in like the white knight to the rescue, is he? Say no more. Pizza and Pepsi pale in comparison. Go for it with The Hunk."

For all the feminist views Val spouted, she had the unliberated attitude that female friendships took a back seat to male ones. Stefanie didn't agree, but at the moment she appreciated Val's generous attitude. She was looking forward to seeing Ryan again that evening.

"Thanks, Val. But I do appreciate the offer. I appreciate your faith in me too. And coming to visit me and being there to lean on . . . everything."

Stefanie opened the back door and stepped aside to let Ryan in, but he just stood there staring at her. Self-consciously, she smoothed the full skirt of the summery flowered dress she was wearing. She'd put it on because she needed its simple prettiness. Now both it and the high-heeled sandals felt too frivolous. She started to apologize, but Ryan cut her off.

"Hey —" He blinked and reared back in an exaggerated double take. "You're a *girl!*"

In spite of everything, she laughed. Ryan had always been able to make her laugh. "I guess I just wanted to get as far away from the jail look as possible."

"You did it."

She took one of his grocery sacks and together they spread his purchases on the counter. Pasta, fresh and canned tomatoes, onions, mushrooms, a packet of Italian spices, olive oil, ground round, french bread, and salad makings.

"What's all this? It looks as if you cleaned out the grocery store."

"I thought cooking dinner together would be more fun than just bringing something from a restaurant."

"And what," she asked, gingerly picking up the most enormous bone she had ever seen, "are we going to make out of this remnant from the dinosaur age?"

"Dogs need bones. An exceptional dog like Sherlock needs an exceptional bone."

Sherlock latched on to the bone with doggy glee. Ryan took dog and bone outside, then wrapped a dishtowel around his waist as an apron. He set Stefanie to chopping onions and mushrooms while he started the sauce simmering.

Their conversation was soothingly normal, skipping lightly from one subject to another. The parking area at his condo was being repaved. His brother's wife was expecting another baby. His sister, Angie, was involved in an ad campaign for a new hair-care company. "I saw her washing her hair on TV a while back. She told me on the phone later that she'd washed it fourteen times for that ad, until she wondered if she was going to have any hair left."

Stefanie appreciated the detour from murder. She contributed mundane bits about Fit 'n' Fun and how Sherlock had already become a fixture there. "He's turned into our official greeter at the door."

They ate spicy spaghetti, green salad, and garlic bread in the dining room. Afterward, Ryan cleared the table and Stefanie filled the dishwasher. Sherlock returned to the kitchen without the bone, but he had the smug look of an investor with important assets stashed away.

Ryan leaned against the kitchen counter. "I suppose I should be going." He'd removed the dishtowel apron, and a wayward spot of spaghetti sauce decorated his Dockers.

But he made no move toward the door, and Stefanie was not eager to see him go. In jail, she'd hungered for the peace and silence of home. She'd ached to be alone.

Now, with vestiges of the invasive search still lingering, the house felt different, no longer a haven of security.

"The offer of my guest room is still open."

"Thanks, but I think . . ."

Stefanie smiled. "That as an accused murderer, I shouldn't do anything further, such as having an attractive man sleeping in my house, to tarnish my reputation?"

Ryan returned her smile. "I already have a room at the Sea Haven."

Stefanie knew that some men might have tried to take advantage of a woman in her vulnerable position. "You're a good man, Ryan Harrison."

"Not good. But forgiven and saved." He softened the small detour into his spiritual beliefs with another smile and didn't press the point. "Look, if you don't have anything planned for this evening —"

"I've decided to abandon my brief, unsuccessful career as a house burglar, so I am free tonight," she said.

He let her attempt at humor go without comment. "How about a walk on the beach? If we hurry, maybe we can still catch the green flash."

Stefanie went upstairs to change from her dress into jeans. When she came down,

Ryan suggested that she not forget where she'd put the dress.

"I like it."

He tucked her hand under his elbow as they walked on the beach. Again, they'd left their shoes behind. Sherlock sniffed and dug and chased sea froth spread by retreating waves. The sun lingered late on July summer evenings, but it faded into a thickening mist as they walked. No green flash that night. Stefanie didn't mind the incoming fog; she was glad Ryan had suggested the walk.

She'd never thought much about freedom, except in an abstract, patriotic sense. Now that she'd lived locked in a jail cell, she realized what a treasure freedom was. Freedom to walk the beach with her bare toes digging in the sand. Freedom to choose if she wanted to run to the store or go see a movie. She could eat when she wanted. Bathe when she wanted. If she wanted to, she could even fling out her arms and turn cartwheels.

I may soon be back in jail, though. The thought intruded even as she tried to keep it at bay. She could be back there not for days or weeks, but years. Unless a jury and judge gave an even harsher penalty.

"Getting cold?" Ryan asked when she shivered.

"No, I'm fine." She stretched up and kissed him on the jaw. "Thank you, Ry."

"Thank you?"

"For being here. For cheering me up. For everything."

They turned around at the creek. When they returned to the stairs climbing from the beach to the parking area, he asked, "How about a cup of coffee? Or cappuccino? I was surprised to see it on the menu at the Julesburg Café."

"Could we just sit here on the steps for a few minutes?"

Ryan whisked sand from a wooden step, gave a courtly bow as he motioned her to a seat, and sat beside her. Sherlock covered Stefanie's toes as he plopped down as close as he could get.

"Would you like to talk about this, Stef? I want to help, any way I can."

Earlier she'd been grateful when Ryan chattered about insignificant matters. Now she was grateful that he sensed the turn of an emotional tide. She did need to talk.

She picked up a twist of driftwood and rubbed the satiny surface with a fingertip. "Twila Mosely told me there were no services here for Trisha, that her family took the body to Tacoma."

"That's what I heard."

"She was shot in the heart. At close range." That still seemed unreal to Stefanie. Beautiful Trisha, so golden and perfect . . . She glanced up from the driftwood. "No, that isn't something I remember. It was in the newspaper. But I feel . . . guilty about her death. As if I'm responsible, even though —" She swallowed. "Maybe there is no 'even though.' Maybe I feel guilty because I am guilty."

"Stef, what is all this about your memory problems?" Ryan asked. "I haven't noticed anything wrong with your memory."

She told him about the accident and the strange periods of lost minutes that had occurred since then. She also told him about her mother's cameo necklace, the ugly scene at the Singing Whale, why she'd gone to Hunter and Trisha's house that Friday night. And what had happened there, right up to the moment Trisha careened down the stairs at her.

"Then you had one of these episodes of 'lost minutes' when you think you could have killed her?"

"No . . . not exactly . . . I mean, I'm not sure! Usually I have warning that an attack is coming. Twice that night I felt as if I were about to have one. But I don't remember feeling anything but astonishment and horror when I saw Trisha racing down the stairs with that broken lamp held over her head. I've always been aware afterward that time was missing. I may find myself in a different place than I last remembered, or someone may tell me about something that happened during the lost minutes. Like when I shoved Trisha at the restaurant. This time it's all just a jumble. I don't know if time is missing or not."

"I know it's difficult, Stef, but try to go back and walk through it. Minute by minute. Look for details."

Stefanie had tried to do that before. But she didn't have Ryan's arm around her then.

She closed her eyes, held Ryan's hand, and took him on the journey with her. "I'm hiding in the bushes . . . entering the house . . . searching . . . hearing someone coming . . . yes, I do see it more clearly now. I'm tangled in the drapes. Trying to find the sliding-glass door. I'm panicking. I feel one of those episodes coming. The light comes on. I know someone is in the bedroom with me."

She clutched his hand tighter. "I hear a click. Then Trisha tells me to come out with my hands up. I do it. She has a gun."

Stefanie's eyes flew open. "I do remember

something else! When Trisha saw me, she was surprised —"

"She had to be surprised to find someone in her bedroom, Stef."

"Yes, but she said something like —" Stefanie squeezed her eyes shut again. "I think she said, 'You! I thought —' like she expected it to be someone else. And was surprised when it turned out to be me."

"I wonder who she could have thought it was?"

Ryan's tone was encouraging. Dig deeper, it said. Look for clues. *Lord, help me remember more! What did I do when Trisha came down the stairs after me? That's what is important. Did I —*

Stefanie cut off the prayer and rubbed her bare feet against the comfort of Sherlock's shaggy coat. "I can't even imagine who she thought I might be."

"What happened next?"

"Then she became agitated and angry and accused me of delaying the settlement on ownership of the company. She said she could shoot me, and it would be self-defense because I'd broken into her home. And I thought she was going to do it."

"So then you ran —"

"I don't remember picking up the gun when I ran out of the bedroom, but I must have, because it was in my hand when I reached the bottom of the stairs. I was horrified that I had it. Then everything is jumbled. I just remember Trisha tearing down the stairs holding that piece of broken lamp as if she intended to impale me with it. After that . . . maybe I did shoot her."

"Try Stef, try to remember!" Ryan grabbed her by the arms. "You're looking up the stairs. She's coming . . ."

Stefanie shook her head. "I — I can't think about that night any more now, Ry. I'm sorry. I just can't."

"That's okay. There's plenty of time." He wrapped his arms around her in a long, reassuring hug. She missed the warmth of his cheek against hers when he released her.

"What about Hunter?" Ryan asked.

"He says he found the body when he came home later that night from a business trip to Eugene. The authorities must believe him because I'm the one accused of the murder."

"But not accused by me," Ryan said. He placed his hands on her shoulders and turned her to face him. "Stef, I'll admit, I wondered about you and the arson at first."

"I know."

"And I admit that after Haggerston's body turned up, I figured someone had hired him to commit the arson, and I wondered if it could have been you."

So that's what he hadn't told her when he left Julesburg. It was not a thought that had occurred to her; she'd accepted the theory that the fire had been a crime of revenge. But a hired arsonist . . . that made perfect sense.

"I had nothing to do with the fire, Ry. Not setting it, not hiring the arsonist. And I still believe in the sacredness of the Bible enough to swear to that on the Bible, if you want me to."

"I know, Stef. I'm sorry I ever had any doubts about the arson."

"I just wish I could swear that I had nothing to do with Trisha's murder." Her head sagged against his shoulder.

He lifted her face and framed it with his hands. "Stef, I believe in you, even if you don't believe in yourself. You didn't do it."

He leaned forward and kissed her. She closed her eyes and let herself drift with the warmth and security of the tender touch of his lips on hers. *I want this to go on. And on and on . . .*

When he finally lifted his head, he tucked a strand of hair behind her ear. "Do you remember what you told me the very first time I tried to kiss you?"

"I remember. I said, 'Don't ever do that again.'" She lifted her hands and twined them around his neck. She looked into his eyes. "I'm not saying that now."

He closed the space between them and kissed her again. This kiss was sweet and caring too, but its depth and passion turned her heartbeat into thuds that shook her body. The first kiss had made her feel secure; now she felt a glorious richness of physical awareness. *I could fall in love with you, Ryan Harrison. Maybe I'm already falling in love with you.*

Stefanie unwound her arms from his neck. With her bleak and uncertain future, she had no right to fall in love.

Ryan instantly felt the change in her, as if she'd resolutely stepped back from a dangerous precipice. *I know what that precipice is, Stef. Because I'm poised on the edge of it too. The difference is that I'm willing to jump off.* But he knew he couldn't rush her.

"Everything's okay, Stef. We'll see this through together, and then —"

"I think I could use that cup of cappuccino at the Julesburg Café now," Stefanie said as she jumped to her feet.

If that enthusiasm is real then I'm ol' Hunter's best buddy. "How about brewing a fresh pot of coffee back at the house instead?"

She didn't admit to relief at not going to a crowded public place, but he saw it in her quick nod. He felt an almost fierce sense of protectiveness toward her. *Maybe we should go out in public. And if anyone so much as looks at her wrong . . .*

They put on their shoes, and Ryan took her hand as they started up the wooden steps. "At this point, is your attorney saying anything about his plans for defense?"

"I'd never realized it before, but I guess it's lawyer policy not to ask a client whether she's innocent or guilty. It's just his job to defend her." Ryan knew this, but she sounded dismayed by it. "Of course, with me, I suppose it doesn't matter. I can't tell him anyway."

"So . . . ?"

"So far he seems mostly interested in my memory problems and medical history. I signed papers so he could get my records, and he said he may need further physical and psychological examinations."

Ryan realized what the attorney had been holding back. Zablonski had accepted the evidence that Stefanie had killed Trisha. He wasn't planning to raise doubts about that evidence; he wasn't trying to find another

291

suspect. He was going for a mental defense, perhaps diminished mental capacity or even temporary insanity.

Objections instantly flared in Ryan's mind. Even if Zablonski got her off legally, there would be a stigma of guilt attached to Stefanie. More importantly, she'd still be guilty in her own mind. A feeling of bleakness rose in him as they climbed the steps.

Lord, help us. Show us what to do to find out who really did this. Bring us something . . . anything . . . to go on!

When they arrived at the house, Stefanie excused herself to go upstairs and take some aspirin.

"I give you a headache?" Ryan joked.

"I think I've had a headache ever since last Friday night," she said ruefully.

Ryan started the coffee while Stefanie was upstairs. An inviting fragrance floated from the pot by the time she returned. She crossed the kitchen and held out her closed hands.

"What?"

"I found this."

He held out his hands, and she dropped something into them.

20

He didn't know what he expected. Perhaps the jade cameo he'd heard about?

"A watch?"

"My watch. The one I wear almost every day."

He felt dense that this seemed so important to Stefanie. He dangled the watch at eye level to inspect it more closely. An inexpensive Caravelle, more utilitarian than decorative. It had a round face, plain black numbers, and a leather band. Then the connection clanged into place.

"So if your watch is here . . . then it can't be the watch the police found near Trisha's body!"

"Bingo." She took the watch back and draped the leather band over her wrist. "I remember now. The battery had gone dead, so I wasn't wearing the watch that night. I'd set it in a nightstand drawer until I could get a new battery. Which is where I found it just now."

"So the watch the police found belongs to someone else who was at the house that night. Which means you, sweetheart, didn't kill Trisha."

Hey, Lord, that's fast action. He'd avoided facing how little hope there was with all the evidence stacked against Stefanie. Now hope took a giant leap upward.

"What we need now is more information about the watch they found so we can figure out who it belongs to."

"My attorney may be able to get a description. I can call him in the morning."

Ryan had another idea. He didn't mention it, but he was out the door after the quickest cup of coffee on record.

The police station was locked up tight. A sign said to call 911 in emergencies or the county sheriff's office for anything else. Ryan saw a police car pull into the Julesburg Café, but it wasn't Ben in the vehicle and he didn't want to discuss anything with the other officer. He found a phone booth and looked up Ben's address in the slim book. 703 Madrona. After a couple of wrong turns, he located the house. It was a one-story ranch with a shake roof. The yard was well kept, the lawn neatly edged. A rose bush climbed a trellis beside the front door.

Ben stepped outside to talk to Ryan rather than inviting him in. Ryan hoped Ben could tell him on the spot what he needed to know, but he wasn't surprised when he had to settle for Ben's promise that he'd try to have the information first thing in the morning. "I'm sticking my neck out again," Ben muttered. But his strong jaw suggested he was not the kind of man to let that deter him.

Back at the house, for the first time since the handcuffs had closed around her wrists, Stefanie's hopes burgeoned. The police would see that someone else had been in the house that night. Even greater than that hope, she realized as she set the watch carefully on the nightstand beside her bed, was the relief. She hadn't killed Trisha.

Lord, are you watching over me after all?

She'd planned to go to Fit 'n' Fun the following morning, but she decided to wait until the attorney's office opened so she could call him from home. In the meantime, she walked down to the post office to collect mail from her overflowing box. There were no home deliveries in Julesburg; everyone had a box at the post office.

She saw only two people: Gina, a clerk at the grocery store, and the town's part-time librarian, Pat Rowland. Their greetings were friendly, but they didn't stop to offer sympathy or support. Yet that didn't necessarily mean anything. Neither was more than a nodding acquaintance and probably wouldn't have stopped to chat under normal circumstances. *It doesn't mean they're dodging me as if I have an "M" for Murderer emblazoned on my forehead.*

Stefanie was at the kitchen table opening the phone bill when Ryan banged on the back door.

"C'mon in."

He came in waving a scrap of paper. He looked as proud and pleased as Sherlock with his bone.

"Got it!"

"Got what?"

"A description of the watch found at the house."

"I'm impressed."

He made an elaborate bow. "Then my day is complete."

Stefanie thought a moment. "Ben?"

"I think he'd prefer to remain anonymous."

She grabbed the paper, but her heart sank a little lower with each word she read. Older Timex watch, quartz movement, oblong face with a diagonal scratch. Gold, expansion type band, broken at the sixth link.

"Does that tell you anything?" Ryan asked.

She set the scrap of paper beside the stack

of unopened mail on the kitchen table and clasped her hands together. "It tells me who the watch belongs to." She lifted her gaze to his. "Me."

"But you showed me your watch —"

"This description is of the watch I had before the one I use now. The face was scratched when a knife slipped in the kitchen. I broke the band while I was gardening. I don't remember seeing it since . . . since I moved out of the house, I suppose. I'm hard on watches, so I don't buy expensive ones. I've never even thought about this one or wondered where it was."

She felt numb. She'd been so certain the watch was a turning point in her innocence. But the evidence didn't point to anyone else; it only pointed to her. Straight as a bullet.

"So how did it get in the living room, near Trisha's body?"

Stefanie glanced up, startled by the simple logic of the question. *Yeah, how did it get there?* Wherever she'd left the watch when she moved out of the house, it was definitely not on the living room floor. And she hadn't been wearing the watch that night.

"How did they decide it was mine to begin with?" she asked.

"I didn't ask Ben about that, but Hunter must've identified it."

Stefanie and Ryan looked at each other, both realizing what that meant.

"There's only one way it could have gotten on the living room floor, Stef. Hunter put it there. Planted it there so he could identify it as yours and incriminate you. And the only reason he'd have for doing that is if he killed Trisha."

Ryan paced back and forth, and Stefanie watched his long strides. He stopped abruptly and wrapped his hands around the top of a kitchen chair.

"Hunter arrives home not long after you run out of the house that night. It looks like a disaster area. He and Trisha have already been quarreling. That's why she wasn't with him out of town. My guess is that he didn't turn out to be as rich a mill owner as she thought, and she'd been scouting for bigger and better prospects. He suspects or has actually found out about that. They get in a violent argument. The gun is right there, loaded and ready. He grabs it. Maybe he didn't really intend to kill her —"

"And maybe he did."

"In any case, now she's dead, and he knows he has to make it look like someone else did it. You're the obvious candidate. Everyone knows how you must feel about Trisha stealing your husband. You've had a

298

public run-in with her at the Singing Whale, complete with what could be interpreted as a threat. It's the perfect solution for him. Trisha has already told him that you were there at the house, so he knows the police will find your fingerprints. As a crowning touch, he adds that old watch of yours to the evidence. Then he calls the police."

Stefanie nodded slowly. It could have happened that way.

"Perhaps she even told him she was leaving him and threw the engagement ring back at him. That would explain why it's missing. More than one murder has been committed on the basis of 'If I can't have her, no one else will.' "

Stefanie doubted Hunter's material-oriented mind ran along the lines of symbolism such as Val had suggested, but his ego would go into a tailspin if Trisha broke the engagement and returned the ring. She was beginning to believe that he had the imagination to scheme his way out of a conviction for murder.

"But what about the gun?" Stefanie questioned. "Why would he get rid of it? He could just wipe off his fingerprints, and the police would assume I'd wiped it to get rid of my fingerprints."

"He may have deliberately tossed it somewhere between his house and here. He's hoping the authorities will find it, and the location will be further evidence pointing to you."

"It must have been a nice bonus for him when the police found my stocking cap, with my hair on it, to further implicate me."

Ryan resumed pacing. "But there's nothing here to convince the authorities that Hunter is involved. It's all speculation, not solid evidence. They aren't going to take your word for it that Hunter planted the watch."

Stefanie felt relief in the certainty that she was not a killer, and she felt a gratitude for Ryan's powerful faith in her. But the chains of evidence were tightening around her again, and this time Hunter was turning the screws. *I'm scared, Lord.*

Ryan stopped and knelt by her chair. "Don't get discouraged, Stef. Just remember that the Lord is bigger and stronger and more powerful than human manipulations."

"I wonder if Hunter's alibi for that night is all that solid?" she asked.

Ryan stood. "Good thought. We'll check it out. How about a housekeeper or cook, someone we might try to get information from about the status of Hunter and Trisha's home life?"

"I think they ate out most of the time, so I doubt they had a full-time cook. I was afraid that night that a housekeeper might be in residence at the house, but I didn't see any signs of one. Of course, I can't really picture Trisha dusting and vacuuming . . . maybe they had a cleaning lady come in a couple of times a week. Tina has a friend who does part-time housework for people. Maybe she'd know something."

"Good. How about a local hairdresser? Don't women always tell their hairdressers everything?"

"Lisa Benedetti has the only beauty shop in town, but Trisha never went there. She always drove over to Eugene to have her hair done. Which rather miffed Lisa."

"Eugene, again."

"Actually, that's where Hunter met Trisha."

"Oh?" Ryan lifted an eyebrow.

"Most of the company business is in Portland or Seattle, but occasionally he deals with some company in Eugene. I suppose I should have suspected something when he suddenly had *a lot* of business in Eugene."

"Okay, I'm going to make a trip over there." Ryan glanced at his watch. "But I need something to go on. Do you remember the name of the company he dealt with there? Names of any friends or business associates? Any special motel where he usually stayed?"

Stefanie didn't know any individual or company names, but she could name the motel he stayed at.

"What do you know about Trisha's life before she came here?" Ryan asked.

"Well, I know she was a secretary with the company Cougar Creek did business with in Eugene. Now that I think about it, I believe it was a plywood wholesaler, something along that line. I'm sorry I don't have more to go on."

"I take it you weren't the kind of wife to hire a detective to dig up dirt on the husband's affairs."

"I didn't know I'd someday be accused of murdering a girlfriend," Stefanie said wryly.

Ryan smiled and looked at his watch again. "Okay, I'll leave for Eugene now —"

"I could come along to help."

"I may have to stay overnight. And since we need to gather all the information we can as quickly as possible, it might be more productive if you'd work on the housekeeper angle here."

Stefanie nodded, but Ryan didn't leave. He just stood there looking at her with a slightly exasperated expression.

"What?" she asked.

"You could be polite and walk me to the door. Otherwise I'm going to be in the awkward position of kissing you while you're slumped in that chair."

Stefanie stood up, but he didn't wait until they reached the door for the kiss. He wrapped his arms around her, and the kiss sent her mind and heart into entwined spirals of joy and regret. *I'm falling in love. But I can't fall in love, not now.*

"Stef, you be careful while I'm gone, okay?" he growled, not releasing her. His arms tightened, holding her hard against him.

"Careful how?"

"Careful when you're asking questions about Hunter and Trisha. Careful about . . . everything. Keep your doors locked. If Hunter wants to talk to you, tell him to go through your attorney."

"Why would Hunter want to talk to me?"

"I don't know. But everything we know so far points to him as the killer. A killer who has no qualms about framing an innocent person. Who knows how far he's willing to go to protect himself? So just be careful."

He kissed her again, and a few moments later she heard the roar of the Blazer's engine. She slumped into the wooden chair beside the table again. Even if Hunter was trying to escape responsibility for a horrifying crime he'd committed, he could have tried to make it look like a burglary gone wrong. But no, he deliberately targeted her to take the blame.

How far is he willing to go to whitewash himself and frame me? Wouldn't it be convenient for Hunter if I suddenly turned up dead? Dead at what looked like my own hand, the guilty suicide of a murderer?

If Hunter would manipulate evidence to make her look guilty, how far would he go to clinch that appearance of guilt and save his own neck?

21

Stefanie hurried down to Fit 'n' Fun. She was anxious to be with people. She wanted to do everyday things, normal things.

But it took only a couple of hours for her to realize that normality was not on the schedule. She could see people trying to act normal. They weren't rushing up to cancel monthly subscriptions. They smiled and made small talk.

"Hey, Stef, these new machines are terrific."

"Do you think those Pilates exercises are worth trying?"

"I love your big old dog. I had one almost like him when I was a kid."

But she could see curiosity lurking in their quickly averted stares, hear speculation in their whispers.

On Tina's lunch break, Stefanie approached her to ask about the friend who did housework. Tina was in the back room eating one of her strange sandwiches. This time it was peanut butter, pickles, and radishes. "No, I'm not pregnant," Tina had assured Stefanie the first time she asked about her unusual eating habits. "I just don't like to get stuck in a rut on what I eat."

Tina nodded in response to Stefanie's question, waving the sandwich until she swallowed. "Betty Young. She worked at the house for a few weeks when Trisha first moved in. But Trisha shorted her on wages a couple of times, claiming Betty hadn't worked as many hours as she actually had." Tina wrinkled her nose. "So Betty quit. But she probably knows who worked there after she left. I'll find out."

Tina had the information by late afternoon. Minnie Hickson had been cleaning at the Blackwell house twice a week. Stefanie threw a wraparound skirt over her leotard and ducked out.

The Hicksons had been around for years, but the only thing Stefanie knew about them was where they lived. Their faded yellow cottage stood on a treeless lot north of the mill. The yard wasn't trashy, but the grass was struggling to survive. Sheets flapping on a clothesline were snowy white and the tiny porch cleanly swept. Minnie Hickson answered the door in worn polyester pants with an elastic waist and a faded button-down shirt. She stood in the doorway with her arms folded. She did not invite Stefanie in, and her sturdy frame radiated a silent hostility. Stefanie caught a glimpse of a man on a sofa, bandaged leg stretched out on a footstool.

Now that she was there, Stefanie didn't quite know how to proceed. She settled on the straightforward approach. "I'm Stefanie Canfield. Perhaps you remember my father, Roger Canfield, and my grandfather? I'm accused of murdering Trisha Duvall, who was the fianceé of my former husband, Hunter Blackwell. I didn't do it —"

"I read the newspapers," Minnie cut in.

"I didn't do it!" Stefanie knew her re- peated denial sounded desperate, but she didn't care. "I understand you worked for Hunter and Trish —"

"I remember your granddaddy, and he was a fine man, but you got no right to be coming here and asking questions and makin' trouble." Minnie braced a foot against the door, as if she thought Stefanie might try to force her way in. "I talked to the police. I don't know anything. Now just go away."

Minnie slammed the door in Stefanie's face. Stefanie fought tears of frustration and disappointment and then raised her hand to pound on the door. *You have to tell me some-*

thing! What stopped her was a sudden awareness that there had been fear as well as hostility in the woman's face. *Was she afraid of me? Or something else?*

Stefanie was still on edge when she stopped at Reedy's to pick up a battery for her watch. Reedy's had a little of everything, from hardware and tools to toys and craft items. She'd purchased the battery and was hurrying across the parking lot to her car when she stopped short. Hunter was headed toward Reedy's door. They were on a collision course.

She remembered Ryan's warning. Could Hunter have followed her there, choreographed this meeting so he could —

Get a grip, Stef. If Hunter had any devious plans for her, he wasn't going to carry them out in a public parking lot. He was, in fact, angling away from her, deliberately avoiding encounter.

Hunter's evasive detour suddenly angered her. The man had once been her husband. Their grandfathers had been partners. And he was trying to frame her for murder. Yet there he was, pretending she didn't exist.

She cut behind a parked car and intercepted him. "I understand an old watch of mine turned up next to Trisha's body."

The challenge forced his gaze to focus on

Stefanie. "If you have anything to say, please communicate through my attorney."

That statement was exactly what Ryan had recommended Stefanie say to Hunter. *You're always one step ahead of me, aren't you, Hunter?* "I didn't kill Trisha, and you know it."

"Innocence or guilt is now up to a jury to decide." He was, as always, the unruffled, crisis-proof Hunter.

"But maybe I won't be the one on trial!" she retorted.

"We'll see." Hunter smiled and nodded to her as if they'd just had a pleasant conversation about the weather.

They both knew who was going to be on trial.

The following morning, Stefanie learned that Hunter had also been a step ahead of her with the Hicksons. Tina had ferreted out an explanation from them.

Buzz Hickson had been injured at the plywood mill and was drawing temporary disability payments on the company's workmen's compensation insurance. Hunter had paid them a visit a few days earlier, expressing concern that they were being properly taken care of. He'd also hinted that if the Hicksons caused trouble for him, they might find their disability payments in jeopardy.

Stefanie and Ryan discussed their days while eating dinner in the kitchen at Stefanie's house. Dinner was an Oriental chicken salad Stefanie had kept ready in the refrigerator until Ryan arrived and a pot of green tea. Sherlock was outside with his disinterred bone.

"A hard man to fight on his home territory," Ryan muttered when Stefanie reported the results of her conversation with the cleaning woman to him.

"Not well liked, I think," he added, "but small-town powerful." Ryan sounded preoccupied, as if some other thought hovered in the back of his mind.

She gave him an uneasy sideways glance. "Is he also powerful in Eugene?"

"No, but most people I talked to seemed well aware they were under no obligation to answer questions from someone without a badge." Ryan's smile held an uncharacteristic hint of cynicism when he added, "But a generous greasing of palms proved helpful."

"And?"

"Hunter's alibi isn't quite airtight, but it's pretty good. About midafternoon on Thursday, the day before the murder, he registered at that motel you named. I couldn't find out where he'd been before that, but I don't think it matters. He spent most of that afternoon at a bank, for what purpose I couldn't find out." Ryan jabbed a chunk of chicken with his fork. "He ate dinner at the restaurant adjoining the motel, went to his room, and apparently stayed there. The next day he went to another bank —"

"This sounds like a man more worried about finances than an unfaithful girlfriend," Stefanie suggested.

"They could be connected. Maybe he figured if his finances were in better shape she wouldn't be unfaithful. That night, Friday night, he attended the annual barbecue of some wood-products industry association. It was held a few miles west of Eugene, at a park owned by a member company. The motel's phone records show —"

"You got into their phone records?"

"That took a very greasy palm. Hunter placed a call to the house in Julesburg, but it was such a brief call that I suspect all he got was the answering machine."

"Which probably made him suspicious that Trisha wasn't home 'in seclusion' as he expected."

"And maybe made him want to rush home to see exactly what she was up to. But he did go to the barbecue, which started at 7:00. Afterward there was dancing to live music and an open bar. It sounds like a pretty rowdy party. When it was over, instead of staying all night at the motel, which would be the logical thing to do, Hunter checked out. It was about 1:00 in the morning. The drive from Eugene to Julesburg takes between an hour and a half to two hours, so that neatly jibes with his 2:45 A.M. report to the police about his discovery of the body."

"Isn't all that airtight?"

"It depends on the details. Whether or not he was actually at the barbecue and dance all evening. I talked to a couple of people who definitely saw him, but they couldn't pin down a time. He could have slipped out at say 8:30 or 9:00, taken an hour and a half to drive to Julesburg, killed Trisha within minutes after you left the house, and then rushed back to the barbecue and dance in Eugene. And therein lies a small peculiarity."

"Peculiarities," Stefanie said, "are beginning to feel like the norm."

"I talked to a waiter from the catering outfit that ran the barbecue. He definitely remembered Hunter being there shortly after midnight. Hunter spilled a drink on a table. When this waiter cleaned up the mess, Hunter gave him a big tip. A memorably big tip. Could be innocent enough —"

"Or it could be a planned accident. A way to be certain he was remembered as being there at that time!"

"Exactly."

"But how could he possibly know this was a convenient night to rush home and murder Trisha . . . and blame it on me?"

"He couldn't know, of course, so it probably wasn't something he'd planned ahead. After the phone call makes him suspicious, he takes his luggage with him from the motel. Then he leaves the barbecue early and returns to Julesburg. But after the deed is done in Julesburg, he rushes back to Eugene and makes a big production of the accident with the waiter to firm up his alibi. Then he does an official motel checkout at that late hour to make it appear as if he was in Eugene all the time."

"That's cutting the timing pretty close." Stefanie visualized the narrow road winding through the mountains to Eugene. "A round-trip drive from Eugene to Julesburg, plus time for a violent enough argument to result in murder —"

"I suspect Hunter's temper was already near the detonation point."

"Even so, he'd have to drive like a maniac to do it all."

Ryan lifted a questioning eyebrow, and

Stefanie nodded. Often, that was exactly how Hunter drove.

"And the authorities have apparently checked with enough witnesses that Hunter's alibi stands up as far as they're concerned," Ryan added. "Several people I talked to had been questioned by the police."

Stefanie pushed her plate away, half her salad uneaten. "So, for all practical purposes, we're back to square one. All we have is speculation about a mad dash to murder, plus a quick planting of a watch to incriminate me."

Ryan nodded. He sipped the tea, appearing to be deep in thought. Finally he said, "Stef, how well do you know your friend Val?"

Stefanie sloshed the tea in her cup in surprise at the question that seemed to come out of nowhere. "Fairly well. Actually, in these past few months, she's been my best friend. Why?"

"Have you talked about the murder with her?"

"Of course. When I was in jail she tried to help me make sense of my memories about that night. We discussed it from every angle. She brought newspaper articles and gossip and sugar-free cookies fresh from the bakery."

"Tell me about her."

"Why?"

"Just humor me, okay?"

Stefanie frowned, but gave him a brief rundown. "She's smart and funny. A bit cynical sometimes, but in a lighthearted way. She's about ten years older than I am. Always struggling with weight and diets and hair color and new cosmetics, but never one to give up the battle. She's also sweet and loyal, the trustworthy kind of person you can count on. Everything anyone could want in a friend."

"Not a Julesburg native, I take it?"

"No. She grew up in California and went to business school in the Bay area. After she married, she and her husband moved up here to Oregon. As lots of Californians do."

"This is the 'Silver-Tongued Rat' husband?"

"Yes, except she isn't calling him that now. His name is Damon Halstead. She's seeing him again, and it sounds like they may get back together." Stefanie still had strong reservations about Damon, but she'd never met him, and her view of him was built on Val's earlier acid-tongued cracks.

"How long ago were they divorced?"

Stefanie considered the question. "I'm not sure. Before she came to Julesburg."

"Which was when?"

"Shortly after Volkman Laser Systems moved their headquarters here. Maybe eighteen months ago. She'd worked for them in Eugene and has a very responsible position as head of their personnel department."

"And you became friends right away?"

"No, we didn't meet until after Hunter and I split up. Val started coming to Fit 'n' Fun about that time. What is all this? Why are you asking all these questions about Val?"

"Did she ever tell you it was Trisha Duvall who broke up her marriage?"

Stefanie gaped at him. "Trisha broke up Val's marriage?" She managed to close her mouth and put down her fork loaded with bean sprouts and bamboo shoots. "What makes you think that?"

"I decided it would be a good idea to see if I could find out something about Trisha's past. There were only three companies listed in the Eugene phone book that sounded like places where Hunter would likely do business. The second company I called, pretending to be an acquaintance of Trisha's from out of town, turned out to be where she'd worked. I was properly shocked when the receptionist told me she'd been murdered. I asked the receptionist if I could take her to lunch so she could tell me more about it."

"You were a busy man in Eugene."

"Not nearly as busy as Trisha was when

she lived there. The receptionist was squeamish about talking about Trisha at first, but she loosened up after a while. She told me that Trisha had, among her various adventures, gone after the husband of one of the receptionist's best friends. Trisha seems to have had a preference for married men. Then Damon Halstead entered the picture. The receptionist didn't know Val, but she knew Trisha broke up Damon's marriage. She'd heard Val had once rammed her car into the side of Trisha's car."

"This all makes for interesting gossip, but I don't see what you're getting at."

"Can't you see? There's a possibility that Hunter's alibi is true, that he didn't kill Trisha. That someone else killed her, and he simply found the body, as he claims. Val had exactly the same motive for murder that the police attribute to you. Trisha Duvall, husband stealer extraordinaire, snatched her husband. If Val is still in love with her ex, her motive may have been even stronger."

"Are you actually accusing Val of killing Trisha?" Stefanie gasped.

"Not necessarily accusing . . . but looking at possibilities."

"Ryan, how do you think it could possibly have happened? Val calls me, finds I'm not home, thinks, 'Oh, she must be over burglarizing Trisha's bedroom. I'll just slip over there, watch for Stef to leave, and murder Trisha before I dash home and watch the late news'?"

"Hold on. I just think we have to keep our minds open. Because I'm afraid this is exactly what the authorities are not doing. We know you didn't do it —"

"We're reasonably certain I didn't do it," Stefanie cut in. "Don't be so eager to get me off that you're willing to incriminate anyone in the vicinity. Especially a wonderful friend like Val who's always been there when I need her."

"I'm sorry, but —"

"Frankly, I'd appreciate it if you'd just drop this line of inquiry, okay? Val may not have told me about Trisha, but it's no big deal."

"Even setting aside her secrecy, there's still the fact that she has a powerful motive."

"And there's still the watch. No way could Val have planted that old watch near Trisha's body. Hunter, and only Hunter, could have done that." Stefanie stood up abruptly and scooped up their plates. "Look, I'm tired, and I'd like to turn in early. Let Sherlock in on your way out, would you, please?"

Ryan found himself outside considerably sooner than he had expected. He waited in the driveway for several minutes, thinking maybe Stefanie would relent and come out. But the downstairs lights went out and the upstairs lights came on.

He felt bad about the sudden cooling between himself and Stefanie; upsetting her and driving a wedge between them was the last thing he wanted. It was why he'd put off bringing up the information about Val as long as possible. He was afraid Stefanie's reaction would be exactly what it was: hostile.

But he couldn't shake the feeling that Val could be involved. He thought about her as he drove toward the Sea Haven. He didn't know Val, of course, but at Fit 'n' Fun she'd struck him as a bold, impulsive person. She'd had no qualms about yanking and inspecting his hair. And her motive was powerful and elementary. If the car-ramming tale was true, it also demonstrated a capacity for violence.

Yet, as Stefanie had reminded him, only Hunter could have planted that watch.

"So don't get sidetracked," he muttered to himself. "Hunter's your man. Don't try to ambush some innocent bystander just because —"

Because I'm in love with Stefanie?

Yes.

★ ★ ★

Stefanie heard Ryan's Blazer pull out of the driveway shortly after she went upstairs. Good! She was glad he was gone.

Accusing Val! All because of a detail Val hadn't told her about her ex-husband and Trisha.

Although it was hardly a minor detail. And why hadn't Val told her?

Stefanie stormed around the room. She snatched up a clump of dog hair and threw it in the wastebasket. She slammed a book on a shelf by the window seat. She would not be suspicious of Val! No one had been more helpful, more supportive, more fiercely loyal than Val. And Val couldn't be a murderer! Val carried daddy long-legs spiders outside rather than kill them. She was vocal against the death penalty.

But Val's hatred of Trisha had so often seemed out of proportion, too venomous, too impassioned, even in support of a friend wronged. Stefanie had sometimes been afraid that Val, in her zeal as a friend, would even do something outrageous, like call Trisha the Liposuction Queen in public. "That woman deserves what she got, and a whole lot worse," she remembered Val declaring after the confrontation between Stefanie and Trisha at the Singing Whale.

Could Val have given Trisha something that *was* far worse . . . a bullet in the heart?

Stefanie picked up the phone and dialed Val's number.

22

Stefanie rang the doorbell at the condo. The nervous dampness of her palms annoyed her. No wild-eyed killer lurked on the other side of the door; it was only her best friend Val.

"Come on in," Val yelled from the kitchen. "Door's not locked."

Inside, the condo smelled fragrantly of cappuccino, and cookie scents, foreign to Val's little-used kitchen, also floated in spicy waves.

"You've decided to turn into a domestic princess?" Stefanie asked, surprised.

Val opened the oven door. "I'm practicing up to impress Damon. I also thought consolation goodies might be called for. You sounded upset on the phone, and I was afraid there might be trouble in paradise with you and The Hunk. These are both sugar and fat free, if you're worried about calories. Someday I'd like to be able to eat stuff that doesn't have all the best parts left out," she grumbled.

Stefanie dropped her jacket and purse on

a stool at the counter separating the kitchen and dining room. "Ryan and I did have kind of a falling out, but that isn't what I want to talk to you about."

"Not upsetting news from the attorney, I hope?"

"No, not really. Although he did call. He wants to see me next week to go over my medical and psychological reports." Stefanie managed a wry smile. "I suspect he intends to remove all sharp objects from his office before I arrive. Just in case I go into one of my spells."

"You're no more a murderer than I am, even if your memory is a little fuzzy," Val declared. "If that guy doesn't believe it, maybe you need a different lawyer."

No more a murderer than I am.

The casually tossed out words unexpectedly jolted Stefanie. She tried to push them from her mind, but she couldn't.

"You okay, sweetie?" Val paused with a cookie on a spatula halfway between the shiny new baking sheet and the cooling rack.

"You never told me it was Trisha who broke up your marriage."

Val eased the cookie onto the rack. "How'd you find out?"

"Ryan went over to Eugene to check out

Hunter's alibi for the night of the murder. He also looked into Trisha's past. And there you were."

"Oh, yes, there I was. And now Ryan is wondering if I was so ticked off about Trisha stealing Damon that I murdered her."

Stefanie didn't reply.

"And you're upset with him about that, aren't you? Stef, sweetie, I don't think you should be mad at Ryan about that. A guy who's in love —"

"Ryan isn't in love!" Stefanie protested. "And he has no right to go around accusing my best friend of murder."

"Did he actually accuse me?"

"He . . . implied it as a possibility. He thought it was very odd that you'd never told me about Trisha."

"He figured the fact that she stole my husband was pretty solid motive for murder. And he's right, isn't he?" Val wiped the baking sheet clean and dropped dough in a whimsical happy-face pattern. She sighed. "The thing with Trisha wasn't something I intended to hide from you, Stef. It wasn't long after she grabbed Damon that I moved over here. They were living together by then, and when the company offered me a transfer, I jumped at it. Then, after a few months here, I heard rumors from a friend back in Eugene that there were some rotten pumpkins in that little paradise and that Trisha was seeing someone new. I didn't realize it was Hunter until Trisha showed up here in Julesburg. Which was one unpleasant shock, let me tell you."

Val grimaced, then smiled. "And, by the way, she did have liposuction on her butt and thighs sometime before she snatched Damon. I got that straight from a friend who worked at the clinic where she had it done. She also had a nose job."

Oddly, rather than feeling satisfaction in knowing Trisha's stunning good looks had been refined by a surgeon's expertise, this revelation made Stefanie blink back tears. She'd always seen Trisha as glossy and golden and perfect. But Trisha had suffered doubts and insecurities too.

"Anyway, when I heard enough local gossip to realize Trisha had done to you exactly what she'd done to me, I looked you up. I guess I thought it would give us this big bond. We'd unite and stick pins into a voodoo doll of her or something. But right away I saw that you were uncomfortable with our having in common the fact that we'd both had marriages shattered by some other woman. You weren't interested in a two-woman 'Betrayed Wives Club.' I figured if you knew it was the same other woman, it would blow your mind. And by then I really liked you and wanted to be friends, so I thought, What does this matter? I'll just keep that ugly detail about Trisha to myself. But I guess it does matter, doesn't it?" Val finished with a sigh.

Stefanie rushed around the counter and wrapped Val in a hug. "No, it does not matter! Because you're right. Back then, it would have blown my mind. And we'd have missed out on a wonderful friendship."

"You're going to miss out on something else wonderful, Stef, if you let this come between you and Ryan. Don't push him away out of a sense of loyalty to me." Val nibbled a crumb of cookie that had fallen on the counter. "Actually, I think you should be proud of him. Smart guy, your Hunk. He uncovered this connection between me and Trisha, which the authorities obviously haven't. And he's going to dig up more facts to prove Hunter's guilt and your innocence, I'm sure of it."

"I thought it was supposed to work the other way around, innocent until proven guilty."

"Unfortunately, sweetie, nothing, from tummy-control pantyhose to justice, ever works exactly like it's supposed to. But you trust Ryan, Stef. He'll get you through this. By the way, did Hunter's alibi hold up?"

"Better than we'd hoped."

"Which is why Ryan wonders if someone else could have done it. And I'm a prime target."

Val obviously thought the suspicion about her involvement in the murder was solely Ryan's. Val assumed Stefanie had as much faith in her as she'd already shown in Stefanie, and Stefanie was ashamed of the crack in her own loyalty.

Val interrupted Stefanie's thoughts with an unexpected laugh. "Hey, did Ryan also dig up something on the infamous car-ramming incident?"

"He mentioned it," Stefanie admitted.

"Oh, he's good. Give that man a gold star! Yep, I did it. Although it was kind of like your incident with the plate of food at the Singing Whale. Mostly accident but maybe not all accident. It happened —"

"You don't have to tell me," Stefanie protested. "I don't think you murdered Trisha."

Val made a little ceremony of rewarding Stefanie with a warm cookie and a cup of frothy cappuccino delivered with a bow of appreciation. "Thanks for the vote of confidence. But I do want to tell you about the car incident, just to get everything out in the open. It happened when I went over to where Trisha worked. This was just after I found out she and Damon were having an affair, before he and I actually split. I had this naïve idea that if I could just talk to her, I could convince her to leave him alone. So I waited in the parking lot for her, but she wouldn't even look at me. She just jumped in her car and started backing up. So I thought I'd nudge my car up against hers so she'd have to stay and talk to me. But my foot slipped on the gas pedal. So there I was, with her car draped over mine like an over-sized hood ornament. And," Val admitted with a laugh, "I wasn't really particularly sorry about it."

"I can understand that," Stefanie said. "If things hadn't turned out the way they did, I might feel a certain satisfaction in dumping a plate of food on Trisha."

"Yeah, I'll bet. And I have to admit that early on I definitely had some murderous thoughts about Trisha. I considered poison in a cup of mint tea. Maybe the prick of a needle dipped in a lethal potion. Or some tiny but toxic insect crawling out of a floral bouquet delivered to her door." Val set her cup on the counter. Her frivolous tone suddenly sobered. "But not a gun, Stef. Not blood and gore and bullets. My thoughts were just wild fantasies, and what happened to Trisha was real and bloody and awful. I couldn't have done that to anyone, no matter how much I hated her."

"Someone could. And did." Stefanie swallowed. "And wants me blamed for it."

Stefanie told Val about the watch that had been found near Trisha's body. The spoon with which Val was stirring the cookie dough clattered to the floor.

"Hunter deliberately planted the old watch there to incriminate you? Oh, that scum! I knew he was a —" Val broke off and tossed her spoon in the sink. "I didn't think even Hunter would stoop that low. What does Ryan say about this?"

"Dialogue between Ryan and me on all subjects has come to a rather abrupt halt."

"Because of me. Oh, Stef, I'm so sorry I never told you everything about Trisha." The faint lines crossing Val's forehead deepened with concern. "I wouldn't for the world come between you and Ryan."

"No big deal," Stefanie assured her.

"Look, this is off the subject, but I was planning to call you this evening even before you called me. Damon is coming over for dinner Sunday evening. I'd like you to come too."

"Me? That's the dumbest idea I've ever

heard," Stefanie declared. "Why in the world would you want me here? In case you've forgotten the old cliché, two's company, three's a crowd. And a crowd is not conducive to romance."

"I want you to meet him, Stef. I've given you a terribly unfair view of him, and I want you to see what a really great guy he is."

Stefanie hedged with a plausible excuse. "Actually, I don't feel much like participating in social events at the moment."

"I know you don't. But there's another, even more important reason for you to meet him. Damon may have important information about Trisha's murder."

"Damon? How could he know anything?"

"I'll just let him tell you, okay?"

"Is this on the up and up? Or just a clever subterfuge to get me to come to dinner when he's here?"

Val flung a hand to her forehead in exaggerated dismay. "Would I do that?"

"You might."

Val smiled. "Okay, I might. But I really do think you should talk to Damon."

"Has he told you what he knows?"

"More or less."

"Why don't you just tell me?"

Val smiled again. "Is 7:00 Sunday evening okay?"

Stefanie tilted her head as she studied her friend. "You really love him, don't you?"

"I really do. I always have, ever since about an hour after I met him at a literary cocktail party a friend took me to."

"Why was he there?"

"I guess I never told you, but he's a writer. He does horror-type paperbacks under a pen name, Knight Ryder. But he also has this really terrific literary novel that he's been working on for several years. He'll publish that under his real name, of course."

Knight Ryder. Not a name familiar to Stefanie, but she was not a reader of horror novels. The fact that he dealt in words gave an unexpected dimension to Val's "Silver-Tongued Rat" name for him.

"What exactly do you mean by 'horror' books?"

"Oh, you know. Demons. Satanic worship. A vampire or werewolf here and there." Val's smile was indulgent, as if she were talking about some little boy's penchant for playing in the mud. "But this is just temporary nickel-and-dime stuff until he gets his big break."

"He doesn't really believe in that sort of thing, does he?"

"Oh, no. It's just what's popular and sells books. You know how low the general public's taste is. Though sometimes he helps get himself in the mood for that kind of writing by burning black candles and incense."

Stefanie felt a strong stirring of revulsion, but Val didn't seem to notice.

"Anyway, I was in love with him before the party was over. I felt as if I was shattering in a million pieces when he left me for Trisha. Saying all those awful things about him was just a way to help me cope. But he's not a terrible person, Stef. He's very intense. His emotions run deep. He was really . . . obsessed with Trisha for a while. But he can see that now. And obsession is not the same as love."

"Why did he and Trisha split up?"

"Money was Trisha's god, you know, and I suspect that the horror-writing business wasn't as lucrative as she expected. So she leaped for the Plywood King, whom she thought stood on a higher rung on the financial ladder."

"Have you ever heard rumors about her and the owner of Volkman Laser Systems? Although I'm sure he's married —"

"No obstacle to Trisha, as we both know. She seemed to prefer married men. Like the wedding ring gave him a seal of approval." Val nibbled a cookie. "I haven't heard that specific rumor, but there could be something to it. The woman was greedy enough to dig up her mother's grave for a buck. Damon sees that now, and whatever the mistakes of the past, he and I are both ready to move on with our lives."

"Good."

"So will you come to dinner please? I think what Damon knows could really be helpful to you."

Possible information about the murder was too powerful a bait to resist. Stefanie nodded, accepting the invitation. She also accepted the sack of cookies Val handed her.

"See you at Fit 'n' Fun tomorrow?" Stefanie asked. Val usually spent an hour or two at the health club on Saturdays.

"Not tomorrow. That's my day to learn how to make the chicken kiev I'm going to impress Damon with at dinner. I've decided to follow that old adage, 'The way to a man's heart is through his stomach.' "

I doubt it was Trisha's cooking that lured Damon into betrayal and obsession, but I hope it works for you, Val.

"Oh, by the way, bring Ryan along to dinner Sunday evening. As you pointed out, three is an awkward number. Four will round out the table nicely."

"You had that little scheme in mind all

along, didn't you, Ms. Valerie 'Matchmaker' Halstead?" Stefanie accused.

"I just think he should hear what Damon has to say about the murder too."

Stefanie hesitated, then turned to go. "Maybe so. But I don't anticipate communication with Ryan any time in the near future."

23

Stefanie spent Saturday morning at the Laurel Cove Nursing Center and the afternoon at Fit 'n' Fun. Val called to ask if Sherlock would be interested in a couple of chicken kiev experiments gone awry. "Sure, bring 'em on. Sherlock's not fussy." When she got home, she found a cardboard carton propped up against the back door. Inside were half a dozen blackened, unidentifiable blobs. Sherlock chowed down cheerfully.

On Sunday morning Twila Mosely called and asked if Stefanie was coming to church. Stefanie hadn't planned to go, but she appreciated Twila's visits to the jail, so she said, "Yes, I think I can make it this morning."

When she arrived in the church parking lot at five minutes to eleven, she saw the board that gave the subject of that morning's message.

"In all things God works for the good of those who love him. Romans 8:28."

Stefanie remembered quoting that to herself when she was putting heart and soul into prayer for her mom . . . and watching her suffer and grow thinner and weaker day by day. She remembered clinging to that verse when her marriage was crumbling. "Please, Lord, make good come out of this. Help us to work through this and come out with a better and stronger marriage."

Stefanie wheeled the car around the parking lot, and the tires spurted gravel as she headed for the exit. She had to slam on the brakes to avoid crunching a dark Blazer turning into the lot.

Ryan rolled down his window. "Going somewhere?"

"What are you doing here?"

"I'm a Christian. I usually go to church on Sundays," he answered. "You aren't worshipping today?"

"I had a change of mind when I saw the topic of today's message."

His gaze followed the snap of her head toward the board. "Maybe we should talk about this. Not here," he added, when a polite toot of horn pointed out that they were blocking the parking lot entrance. "How about a drive?"

"Shouldn't you stay for church?"

"I'll square it with God later."

"No, thank you."

"I'm not moving my car until you agree, and you can't get out of the parking lot until I move. Which is going to make it rather inconvenient for any member of the congregation who would like to get into the parking lot today." Another toot emphasized his point. Ryan merely smiled.

You didn't outgrow your stubbornness, did you? Stefanie let her car roll back into the parking lot. Three vehicles immediately scooted through the entrance. She pulled around to the last row of spaces.

"We'll take my car," Ryan called.

His vehicle was comfortably messy. A Snickers wrapper lay crumpled on the dashboard, and a crushed 7-Up can was jammed into the ashtray. Ryan remained silent until they crossed the bridge over Wandering Creek.

"I'm sorry for upsetting you about Val. My suspicions were way out of line, and I apologize. As you pointed out, only Hunter could've planted the watch to incriminate you. And the only reason he'd have for incriminating you was if he killed Trisha."

"Val explained why she hadn't told me about Trisha." Stefanie repeated Val's explanation.

Ryan nodded. "I can understand that."

Stefanie felt her attitude toward Ryan

softening. His accusation hadn't angered Val; Val had seen it as protective. Perhaps she should too. And he did say he was wrong and apologized.

Tentatively she said, "Val invited both of us to dinner this evening. She wants us to meet her ex-husband, Damon."

"I know. She called me at the motel about an hour ago."

"She's playing matchmaker, you know."

"An honorable calling."

"What did you tell her?"

"I accepted, of course."

"I wouldn't have thought meeting a horror writer dealing in vampires and were-wolves was high on your list of priorities."

Ryan shrugged. "It isn't. But I wasn't going to pass up an opportunity to have dinner with you." He looked over at her and smiled. "Considering our last parting, I didn't see any dinner invitations from you in the near future."

Stefanie let the teasing comment pass. "Did she tell you Damon claims he knows something about the murder?"

Ryan nodded. "What do you think?"

"I think Damon Halstead is an egotistical, slick-talking, cheating-husband shyster who deserves the 'Silver-Tongued Rat' name Val gave him. I think he's just trying to build himself up and look more important than he is."

Ryan lifted an eyebrow at the harsh assessment. "Given that attitude, dinner may be an interesting experience."

"For Val's sake, I'll try to keep my opinions to myself. And I could be wrong, of course. I suppose it's unfair to form an opinion before meeting him."

"Yeah, you're probably right about that. Hey, did Val tell you that he's specific about the subject of his information? He says it has to do with Hunter."

Stefanie sat up straighter in the seat. "She didn't tell me that." She paused. "But if Damon really knows something important, why hasn't he gone to the police?"

"Good question. Perhaps we should ask him tonight."

Ryan pulled the Blazer off the highway at an overlook high above the water. Jumbled rocks sloped steeply to a narrow crescent of beach below. Seagulls swooped and shrieked. Waves exploded through a hole in an offshore rock. The irregular crash rose above the steady roar of surf. Ryan leaned his forearms against the steering wheel.

"I gather you take exception to Pastor Gordon's scheduled message at church, that all things work together for good for those who love God." His tone was conversational, his glance across the front seat of the Blazer interested rather than confrontational.

"I don't see any evidence that it's true."

Stefanie kept her gaze on the hole in the rock. Not every wave crashed through in an explosion of spray. Some rolled gently. *Isn't every seventh wave supposed to be larger than the others?* She tried to count waves to predict which wave would rise and surge through the opening. One, two . . . It didn't work. Some waves exploded; some didn't. As in life, if there was a pattern, she couldn't find it. Sometimes there was just one crash after another.

"Can you look at all the terrible things that happen to faithful Christians and honestly say good comes out of every one of them?" she challenged.

He didn't answer immediately. "I think, in the long run, it does," he finally said. "But that good may not be apparent for a long, long time. The bottom line of being a Christian is not carried out here in earthly rewards and punishments. It shows up in eternal salvation in the life beyond this one. We may have to wait until we see Jesus for some answers."

"But can you in any way see good in what

my mother went through? She *suffered,* Ryan. Pain, nausea . . ." Stefanie shook her head.

"No," Ryan admitted. "I can't. But —"

"Is there good in Trisha's murder? And in my being accused of that murder?" Stefanie's knuckles whitened against the seat belt as she squeezed it.

"I can't see it now," he said.

"So often it's seemed that whatever I prayed, exactly the opposite happened. Sometimes I feel like our lives are just a cruel game with God. 'Look at all those foolish people down there. I can crush them if I want to. Maybe I will.' "

"But he cares, Stef. About each and every one of us. Statistics say there are six billion of us on earth now, and if each one of us were to cry out to him at the very same moment, he would still hear every cry. And care. Don't give up on him, Stef. I know it doesn't seem like it at the moment, but we can go to his Word —"

"You think there's a Bible verse for every occasion?" she snapped.

"Actually I do."

Three waves in a row blasted through the hole, like some out-of-control chain reaction. Stefanie clenched her hands.

"Actions speak louder than Bible verses.

Sometimes silence speaks just as loud. I see God as the ultimate expert at silence. If he does listen and care, why do such terrible things happen, not only to me but to Christians everywhere?"

Ryan shook his head slowly. "That's right up there at the top of any list of 'How come, Lord?' questions. Because we know he's all-powerful, and he could intervene. And often he does —"

"And often he doesn't. Sometimes I think of that verse in Matthew that says if you have faith as small as a mustard seed, you can say to the mountain, 'Move from here to there,' and it will move, that nothing will be impossible for you."

"And no mountain moved for you."

"That's right, no mountain moved for me." Stefanie's hand ran up and down the seat belt. "Will one move now? If I get down on my knees and pray long and hard enough that I won't be convicted of a murder I didn't commit, will it happen? Will the real killer suddenly come forward? Or will I wind up spending my life in a jail cell?"

"I don't know, Stef. I wish I could know, but . . . I can't. The Lord sees a bigger picture than we do —"

"You know the picture I see? Years ago, we were exploring on Lighthouse Hill. It was raining and the wind was blowing like a banshee, and we were the only ones up there. Remember that day? We went off the trail and way beyond the sign that says, 'Danger! Do Not Trespass Beyond This Point.' "

"I remember. It was a stupid thing to do. We crawled out to the edge of a cliff that was so slippery we had to hang on to each other to keep from getting blown off it. And it was so crumbly that pieces were breaking off under our feet."

"And we could look down and see a whirlpool among the rocks and waves down there. I got dizzy. I felt it . . . pulling at me. As if it had a will and wanted to suck me under. That's how I feel now, Ry. As if I'm caught in a whirlpool and everything is out of control and I'm going under."

He scooted across the seat and put his arms around her. He soothed her with a stroke of his hand on her arm and a touch of his lips on her hair. "The Lord has promised that he'll always be with us. He'll never leave us or forsake us."

"But he doesn't always save us from the whirlpool."

Ryan let her out at the parking lot. Except for her car, the lot was empty. He watched until she drove away. He pulled around until the Blazer faced the small church. It was a modest building. White clapboard with an old-fashioned steeple and the newer addition of a ramp for wheelchair use. He closed his eyes and rested his head on the steering wheel.

Lord, I didn't handle that very well, did I? I want so much to help her find her way back to you, but I fall short. I pray you'll move in her heart. Guide her out of this whirlpool in her life.

And what should I do about this unfair accusation against her? She didn't murder Trisha. You and I both know that. Lord, I pray for your mercy and compassion on her. My own faith doesn't falter, Lord, but sometimes I don't know the way. Show me.

Ryan picked Stefanie up at the house at ten minutes to seven. He was dressed in chinos and a sports jacket. Stefanie didn't feel much better than she had that afternoon, but the outburst with Ryan seemed to have cleansed something in her.

No other car was parked in Val's driveway when they arrived at the condo.

"The honored guest apparently hasn't arrived yet," Ryan observed.

"Maybe he won't show." *I don't want Val to be disappointed . . . but maybe she'd be better off*

344

if this cheating ex-husband did pull a no-show act tonight.

Val answered the door in a head-turning outfit. Her black blouse was low cut and clingy. Black velvet pants made her legs long and lean. And no bare feet for Val tonight; her barely-there sandals were stiletto heeled and lipstick red. Her only jewelry was the pair of ruby earrings Damon had once given her. They glittered like glistening drops of blood at her ears. Tendrils of hair framed an artful disarray of freshly-auburned curls. Her makeup was not over the top, but pushing the limits. Stefanie wondered if the brightness of her eyes had the aid of a drink or two before they arrived.

"Hey, how come you didn't tell me this was go-for-the-glamour night?" Stefanie asked. Not that she owned anything in a class with that outfit. "You look gorgeous, and here I am, all dull and dowdy."

"You're my best friend, sweetie, but that doesn't mean I want Damon staring at you instead of me," Val said with cheerful honesty.

Stefanie didn't mind being out of the glamour competition. The last thing she wanted was any show of interest from Damon Halstead's roving eyes.

"I also want him concentrating on this

dinner I've knocked myself out to produce."
With a roll of the eyes, Val added, "I've
made chicken kiev enough times to allow
some chicken farmer to retire in style. By
the way, there's another box of discards in
the kitchen for Sherlock."

Ryan presented the gladiolas he'd
brought for Val. Val arranged the flowers in
a vase and set it on the coffee table. An elaborate centerpiece of candles and deep red
roses clustered among ferns already decorated the dining table.

"I have champagne, but it's juice cocktails
for both you teetotalers, I presume?" Val
said, teasing.

"Please," Ryan said, and Stefanie nodded.

Val brought the frothy orange drinks in
tulip-shaped glasses on a tray. Her own glass
appeared to be filled with something
stronger. She sat in a chair across the coffee
table from where Stefanie and Ryan sat on
the sofa. Val gave an airy wave with the glass.
"Damon should be along soon. Promptness
is like broccoli with Damon: not a high pri-
ority."

"It's hard to estimate driving time," Ryan
offered.

He could have done it if he'd tried.

Val chattered vivaciously about her dinner
problems and soon had them all laughing.

"You know how you're supposed to tear lettuce instead of cutting it?" She rolled her eyes. "Forget it. My lettuce looked like two maniacal rabbits waged a battle over it. And radish roses. Have you ever heard of anything more ridiculous? Mine turned out looking like a row of tiny little dismembered body parts. Ugh. And did you ever make a mistake and put something metallic in the microwave? Let me tell you, there's a reason they say not to do that."

But Val's vivaciousness began to droop after a half hour. She jumped up and looked out the window at the driveway every few minutes. *Oh, Val, don't let him do this to you. He isn't worth it.* After forty-five minutes, Val tried Damon's number in Eugene. The answering machine picked up. "That means he's on his way," she said brightly.

At three minutes after 8:00, fully an hour late, the muted roar of a powerful car sounded in the driveway. Val jumped up, and her drink sloshed on her velvet pants. She didn't notice.

"There's the Rat now," Val said. She grimaced, but her relief was so patent that Stefanie's heart ached for her. *Don't let it mean this much to you. Please.*

Val put a scarlet-tipped finger to her lips. "Not a word about my dinner troubles, okay? I want him to think I can do this with a snap of my fingers. I neglected this sort of thing when we were married, and Damon is not a tuna casserole and corndog kind of man."

Then the man walked through the door Val held open, and Stefanie's preconceived images of the Silver-Tongued Rat tangled with the high-powered reality of Damon Halstead.

24

"Guess who feels dull and dowdy now," Ryan murmured. He fingered a button on the cuff of his sports shirt. "Maybe I should have traded in my chinos for something Armani."

Stefanie had envisioned Val's ex-husband as a slick-looking, hot-talking salesman in polyester. When she learned he wrote horror fiction and had an ambition toward literary novels, she pictured him in something tweedy with leather elbow patches. Or perhaps, in more facetious speculations, a vampire cape and fangs.

Damon Halstead put those cheesy conjectures to shame.

His perfectly tailored charcoal suit, white shirt, and burgundy-and-silver striped tie discreetly proclaimed expensive good taste and elegant masculinity. Silver streaked the temples of his dark hair, and his eyes were almost startlingly blue in a dark-complected face. He wasn't tall, nor was his build muscular, but he projected power and a black-cat grace. Maybe even a small, tantalizing hint of danger. He was a man with a high-voltage *presence,* one who would draw eyes, both male and female, even in a roomful of taller, more muscular hunks. As Val had said, not a tuna casserole and corndog kind of man.

Ryan jabbed her lightly in the ribs. "Put your eyes back in their sockets," he muttered. "Before you trip over them."

Stefanie gave him a quick, embarrassed smile.

Val made introductions. Stefanie had a preconceived aversion to Damon, but that didn't keep her from seeing that his smile was potent enough to flutter heartbeats. His gaze riveted on Stefanie when they shook hands. "I've been looking forward to meeting you."

He makes it sound as if he's been holding his breath and waiting a lifetime to meet me. Silver-Tongued Rat. But Damon's smile wasn't just for her — Ryan received the same intense focus of attention when he and Damon shook hands.

"I understand you're an arson investigator." Damon also gave the impression he'd been waiting a lifetime to meet an arson investigator, Ryan in particular.

As soon as they were all seated and Val had brought Damon a drink, Damon gave

Ryan a long chemical name and asked about using the substance in a future book he was planning. She heard respect for the man's knowledge in Ryan's answer, and they continued with a discussion of other chemicals.

Stefanie would've preferred to dump Damon in the 'Big Phony' category, but she couldn't doubt that the intensity of his focus on one person was genuine.

"I apologize for jumping right into shop talk," Damon said. He directed another of his easy, dazzling smiles at Stefanie, then looked at Val. "Something smells wonderful."

He hadn't spoken more than a few words to Stefanie, but already she found herself reluctantly intrigued by the man. And he was very good looking. Val hadn't exaggerated. When Damon wasn't smiling, his face had a dark, smoldering quality, like an old James Dean poster. And when he did smile . . .

"Dinner is ready," Val said, "but if you'd like another cocktail first . . . ?" Ryan and Stefanie's glasses were empty, but Val directed the question to Damon.

"Considering how late I am, why don't we skip the cocktail and eat right away?" Damon suggested.

Stefanie approved of his considerateness. She knew Val must be worrying that her chicken kiev was shriveling to leather. *Perhaps I've misjudged the guy. Everyone makes mistakes. Maybe his mistake with Trisha was just more devastating than most, and he's really a great guy otherwise. Keep an open mind.*

Of course, she couldn't help thinking as they took seats at the dining table that Damon had offered neither apology nor explanation for his lateness.

Val served the dinner. The chicken kiev may have suffered a bit from the delay but it was still delicious. Damon was generous with compliments. "The chicken is incredible, Val. I didn't know you could do this. And the hollandaise sauce has just that right tang I love." He made a little circle with forefinger and thumb and winked at her. "Been hiding talents from me, haven't you?"

Damon seemed in no hurry to get to the subject of Hunter and the murder, and Stefanie was thankful for that. She was impatient for his information, but it was not an appropriate side dish for the asparagus tips and pasta. He instead regaled them with stories about book tours, eccentric editors, and strange fan mail he had received.

"The letters signed in blood are the ones that remind me why I use a pen name." Damon's chuckle and wrinkle of nose gave his darkly handsome face a boyish charm.

"And then there are the marriage proposals." Val rolled her eyes. "He has a special allure for women who claim to be witches. Plus the occasional female werewolf."

"I have this fear one of them will discover my real name and home address and show up at my door. Not necessarily in human form. Makes a man appreciate a nice, normal woman who merely nags about taking out the trash." Damon's glance at Val seemed affectionate.

Damon dominated the conversation during dinner. Val had little to say. Her feverish chatter had ended with his arrival. Mostly she just smiled and looked at Damon. Stefanie had the feeling Val was so eager to please Damon that if he'd asked her to cartwheel across the dining table she'd have jumped to comply.

But Val aside, Damon passed all the tests for a pleasant dinner companion. Perhaps a bit self-centered, if one wanted to be picky, but with enough entertaining anecdotes and insider's knowledge about the literary world to be fascinating. Only once did the lively dinner conversation veer in a direction that put Stefanie on edge.

"You're working on a new book now, I suppose?" Stefanie asked.

"Yes. The working title is *Mirage in Cold Blood*. I see a stark black cover with a single pool of glistening red blood." Damon's hands outlined a graceful swirl, at odds with the gory description.

Stefanie wasn't sure she wanted to hear more, yet courtesy seemed to require that she not drop the subject immediately. "Will it be available soon?"

Damon murmured something noncommittal about delays.

Val jumped in. "Being a writer isn't like being a plumber or an accountant. Writing is so demanding, so intensively creative, that a writer can't just leap in and do it the way a plumber can always fix pipes or an accountant juggle numbers —"

Val broke off abruptly when Damon glanced at her. His expression revealed nothing to Stefanie, but Val apparently read something in it. She became very busy cutting her asparagus into green slivers.

With an exaggerated sigh, Damon said, "Writer's block. It's like a concrete wall falling over the well of creativity blocking the flow of words. The bane of every writer's existence."

His smile suggested it was a minor problem, a temporary setback, but Stefanie couldn't help wondering how long the block had existed. Since as far back as when Trisha walked out on him?

"But the time hasn't been wasted. I do know this story will be about a survivalist existing on a deserted island. The kind of man trained to kill silently with his bare hands. The kind of man who enjoys killing with his bare hands. I've had time to do a lot of research."

Damon picked up a roll and began buttering it. Stefanie looked at his hands. They were well-groomed, but not as long-fingered and elegant as she would have expected. The fingers were thick and blunt. Capable looking.

Damon looked up and smiled. "Of course it can be tough killing a not-quite-human adversary. My fans expect a good fang-baring, claw-raking, Satan-in-disguise fiend, bless their bloodthirsty little souls."

Dinner moved on. Val successfully managed a flaming dessert, and afterward they moved into the living room with coffee. Damon remarked on the great view and what a nice small town Julesburg was. It might have been any ordinary intimate dinner party among friends, but Stefanie sat there with her hands in her lap, trying to keep them from fidgeting nervously.

Something about Damon or the evening was . . . off. She couldn't put her peculiar feeling in a mental frame and hold it up for inspection, but it was there. An unwanted male interest? No. Damon had offered no more than a subtle acknowledgment that she was an attractive woman. Perhaps it was that his dazzling smile moved only his mouth; the easy laughter never warmed his eyes. Behind those smiles, beyond the entertaining conversation lurked something dark and disturbing.

Finally she pinned it down. It was a watchfulness, as if another Damon existed somewhere behind those eyes. And that unsmiling Damon was sizing her up, weighing her worth.

Stefanie shivered and squirmed on the sofa. She tucked a foot under her. She found a pinpoint of lint to pick off her skirt. She wanted to leave, but she had come to hear what Damon had to say about the murder, so she forced herself to sit on the sofa and sip her coffee.

Damon inquired about the tale of a long-ago murder at Julesburg's closed theater, the Nevermore. Stefanie told what she knew about the murder of the man and the later suicide of the woman who'd owned the theater at the time. "And there have been other

. . . oh, odd things that happened to people connected with the theater."

"Some people say some evil entity inhabits the theater," Val added. "Just your kind of place." She gave Damon a flirty sideways glance, but he didn't respond.

He leaned forward and set his cup on the coffee table. "And this was Julesburg's only murder . . . until now?"

Stefanie met Damon's eyes and realized that he had manipulated the conversation to fit his time frame. "Yes, I believe that's true. Julesburg's only murder. Until now."

"Hunter killed her, of course," Damon said, tossing the statement out casually.

Stefanie felt let down. *Is that all you have? Surely you don't think Hunter's guilt has never occurred to me. Let's see some proof.*

Damon smiled faintly as if reading her skepticism.

"Trisha kept in touch with me off and on even after she moved over here with Hunter," Damon said to Stefanie; Val and Ryan had apparently become irrelevant to the conversation. "We had lunch occasionally when she was in Eugene having her hair and nails done."

Had Val known that before now? Stefanie angled a sideways glance at her friend. Then she looked back at Damon, puzzled. Why would he have been in contact with a woman who had betrayed him? Damon did not strike her as a man who would settle for crumbs.

"It wasn't something I encouraged." Damon smiled again. "Although I have to admit to a certain petty satisfaction in hearing Trisha's complaints about Hunter. I was long over whatever feelings I'd ever had for her, but I was concerned about the increasing level of fear she was expressing about Hunter. She even said she'd bought a gun for protection."

"Why would she be afraid of Hunter? He showed every evidence of being totally smitten with her."

"Trisha could be an infuriating woman, and Hunter had a violent temper." Damon lifted an eyebrow, head tilted toward Stefanie.

He expects me, the ex-wife, to confirm that statement. She hesitated. Even though Hunter had been sly and underhanded with her, he'd never directed physical violence at her.

But . . . there was one time they'd had a heated argument about selling a property that had been in Stefanie's family for years. Later she'd found the mirror in the bathroom smashed. She'd wondered then if his usual veneer of calm concealed a violent nature. And the term "road rage" might have been invented to cover his style of driving . . .

Stefanie gave a tentative nod of agreement.

"Hunter was in desperate need of money, of course," Damon went on. "Trisha said any little financial setback might send him into a fury. Then he'd make some extravagant purchase for himself or her to make up for it and be in more financial trouble than ever."

True. Hunter has always been one to prove his worth with a show of his possessions. "What about another man?" she suggested. "Was Hunter jealous of someone?"

"Perhaps. Although, if that were the only cause of his anger, I suspect he'd have aimed his bullet at the rival, don't you? In any case, Trisha discovered that Hunter had found a way to get out of his financial black hole." He paused. "He hired a man to burn down the mill."

Ryan leaned forward. "Is there any proof of his connection to the arson?"

Damon blinked, as if surprised to find someone else in the room. "There is no proof at the moment, no."

"Why would she tell *you* all this about Hunter and the arson?"

"At the time, I presumed it was simply because she had no one else in whom to confide. Trisha didn't make close friends easily —"

"Especially not women friends," Stefanie cut in. "She was too busy stealing their husbands."

Ryan and Val both looked shocked at the catty remark. Stefanie put a finger to her mouth, shocked at herself. "I'm sorry —"

"But correct." Damon smiled and his head dipped in a deferential nod. "In any case, for whatever reason, she did tell me. She also said she didn't feel Hunter should get away with arson and insurance fraud. It wasn't right, and she'd decided to expose him. But she feared he suspected what she planned and would resort to violence to stop her."

Yeah, right. Trisha with some noble sense of duty, some virtuous concern about right and wrong? I could never believe that! Concern about moral accountability was as foreign to Trisha's self-centered character as heed for the women whose husbands she stole.

"Isn't it considerably more likely," she suggested bluntly, "that Trisha planned to blackmail Hunter about the arson?"

For the first time that evening an unplanned expression broke through Damon's smooth façade. His jaw dropped a fraction of an inch. Stefanie wondered if Damon would try to defend Trisha, but after a long silence, he nodded slowly.

"Yes, that's possible. And perhaps an even greater motive for Hunter to kill her." He nodded again. "Yes, that's it. Exactly. She threatened to blackmail him, and he killed her!" The look he awarded Stefanie elevated her to a place at the top of the class.

"But if she was so afraid of him, why didn't she simply leave during those days Hunter was away from home just before she was shot?" Ryan asked. "It would have been a logical time for her to escape."

"She may have been trying to collect more proof about the arson," Damon said.

"The better to blackmail him with," Stefanie murmured.

Damon tilted his head, his gaze on Stefanie. "There's also a possibility Hunter hired someone to actually commit the murder, as he did with the arson. Or had a willing accomplice."

Damon's eyes locked with Stefanie's and did not look away. Was he suggesting she could be involved with Hunter in Trisha's death? The police had evidence against her. As co-owner of the mill she possibly stood to gain from an insurance payoff. Was

Damon there not to prove Hunter's guilt but to ensnare her?

A faint smile played across Damon's face as he watched her, as if he enjoyed the chaos he'd created within her.

"Why haven't you gone to the authorities with this?" Ryan demanded.

Damon's elegantly clad shoulders lifted in a shrug. "Because all I have at the moment is what Trisha told me. Hearsay evidence, I believe it's called in legal terminology. Of no value in court."

Again Stefanie felt Damon's watchful gaze. Like a hunter studying prey through a telescopic sight, aligning her in the crosshairs . . .

"But I don't think Hunter had help." Damon folded his hands behind his head and smiled at Stefanie as he freed her. "Hunter killed Trisha, and I have no doubt but that he did it alone. Shot her in cold blood. And from all appearances, he's getting away with it." A momentary incandescence of fury burned in his blue eyes.

Somewhere in the back of her mind Stefanie noted that Damon showed no concern that *she* stood to be blamed for the murder, only anger that Hunter was not going to pay for what he'd done.

"Hunter planted an old watch of

Stefanie's so that it was found near Trisha's body. He did it to incriminate her," Val said suddenly. "He's the only one who could have killed her."

Damon looked at Stefanie. "Is that true?"

"Yes."

"A very clever man, our Hunter Blackwell. He burns the mill but keeps his hands clean. With a shot to the heart, Trisha the blackmailer is dead. You, the greedy and troublesome ex-wife," Damon bowed his head to Stefanie, "are convicted of the murder. Hunter wipes his bloodstained hands, collects the insurance money on the mill, and lives happily ever after."

Stefanie agreed with the grim scenario, but at that moment, all she wanted was *out*. Out and away from the feeling that Damon was manipulating all of them, that he was working on some agenda outside her comprehension. She stood up. Her leg, numb from how she'd been sitting, gave way and she stumbled against the corner of the coffee table. Ryan jumped to grab her elbow and didn't let go.

Stefanie tucked a strand of hair behind her ear and forced a polite normalcy into her voice. "I think you should go to the authorities. Even if what Trisha confided in you isn't evidence that will hold up in court, it might force the police to investigate Hunter more thoroughly and uncover the truth."

Damon also rose. The momentary glitter of blue fury was gone and the watchful calculation had returned. "Have you gone to the police about the watch?" he asked.

"No. It was an old watch. I'd left it at the house when I moved out. But I can't prove that. Or that I wasn't wearing it that night."

"So, again, we come back to the matter of proof."

Ryan's hand tightened on Stefanie's arm. "We really should be going." He turned to Val. "Thanks for a fantastic dinner."

Stefanie echoed the thanks. They retrieved their jackets and moved toward the door. Stefanie wanted to run, but Damon was small-talking, almost playing the host.

"I'm so pleased that I had the opportunity to meet both of you. If you can get over to Eugene sometime, we'll have dinner at my place. Not as sumptuous a meal as this, but I'll whip up something."

Val slipped into the kitchen and returned with a neatly tied carton. "A present for Sherlock," she murmured in a conspiratorial whisper to Stefanie.

At the door, Damon shook hands with them again. "It's been a pleasure meeting both of you."

"I'll call you," Val said as Stefanie and Ryan walked out the door to the car.

Ryan edged the Blazer around Damon's car, a dark-colored, foreign make that Stefanie couldn't identify. He drove without speaking until they reached her driveway. She was grateful for the silence; she felt like a spring too tightly wound. She needed time to unwind before the spring snapped. Ryan parked under the yard light and turned off the engine.

"So, what do you think?" he asked.

Stefanie knew he was talking about Damon's revelations about Hunter's guilt in both the arson and the murder. She shivered, and her answer jumped down a different path. "I think Val should reconsider wanting that guy back. I think she should save her chicken kiev and flaming desserts for someone more worthy of them." Her voice took on an urgency she hadn't realized was there. "I think she should send him packing . . . or run like crazy."

In the semidarkness of the yard light, she saw Ryan lift an eyebrow. "Oh? I thought you were quite taken with him. Movie-star good looks, successful writer, charismatic personality. The way you hung on his every word, I was beginning to get a little jealous."

"I hope you're kidding," Stefanie said.

"But he is . . . intriguing. I can see why Val fell for him. But I definitely am not taken with Damon Halstead."

To let him know she really meant it, she leaned over and kissed him lightly on the cheek. "I'm glad you were there tonight."

"So am I." He grinned and pulled her across the seat. "But you're not going to get away with that skimpy little peck of a kiss."

He wrapped his arms around her and kissed her, his mouth warm in the damp coolness of the car. It was no skimpy little peck of a kiss. Stefanie hadn't known she needed it, but now, with his lips on hers, she knew the kiss was exactly what she needed.

When he finally lifted his head, Ryan smiled at her. "I'm glad to know you were not overly impressed with Damon Halstead."

"Who?"

Ryan laughed. "Okay, don't lay it on too heavy, or you'll have me wondering again."

The bucket seats did not make for comfortable snuggling, but Stefanie reached for his hand again when she settled back in her own seat. "I wonder quite a few things about Damon." She tapped Ryan's fingers thoughtfully. "Val once told me that he was obsessed with Trisha. I can see now how that was probably true."

Ryan nodded. He didn't ask for an explanation. Stefanie wasn't sure if she could explain; she just knew. There was something about the intensity of Damon's personality, something about his voice when he said Trisha's name.

Ryan's fingers played an absentminded game of twist and weave with hers. "Obsession . . . and love and hate . . . can make a strange triangle," he reflected.

Stefanie felt a shiver unrelated to the cool of the car. "And I'm not sure which side of the triangle we're dealing with here."

"Do you get the feeling," Ryan asked slowly, "that Damon was holding something back tonight? That he wasn't telling us everything he knew?"

"Yes, I did." *Damon is definitely holding something back.*

25

Over the next few days, several important events occurred.

Using a photo of Hunter supplied by Stefanie, plus a lot of leg work, Ryan located a neighbor of Greg Haggerston's in Dutton Bay who said that some weeks previous someone resembling the blond man in the photo had mistakenly rung her doorbell and asked for Greg.

Stefanie came across one of Damon's older books in a rack at the grocery store. The cover showed a cat-creature's head with its red mouth wide open, an image of a hideous demon peering through the bared fangs. The blurb on the back described a story of supernatural violence and demonic sex. She replaced it on the shelf with a strong feeling that she needed to disinfect her hands. The question Ryan had raised the night of the dinner nagged at her again. Did Damon know more than he'd told them? Was he playing some strange game? Or treating the murder as if it were some plot to be manipulated like in one of his books?

A gun was found by some boys wading just above the bridge over Wandering Creek. It was not immediately identified as the murder weapon, but as the news spread across town, there was no doubt in anyone's mind that it was. That evening a central coast newspaper, peppering the article with the protective word "alleged," pointed out that the meandering creek flowed within a few hundred yards of Stefanie Canfield's home. An "expert" suggested the time between the murder and then was commensurate with how long it might take an object the size of the gun to wash downstream from near the house to the bridge.

Stefanie's lawyer called and said the DNA tests confirmed that it was Stefanie's skin under Trisha's fingernails.

On Wednesday the grand jury met to consider the prosecution's case against Stefanie. Arthur Zablonski called her at Fit 'n' Fun. She knew the decision might come that day, and Ryan was with her. The news was not unexpected, but it stunned her anyway. She clutched the phone.

Indicted for murder.

She felt the whirlpool tug at her again. A clammy coldness settled over her and her lungs seemed to have not enough space for air. She tried to stay afloat as the attorney explained the proceedings to her. She shaded her face with one hand as she listened. The prosecution had called sixteen witnesses. Hunter and Ben. The driver who'd seen her fleeing on the road that night. Various fingerprint, gun, DNA, and hair experts.

Zablonski could call no witnesses to defend her. She had no opportunity to explain the fingerprints or the stocking cap or the watch or how her skin got under Trisha's fingernails. She had no chance to direct their attention to some other suspect.

But that was how the system worked, Arthur Zablonski had said. A grand jury didn't decide guilt or innocence; it merely determined whether the prosecutor had enough evidence to take the case to trial. And this prosecutor had proved her point.

Stefanie didn't realize she was still holding the phone until Ryan gently lowered her hand and pried it out of her grip. Not letting go of her hand, he circled the desk. He nudged her gently to the easy chair in the corner of the office and pulled her into his lap. One arm held her waist. With the other he stroked her arm.

"This isn't anything final, Stef. It's just

another formality in the legal process." Protectiveness roughened the tenderness of his voice. "They're a long way from convincing a jury that you did it. You're still out on bail, and we're going to find out who really murdered Trisha."

Stefanie rested her head against his shoulder. She couldn't remember the last time she'd felt the sweet security of sitting in someone's lap. With her mother, maybe, in that old rocker in her bedroom. Of course, the feeling in Ryan's lap was different, what with his hard-muscled chest, strong male arms, and a hint of sun-and-sea aftershave. But the security was still there. Yet suddenly she jerked upright.

"Do you have any doubts about me, Ryan? Any doubts at all?"

"None." He kissed the tip of her nose. "*None*. I love you, Stef."

The words warmed and thrilled her, but she didn't feel completely secure. "And that's why you think I'm innocent?"

"I'd think you were innocent even if I weren't in love with you, because I know what kind of person you are. I know you aren't capable of killing anyone."

She relaxed against him again. He loved her. But she couldn't say the words back, not with a murder indictment hanging over her head . . . and her future hanging in the balance. But with a fingertip she wrote the words across his heart.

"God loves you too, Stef. He knows you're innocent. Don't ever forget that. He's there to lean on. Will you pray with me so we can ask for his help and guidance?"

Is your faith strong enough for both of us, Ry? I hope so. She nodded and remained quietly in his arms while he prayed. She kept one hand tucked against his chest where she could feel the strong beat of his heart.

"Father," he began, and the word jolted Stefanie with an unexpected homesickness. It had been a long time since she had felt that personal a relationship with God. "Father, we don't know why all this has happened, but we pray that you will guide us in this battle that has come upon us. We pray for strength and wisdom. We pray you will guide us to the facts we need to overcome misleading evidence. And we pray that you will help us stay united with each other and with you in this." He paused, then added softly, "And we pray that whoever committed this evil act will not be allowed to triumph."

He kept his eyes closed for a few moments more as he continued in silent prayer.

"Now what?" she asked when his eyes finally opened.

He set her on her feet, his motions gentle but brisk. "Now I'm going back to Portland."

"You're *leaving?*"

He clasped her upper arms. "I'm supposed to be back at work tomorrow, but I'm not abandoning you, Stef. *Never.* I'll drive up there tonight so I can wind up some loose ends at the office. Then I'll arrange for an indefinite leave of absence and be back here within two or three days at most."

Stefanie was relieved he would be returning, but she couldn't help but think that it didn't change her situation. Even her attorney thought she'd killed Trisha, and he was exploring some other defense or plea bargain for her.

"Don't get discouraged, Stef. If Trisha managed to find out Hunter hired the arsonist, I should be able to do it too."

"Hunter may simply have told her about it, not realizing she'd use the information against him. Or maybe she snooped in his private papers, which you can't do. And even if you turn up something about the arson, that doesn't prove anything about the *murder.* It goes to trial in six weeks."

That was a considerably shorter time than usual, Arthur Zablonski had told her. The prosecutor was rushing the trial, just as she had the indictment. Stefanie's conviction meant votes.

"Maybe we should contact Damon again," she said.

"I'm not exactly comfortable with Damon." Ryan hesitated, then smiled and kissed her on the nose. "And it's not because I figure all his razzle-dazzle will sweep you off your feet. It's just that . . ." He frowned, as if he couldn't explain the feeling, but Stefanie knew what he meant. There was something about Damon that was disturbing. "But we will contact Damon again if it looks like the right thing to do, okay?"

Stefanie felt at loose ends as the day dragged on after Ryan left for Portland. *I'm indicted for murder; shouldn't I be doing something active and meaningful? Running down clues, finding new evidence, cornering witnesses?* Yet there she was, bouncing and kicking, teaching a rah-rah class of potential cheerleaders, of which there were only about half as many as usual. But at least some of the townspeople still believed in her.

Val dropped by after work for a session on the treadmill. She seemed more subdued than usual, although she was ecstatic that Damon had sent a bouquet of flowers the day after the dinner. Stefanie wondered if

Damon had spent that night with Val, but decided she didn't want to know. She knew, however, that she wanted to scream, "Don't get tangled up with him again, Val!" Yet at the same time, she couldn't come up with concrete arguments why, especially none that could compete with starry-eyed love.

At closing time, Tina, knowing Stefanie hadn't brought her car, offered her a ride home, but Stefanie decided to stay to do some office work. When she finally started home almost an hour later, fog laced with a scent of wood smoke hung in the air. She wished she had brought her car. She'd never felt uncomfortable with walking at night or in the fog in Julesburg, but that was before she had been indicted for murder.

"You'll protect me, won't you, fella?" she murmured to Sherlock. He'd put on almost seven pounds, and his sturdy body brushed her thigh with each step. "You'll jump right in and slurp any mean old attacker to death, won't you? I don't know what I'm so worried about, anyway. People are probably more afraid I'll attack them."

At home, she fed Sherlock and had just put a load of laundry in the washer when the phone rang. She made a leap for it. Ryan!

"Stefanie?"

Her first impulse was to say, "Sorry,

wrong number," and hang up. But that would be foolish; it was just a phone call.

"Yes, this is Stefanie."

"Damon Halstead here."

"Yes?"

"There's something I'd like to discuss with you."

She peered out the window, irrationally fearful that he was standing on her walkway with a cell phone. "Where are you calling from?"

"I'm at my apartment, in Eugene. But I can drive over to Julesburg tomorrow evening. It's extremely important that we discuss something."

Stefanie hesitated. She didn't want to see him, but it might be an opportunity to find out what Damon Halstead was holding back.

"Look, Stefanie, I'm not hitting on you, if that's what you think." Damon sounded impatient. "This is about murder."

"I thought we discussed that at dinner."

"This is something that concerns just you and me. I think you want Hunter brought to justice as much as I do, and together we can do it. Or am I wrong about your feelings toward Hunter?"

"No, you're not wrong."

"Then I'm sure you'll find this worthwhile. I can be there about 8:00 —"

"I'll be busy at Fit 'n' Fun until 9:00."

"Very well, then, 9:15. That will give you a few minutes to get home. You're halfway up the hill, on Luther Street?"

"No! Not here at the house. I'll meet you at . . ." she grabbed for a familiar, friendly location, "the Julesburg Café."

"No, that's too public."

"What's wrong with public?"

He laughed. "You'll understand after we talk. Actually it's probably better that I don't come to your house anyway. I don't want my car spotted there. Perhaps we could meet somewhere out of the way in our vehicles," he suggested.

Stefanie thought rapidly. No way was she going to meet Damon Halstead in some dark alley. Yet she had to know what this was about.

"All right. I'll meet you in the parking lot at the Calico Pantry." The parking lot lights, plus a fluorescent glare streaming through the big windows, lit up the area as brightly as the gym at Fit 'n' Fun. "You can park around the corner and come to my car. It's a white Toyota. No one will notice us."

"I'd rather — no, that's okay. 9:15," he repeated.

"Okay."

"By the way, this is strictly confidential. No Val, no Ryan."

The restriction startled her. "They want to see Hunter caught too —"

"I'm sure they do. But, for the moment, this can't go beyond the two of us." She heard a finality in his voice. If she didn't agree, she'd never find out what he wanted to tell her.

"How do you know I won't promise and then tell one of them anyway?" she challenged.

"You won't do that." He sounded sure of himself. Was that why he had watched and weighed her the other night? Did she pass some invisible character test, and now he felt he could trust her?

She hesitated. The whole idea troubled her. Yet it wasn't as if she was agreeing to something underhanded or dangerous. It was just a meeting in a perfectly safe place to talk about . . . something.

"Okay, I'll keep this to myself."

"Good."

Five minutes later, that promise was tested. Ryan called. His drive home had been uneventful. Everything was fine at his condo. "I'm hoping I can get back down there as early as day after tomorrow," he said.

378

Ryan's voice made Stefanie feel guilty about keeping a secret. She couldn't go back on her word and tell Ryan about Damon's call, but she wouldn't meet Damon alone. She'd simply call him up and tell him the meeting had to be postponed for a few days and that Ryan must be included. Then they could schedule a three-way meeting, and Ryan would know a more appropriate location than a parking lot.

Ryan, sharp as always, read something into the brief silence. "Everything okay?"

"Sure, everything's fine." She forced a frivolous lightness into her voice. "A sore hangnail. A computer mistake on my bank account. An indictment for murder. Just an ordinary day."

"I doubt we'll ever look back and see this as 'ordinary,' but God will see us through it. And I love you, Stef. Don't ever forget that."

After Ryan's phone call, Stefanie felt better. While her trust in God was shaky, her trust in Ryan was rock solid.

Stefanie's plan to call Damon and postpone the meeting fizzled — she couldn't get his unlisted number from Information. *Why didn't I ask him for it?* She knew she could get the number from Val, but she was reluctant to do that. Val would be inquisitive; Stefanie would have to lie.

By morning, she decided the solution was simple: She'd skip the appointment with Damon. That would send him the message that she didn't go for sneak-around tactics.

But despite her decision, she had the jitters all day. She took a fall in an aerobics class and made a computer mistake on a billing that took her an hour to correct. She drove her car to Fit 'n' Fun in the evening because she didn't want to be walking home and unexpectedly encounter Damon prowling around.

But everything's fine, she told herself after work as she opened the door for Sherlock to jump into the passenger's seat. *I'll just drive home, take a soothing bubble bath, and hit the sheets. By the time Damon figures out I'm not keeping that appointment, I'll be sound asleep.*

A fine plan . . . unless Damon decided to track her down at the house. Which was exactly what he'd do, she suspected.

Reluctantly she swung around to the main street and drove a few blocks to the brightly lit Calico Pantry. She'd just get it over with fast. She'd tell him that Ryan had to be included and end it right there.

She saw nothing resembling Damon's car in the parking lot. *Good. Maybe he isn't coming.* Yet within seconds he materialized beside her closed window, a dark-clad figure in black jeans and jacket, dark hair gleaming with beads of moisture, handsome face unsmiling. He put a hand on the handle of the car door, and she was glad it was locked.

Because a shocking thought that had eluded her conscious awareness rocketed to the surface: Damon Halstead was an obsessed man. Damon Halstead was . . . strange. And Damon Halstead was not without motive in the murder of Trisha Duvall.

26

Stefanie stared at Damon through the glass.

Obsession . . . love . . . hate.

Trisha Duvall had torn Damon's life apart when she abandoned him for Hunter. She'd humiliated a man with a powerful ego, rejected his obsessive love, and plunged him into a paralyzing writer's block. And then expected him to have lunch with her and commiserate about her problems with her new love.

Would Damon let her get away unscathed after all that? About as much chance as there was of his turning from horror books to tender poems about puppies and rainbows.

He'd bided his time. He'd watched and waited, keeping track of Trisha, his obsession with revenge growing. Until a night came when he knew Hunter was away and Trisha was alone at the house, a night when he may have planned to kill her with his bare hands, but a gun conveniently fell into his grasp. And Trisha's missing diamond engagement ring. Damon would have pulled it off her finger as a final symbol of his fury at her for abandoning him and pledging herself to another man.

Startled, Stefanie realized Damon was pounding on the window with his fist. She felt a stab of fear. Had he lured her here to —

But Damon couldn't have planted the watch at the murder scene to incriminate her. Hunter, and only Hunter, could have done that. She edged the window halfway down.

"Open the door on the other side." Damon peered at Sherlock sitting in the passenger's seat. The dog wasn't growling, but a ruff of fur stood out as if electrified around his neck. Damon changed his mind about getting in the front seat. He grabbed the handle of the rear door behind Stefanie. "I'll get in back and we can go somewhere else to talk. This place is lit up like an operating room."

Stefanie poised a fingertip over the button to raise the window. "Ryan will be back in town in a couple of days. I think we should wait and —"

"There isn't time to wait," Damon cut in. "Hunter may find and destroy the evidence by then."

Evidence?

Damon glanced from side to side. Only

one other vehicle was in the parking lot, an empty pickup with a flat tire. Inside, Mrs. Maxwell sat at the cash-register counter watching a tiny-screen TV.

"Trisha told me she kept a journal, and in it she had all the details about Hunter's involvement in the arson, along with enough incriminating information about his financial affairs to keep the IRS busy for months." Damon spoke rapidly, and Stefanie had to lower the window farther to catch every word. "She can't tell us in the journal that Hunter killed her, of course, but there will certainly be something about the gun and how afraid she was of him. There'll be enough to prove Hunter killed her to keep her quiet."

"But Trisha didn't seem like the type of person to keep a journal."

"She expressed some ambitions about writing when we were together. I told her a journal was a good way to become familiar with putting thoughts on paper." Damon passed off the explanation with an impatient gesture of his gloved hand. "I think there may be more than her writing in the journal, however. Possibly even actual incriminating physical evidence against Hunter."

"But even if there is a journal, if no one knows where it is —"

"It has to be somewhere in the house."

"Not in the bedroom," Stefanie stated flatly. "If it were there, I'd have seen it."

"Then somewhere else. Somewhere she'd be sure Hunter wouldn't stumble across it. Her car?"

Stefanie shook her head. "Hunter drove the Mercedes occasionally, so I doubt she'd keep anything confidential there." Where would *she* put something in the house if she didn't want Hunter to see it? She'd hidden his Christmas present one year, a silk robe, in a place where she was sure he'd never look: an upper shelf of a kitchen cabinet.

"The kitchen," she said. Hunter's interest in the kitchen was limited to an occasional prowl through the refrigerator. "He never goes there except to grab something out of the refrigerator or pass through on his way to the garage. Not that Trisha spent much time there either, but —"

"Yes. The kitchen!" An uncharacteristic excitement rippled Damon's words.

"You want to get the authorities to go in and search?"

"The authorities?" Damon's mouth twisted with scorn. "Are *you* satisfied with how the authorities have handled this case so far?"

"Not exactly."

"Neither am I. So we need to get that

journal first to make sure it's properly presented as evidence against Hunter. We have to make certain nothing happens to it along the way."

"But if it's hidden in the house . . ."

He put a hand on the window, dark-gloved fingers curling over the glass. What she read in his slight smile made her gasp.

"You want me to — No way! After what happened when I went to the house before, no way I'd ever —"

"I'm not asking you to go to the house. I'm just asking you to help me get inside. And then to make certain that Hunter doesn't come home and catch me there, like Trisha caught you."

"How could I possibly do that?"

"You had a key to the house, right?"

"The authorities took it. I'm sure it's part of the evidence against me now."

"Okay, it doesn't matter. The key isn't all that important. I've researched enough break-ins that I can handle it." Damon looked at a car passing on the side street and angled his body so the driver couldn't see his face. "The important part is this: I need you to get Hunter away from the house. I need you to keep him away for at least an hour or more while I search for the journal. And then, when he does leave your house, I need you to dial the phone at his home, with a signal we arrange, to warn me that he's coming so I can get out."

"Damon, this entire scheme is . . . preposterous!" She rolled the window all the way down. "Hunter won't even speak to me, let alone come to my house. He told me if I had anything to say to him to go through his attorney."

"He'll talk to you and he'll come to your house if you tell him you're willing to make big concessions on dividing the company. That you might even sign all the insurance money over to him. But only if the two of you can get together and settle it between yourselves, because you think the attorneys are the ones causing all the problems between you. He's a greedy man. He'll go for it."

Stefanie felt a grudging admiration for the scheme even as it appalled and frightened her. Hunter was greedy. And opportunistic. He might go for it. But if something went wrong and she was found involved in a conspiracy to break into Hunter's house again, the trial would be no more than a formality.

Although it could be no more than that anyway . . .

"Get someone else to help you. Val would be happy to do it."

"Hunter isn't going to be interested in a

meeting with *Val.* At the moment, you're the only one who has something he wants."

Stefanie heard the urgency in his voice and wondered why he was willing to go to such dangerous lengths to obtain evidence against Hunter. Not for her sake; she was simply a tool, like the key to the house.

"Make up your mind, Stefanie," Damon snapped. He tapped the window frame with his closed fist. "You're in more desperate need of this evidence than I am. I want to see Hunter behind bars — or in the electric chair — where he belongs. But you're the one who has the most to lose if no evidence against Hunter is ever found."

Stefanie swallowed and rubbed a knuckle across her dry lips. "When . . . when did you have in mind doing this?"

"As soon as possible. I don't know if Hunter knows the journal exists, but if he does, you can bet he's searching for it. And maybe we're too late. Maybe he's already found and destroyed it."

"I — I could try to contact Hunter tomorrow. And then let you know if and when he's willing to meet with me."

"Good." Damon pulled a small spiral notebook out of his jacket pocket. He wrote his phone number on a page and thrust the scrap at her. A noise rumbled low in

Sherlock's throat when Damon's hand came through the window. "Now, about the best window for possible entry —"

"I have another door key. One the authorities don't know about."

Damon lifted his dark eyebrows. "Good girl."

Good girl? Stefanie's hand shook as she stuffed the slip of paper in her own pocket. What would Ryan think?

But wasn't it exactly what Ryan had prayed for? She felt a flare of hope and excitement. He'd asked for the Lord's help in providing a way to overcome the misleading evidence against her . . . and there it was!

"I — I'll call you as soon as I've arranged something with Hunter."

"I'll be waiting to hear from you." With another quick look around, Damon melted into the shadow of a hedge of rhododendrons on the edge of the parking lot.

Stefanie waited several minutes before driving away. Her nerves felt frazzled. *Have I made some disastrous mistake agreeing to this? So many things could go wrong . . .*

But it's my only chance.

She drove several blocks north until she could see the glass-walled house on the ridge overlooking town. It wasn't lit up the way Hunter often kept it to impress people, but the living room and bedroom lights were on. Back at her house, quickly, before her nerve vanished, she dialed the number.

"Hunter Blackwell."

"Hunter, this is Stefanie. I'm sorry to call so late —" She could've slapped herself. Apologizing! To Hunter! She started again. "I've been thinking about the complications with our ownership of the company —"

"As I've told you before, if you have anything to say, go through my attorney." Hunter's tone was crisp and impatient. "I think it's highly improper for us to have even this much of a conversation."

Stefanie wished she'd scripted the dialogue better before making the call. Too late. She barreled ahead with what Damon had suggested. "I know it's irregular, but I'd like to discuss settling our problems with ownership of the company directly with you. Under the circumstances . . ." She gritted her teeth. Under the circumstances that he was trying to frame her for murder. "Under the circumstances, I'm willing to sign off on the company completely. But only if we can have a calm, nonconfrontational meeting that doesn't involve our attorneys."

"I don't think that would be a good idea," Hunter said.

But Stefanie sensed he was weakening. "I'm also willing to discuss my giving up claim to proceeds from the insurance company. And I can cancel all claims my attorney has made that there were irregularities with papers I signed while we were married."

"Why?" he asked bluntly.

"I didn't kill Trisha."

But you know that don't you, since you killed her?

She kept her voice sweet and sympathetic. "But someone did, and I know how you're hurting and how difficult all this has been for you. We've had our differences, but I'd like to make things easier for you if I can. Sometimes I think our adversarial attorneys have been more hindrance than help in solving our problems, and we can do better without them."

"The longer they can drag this out, the more they make in legal fees, that's for sure."

"Exactly," she agreed. "I thought perhaps you could come here to the house tomorrow evening?"

"Let's see, that's Friday . . ."

With sudden inspiration, thinking that it might give Damon more time at the house, she added, "I could fix a light supper?"

"Sure. Why not? That'd be nice, Stef. No

need to be at each other's throats, is there? We can let bygones be bygones."

They settled on 8:00.

Stefanie was surprised at the momentary flush of guilt she felt when she set the phone back in its cradle. Leading Hunter on, baiting the trap to ensnare him . . . She felt like one of those sirens of mythology who lured sailors to their deaths on the rocks.

Stefanie allowed Damon a couple of hours to get back to Eugene, then dialed his home number.

"Damon Halstead."

She told him that Hunter had agreed to meet with her at 8:00 the following evening. Damon said he'd be waiting near Hunter's house so he could slip inside as soon as Hunter drove away. She'd leave the key to the house in the paper delivery box at the bottom of her driveway; he'd make a casual stop there to pick it up. They arranged a signal to warn him when Hunter left her house. She'd dial the number, let it ring twice, hang up; dial, let it ring twice more, hang up; and dial for one final ring.

"I'll contact you later in the evening to let you know if I have the journal," Damon said.

"Hey, Damon?"

"Yes?"

"While you're looking for Trisha's journal, keep an eye out for a jade cameo necklace, okay?"

He chuckled. "Will do."

Stefanie hung up. Her hands were damp with nervous excitement. By the time Ryan returned to Julesburg, they'd have the evidence he'd prayed for.

27

When he left his Portland condo before 7 A.M., Ryan had his plans organized like tin ducks, gliding across a shooting gallery.

Arrive early at the office and clean up details on whatever old cases remained on his desk and computer. As soon as his boss, Steve Richter, arrived, arrange for the leave of absence. Work as late as necessary to finish up paperwork. And then leave for Julesburg at the crack of dawn in the morning.

But the ducks did not glide smoothly across his shooting gallery.

He found three new files stacked on his desk, along with a note from Steve: "Welcome back to the rat race! The firebugs have had a field day while you were away. We need you in Yakima by Saturday morning."

Then he discovered someone had messed up several of his case files on the computer. He spent over an hour putting them back together.

The big frustration came when he hurried to Steve's office at 9:00. The secretary said

Steve was out of town until some time the following afternoon.

Okay, stay calm. This is just a one-day delay, nothing earth shattering.

Yet he found his concentration on cleaning up the old cases shot full of holes by worry about Stefanie. He also found thoughts of Damon Halstead rattling around in those holes.

I don't like the guy. At dinner, Damon had been the perfect gentleman toward Stefanie. Damon had also been pleasant to him. But Damon certainly could have been more attentive to Val.

The information Damon had acquired from Trisha, that Hunter had hired the arsonist, supported what Ryan had suspected all along. Silencing Trisha offered a powerful motive for Hunter to commit murder. But of what practical use was Damon's information? It was no more than what they already had: hearsay, suspicions, and theories.

Ryan settled down to read a claimant's account of how a garage fire had started. The long explanation was so full of contradictions and discrepancies that he could only shake his head. Politely, it might be called a creative reconstruction of events. Less politely, it was simply . . .

Lies.

Lies. What if there was no truth in anything Damon had told them? What if it was all just as fictional as his horror books?

Oh, come on now, just because you don't like the guy. Okay, I've admitted I don't like him. Why would Damon lie about such a thing?

But from the very first it had seemed unrealistic that Trisha would have entrusted such incriminating details about Hunter to Damon, the old lover she'd dumped. Ryan also had a strong feeling that Damon was holding something back.

Put them together and . . . what?

Damon himself had a powerful motive to kill Trisha. An obsessive love distorted by rejection to an equally obsessive fixation on revenge. A bullet to take vengeance . . .

Sure, Damon had motive for murdering Trisha. But what reason would he have for making up a story about Trisha telling him all those incriminating details about Hunter? He didn't need to deflect suspicion from himself; no one suspected him of anything. If he'd killed her, it would be pure stupidity to get involved in any way. He could just hide quietly in the background and smirk when Stefanie was convicted of the murder.

Of course, how much more satisfying would it be for Damon if *Hunter* were convicted for a murder Damon himself had committed. He might even see poetic justice in such a twist, a worthy ending for a plot to take vengeance on both Trisha and Hunter for what they'd done to him.

And Damon was a man experienced with plot twists . . .

But if he had a scheme for revenge, wouldn't a man as clever as Damon provide stronger, more solid proof to back up his accusations? All Damon had done was toss out suspicions. Where was something in the way of evidence to make such a scheme for revenge work?

Ryan's thoughts suddenly jumped to a different track. Did an unseen danger for Stefanie lurk in here? He gave this several minutes' thought, then relaxed. Even if Damon had dark secrets and an agenda of his own, he had no reason to harm Stefanie. And there was still the matter of the watch. It had to have been planted by Hunter to incriminate Stefanie. Considering the situation with detached logic, the watch surely eliminated Damon from involvement in Trisha's murder.

Okay, get off Damon's case. There's no way he could've planted the watch. Only Hunter could've done that. Damon's goal was simply as he'd presented it: Hunter was guilty and Damon wanted to prove it. So perhaps they should, as Stefanie had suggested, contact and try to work with him.

Ryan looked at his watch again. He was tempted just to leave Steve a note and go, but even a valued employee couldn't drop out on an unauthorized leave of absence. Steve might even have to run it through someone higher up for an official okay.

One day wasn't all that vital. He'd be back in Julesburg by midday Saturday at the latest.

Ryan tried to call Stefanie late that evening but received no response. The answering machine didn't kick in, but that didn't surprise him. After receiving a couple of crank calls, Stefanie sometimes left it disconnected. She'd probably unplugged it and gone to bed.

He had his desk almost cleaned off by noon on Friday, the following day. Steve wasn't going to be happy that Ryan couldn't be in Yakima on Saturday, but Pozzeri could take care of Yakima. Ryan went down the hall to Steve's office at 1:00. "Not in yet," the secretary said cheerily. Still not in at 1:30. He was ready to make the trek a third time when Steve stuck his head in Ryan's office.

"Hey, buddy, good to see you."

"Steve, I have to —"

"So tell me about this mysterious vacation. Maybe it's a place Marie and I would like to sneak away to."

Ryan cut his explanation about the "vacation" to the bare-bone facts of what had happened in Julesburg. "So, starting immediately, I want to take a leave of absence until we get things straightened out down there. The trial starts in six weeks."

Steve was perched on the corner of Ryan's desk with one foot on the floor, the other swinging. He frowned.

Ryan's thoughts jumped back to the first day he'd arrived in Julesburg to conduct the investigation on the mill fire. He remembered feeling that he was standing at a crossroads. He'd scoffed then . . . what possible crossroads could there be in Julesburg? Now the feeling lurched back. Steve was not saying, as Ryan had expected, "Sure, buddy, I understand. Take all the time you need."

Ryan added, "I'm also strongly suspicious that Hunter Blackwell hired the arsonist who burned the mill. I can put in time investigating that further while I'm down there."

"Blackwell connected to the arsonist? That's interesting. And it warrants further investigation —"

"Thanks, Steve. I'll —"

"But not right now. Look, I can see you're really concerned about this old friend of yours. It sounds as if she may be getting a raw deal. But there's no way we can spare you right now. Pozzeri starts his vacation Monday, so he can't take up the slack and fill in for you at Yakima."

"It's important, Steve. Really important." Ryan hadn't intended to go into personal details, but he couldn't hold back. "Stefanie Canfield isn't just an old friend. I'm in love with her. I want to marry her. And she goes on trial for murder in six weeks."

"I see." Steve tilted his head. He jiggled the leg hanging over the corner of the desk. "Busy guy on your vacation, weren't you, falling in love and everything?"

Ryan didn't reply. He knew Steve was stalling for time.

"Okay, look, we can do this. You head on up to Yakima. This is a cabinet shop fire, very suspicious looking. You handle that, then hang around for the next two weeks, taking care of whatever comes up, until Pozzeri gets back. Then I'll get you your leave of absence."

Ryan appreciated Steve's effort, but two weeks? "You could hire an outside investigator. We've done it before when we were overloaded. I won't be on the payroll, so that money will be available."

Steve shook his head. "That isn't an option this time. We need you here for at least the next two weeks."

Ryan hesitated. In two weeks, he'd still have close to a month before the trial to nail Hunter. But Hunter hadn't made any mistakes so far. Was a month enough time? He looked back at Steve.

"You haven't said what happens if I don't go along with this. I get the feeling there's a definite 'or else' in there."

Steve's laugh sounded strained. "Well, sure, there's always an 'or else.' A guy can't just take off in the middle of a crisis and expect his job to sit here waiting for him."

Ryan restrained an explosion of impatience. "This isn't any more of a crisis than our usual day-to-day work. We're always in a crisis!"

Steve acknowledged that remark with a shrug. "Look, you'll still have close to a month to work on Stefanie's case. And six weeks is an incredibly short time to allow before a trial. A good lawyer can surely get it postponed, maybe even for months."

What Steve didn't point out, but what Ryan knew he must be thinking, was that Ryan was in line for promotion to Steve's job when Steve retired next year. It was a promotion that would mean a bigger paycheck, better benefits, and much less away-from-home travel.

"This company's been good to you, Ryan."

"I've been good to the company too." *How many thousands of dollars — almost a million in one case — have I saved this company in phony claims?*

"Right. You're one hotshot investigator." Steve stood and added an encouraging slap on Ryan's shoulder. "Which means you can turn things around down there for her in a month. If you're going to spend time on the mill fire, I'll even see you stay on the payroll. Okay?"

Perhaps Ryan could turn things around in a month. Perhaps Zablonski could get the trial postponed. But if not . . .

Am I willing to take that chance?

"Take time to think it through, Ryan. This is your future you're kicking around here."

Stefanie's future too.

Crossroads.

28

Stefanie heard the smooth purr of Hunter's Porsche in the driveway and nervously wiped her hands on a kitchen towel. She let the doorbell ring before she went to the front door.

She felt a small jolt when she opened it. Sometimes she forgot how good-looking Hunter was, how impressive his royal blue eyes and crisp blond hair were. He wore slacks and a knit sports shirt. A jacket draped over his shoulder added a note of casual self-confidence.

"Hello, Stefanie."

His smile was congenial, the kind of smile she hadn't seen from him in a long time. Had he heard the news that the gun found in Wandering Creek had been positively identified as the murder weapon? It had revealed no fingerprints, but the authorities hadn't said whether that was because fingerprints had been wiped off or if immersion in the creek had destroyed them.

She looked over his shoulder at the

flaming sunset silhouetting his figure in the doorway. For several days, summer fog had clung to the town but that evening a spectacular display of gold and red streaked the western sky. At the moment, however, she didn't appreciate the glorious sunset. Heavy fog would make a better cover for what Damon was doing. She'd spotted him making a discreet stop at her newspaper box to pick up the key an hour before. If he'd been watching for Hunter to leave, he should be inside the house.

"Is something wrong?"

Stefanie realized she was just standing there, her body a tense barrier across the doorway. She stepped back and gave him a high-wattage smile. "I'm sorry . . . come in! I guess I'm just awestruck by this marvelous change in the weather."

"Perhaps it's indicative of other changes as well."

He looked around when he stepped inside, a quick, dismissive glance. She hadn't changed much in the house since her mother's death, and Hunter had little use for anything not new, modern, and expensive. He noticed Sherlock standing beside her.

"You have a dog?"

Stefanie knew Hunter had almost a

phobia about getting animal hair on his clothes, but she didn't make any move to put Sherlock in the backyard. "I'm keeping him temporarily for a friend."

Sherlock waved his tail. When Hunter didn't offer a pat on the head, the dog padded off to his favorite spot in the kitchen.

"Would you like something to drink? Our dinner is Mexican, so I made gazpacho. Or there's sparkling apple juice."

Surprisingly, Hunter seemed in no hurry to jump into business dealings, and he made no derogatory crack about her lack of alcoholic beverages. "Gazpacho sounds terrific." He tossed his jacket on the arm of the sofa.

He sat on the sofa and she went to the kitchen. She returned with two chunky glasses filled with the spicy tomato drink. She set one in front of him. She sat on the far side of the coffee table and twisted her own glass nervously.

Now what? She took a sip of the thick gazpacho. It slipped down the wrong pipe. Only a frantic swallow kept her from choking. Hunter leaped around the coffee table and patted her on the back.

"Are you okay?"

Stefanie didn't know whether to be

pleased or apprehensive about this solicitousness. She took another sip. "I'm fine."

Hunter returned to the sofa. After an awkward minute of silence he said, "I understand a sale is pending on the old Nevermore theater."

He was willing to small talk. Good! "I wonder if the new owners plan to reopen it as a theater?"

"I doubt if Julesburg could support a theater, what with all the inexpensive videos available. And the equipment would surely need some high-priced updating."

"Someone suggested it would make a good site for a minimall for crafts or antique vendors."

"An interesting possibility."

Stefanie wondered what his plans were concerning rebuilding the plywood mill, but that was not something she wanted to explore at the moment.

She thought about Damon. What was he doing now? Standing on a kitchen stool so he could peer into the upper cabinets? Digging through drawers?

The cabinet of cleaning supplies in the laundry room! I should have mentioned that as a possibility to Damon. Trisha could have hidden a dozen journals in there, and Hunter would never have run across them.

". . . success you've had with Fit 'n' Fun." Hunter smiled, and Stefanie realized she was completely adrift in the conversation. She heard a surprising intimacy in Hunter's voice when he added, "And you're looking absolutely fantastic, Stef."

A buzzer sounded in the kitchen. Stefanie jumped up. "That means the casserole is done. If you'll excuse me."

In the kitchen Stefanie grabbed a couple of potholders and eased the casserole out of the oven. She wrapped tortillas in a damp towel and slipped them in the oven to warm. She jumped, startled, when she realized Hunter was standing right beside her.

"Hey, isn't this that chiles rellenos casserole you used to make?" Hunter leaned over to sniff the spicy fragrance of the dish.

"I remembered it was one of your favorites."

Maybe it was a mistake to make his favorite food, but she wasn't certain why.

"I've eaten out enough in the past year to last a lifetime," he said. "It's wonderful to have a home-cooked meal."

"I'll just get the salads out of the refrigerator." She turned to open the refrigerator, but he blocked her path with his arm.

"This is nice of you, Stef. I'd forgotten how sweet and thoughtful you are. Sometimes men get . . . sidetracked."

"It's just a casserole. Peppers and cheese and —" She tried to duck under his arm, but he lowered his hand, catching her lightly at the waist.

"Remember how we used to talk about sometime flying down to Acapulco or Cozumel and sitting in the sun and stuffing ourselves on shrimp tacos and enchiladas and sangria?"

"That was a long time ago."

He leaned forward. His warm breath brushed her cheek. His gaze dropped to her mouth. "We could still do that . . ."

His hand slid around her waist and pulled her toward him. She stared at him, too astonished to resist. He was coming on to her? He'd killed the woman he left her for . . . he was trying to frame her for the murder . . . and now he was suggesting they get back together and take a fun trip to Mexico?

She put her palm against his chest. One shove and he'd be *in* that casserole —

Hunter misinterpreted the touch and clasped her hand. "I'm really glad you suggested we get together tonight."

Or maybe he had something short term in

mind, she realized as she saw the smoky heat in his eyes. Something such as a quick trip upstairs to the bedroom.

She slashed her forearm down on Hunter's arm. He stepped back, frowning slightly as he rubbed the swatted arm. Sherlock had taken an unfriendly stance between them, amber eyes on Hunter. Stefanie swallowed and tried to collect her composure. She gave the dog a reassuring pat. No matter how angry she was, she couldn't blow it. Her future, her life, depended on Damon having enough time to find that journal.

Injecting false calm into her voice, she said, "I — I think this is rushing things."

"Yeah, I suppose that's true." Hunter sighed. "Okay, I'm sorry, Stef. It's just that it's been so long, and being so close to you I just . . . got carried away."

What she wanted to do was tell him to carry himself far, far away. And never come back. Instead she forced herself to say lightly, "Dinner's ready, so let's eat now, shall we?"

Stefanie ferried a pitcher of gazpacho, the salads, the casserole, and warm tortillas to the dining room table. She'd already set the table with colorful pottery and a cactus centerpiece. Now she added salsa and a choice of dressings for the salad. Hunter was complimentary as he ate. "I haven't had anything this good in a long time, Stef."

He had two big helpings of the casserole. Even so, dinner did not take nearly as long as Stefanie had hoped. She pushed her own food around on the plate, making canals and mountains of it rather than putting it in her mouth.

She sneaked a look at the grandfather clock at the end of the room. Dinner was indeed going too quickly, but they hadn't started talking about Cougar Creek Timber Products yet. She could drag that out for another hour. Damon would have plenty of time for a thorough search.

"Coffee and dessert?" she suggested. She stood, poised for a trip to the refrigerator. "It isn't Mexican, but it is homemade cherry cheesecake."

He stood up and circled the table. "Another of my favorites. But you always know what I like, don't you, Stef?"

The touch of his hand on her hip flooded her with nausea. *I can't believe this. Trisha has only just died, and —*

"We could save the cheesecake until later. . . ."

Stefanie manhandled an urge to kick him in the shins. She tried to extricate herself,

410

but his other hand slid up her arm and curved around the back of her neck.

"Maybe I am rushing things, Stef," he whispered, "but we have a lot of time to make up for." He brushed his lips against her throat.

"Hunter, stop that!"

He straightened up, annoyed. "Oh, come on, Stef, it's a little late to go all righteous and indignant. We both know why you invited me here, and I'm quite willing —"

"I asked you here to discuss finalizing the division of our business relationship!"

"Yeah, right. You sweet-talk me into coming over. You tell me you don't want lawyers around. You cook my favorite foods and meet me at the door looking gorgeous. And now you go all huffy when I respond?"

Now she knew why making the Mexican casserole had been a mistake. Corned beef, which he hated, would have been a better choice. "I'm sorry if you got the wrong impression, but all I want is to discuss our business relationship." She kept her tone as stiff as her rigid body, but embarrassment flushed her cheeks.

She sneaked another glance at the clock. Much as the situation disgusted her, she had to keep him there a little longer. "This would be the time to get started on that discussion, don't you think?"

"I don't appreciate being yanked around, Stef." He clenched his teeth. "You pull the old tease routine —"

"Tease!" she gasped. "Hunter, you always have been and still are the most arrogant, boorish, conceited, self-important, egotistical, self-centered —"

He snatched his jacket off the sofa and stalked to the door.

No, not yet! Damon needed more time!

"Wait!" She stretched a hand toward him. "We really do need to talk about —"

"Talk to my lawyer." Then Hunter paused and smiled. "But I really don't need your concessions, Stefanie. Because in about six weeks, you're going to be convicted of murder."

When she heard the Porsche screech out of the driveway, Stefanie jumped for the phone. She dialed the number. Two rings. She broke the connection with a stab of her finger.

The phone rang beneath her hand. *No, not now! I can't get stuck talking to someone.* But she couldn't let it ring either; some persistent salesman might hang on for a dozen rings, and she didn't have time for that.

She lifted the receiver. "I'm sorry. Please call back later. I'm —"

"Stefanie? What's wrong?"

"Val! Oh . . . nothing. But I can't talk now; I'll call you back —"

"Stefanie, you tell me right now what's going on! Is someone there, threatening you or something? I'll call the police."

The police. Ben. Just what she needed, an interview with the police, while Damon was a sitting duck, not knowing a furious Hunter was on his way home.

"Just get off the phone, Val, please? I have to call someone."

"You *are* in trouble!"

"No! But . . ." She hesitated. If she slammed down the phone, Val would dial right back. "Val, I can't explain everything now, but Damon is at Hunter's house. He's looking for a journal Trisha left that incriminates Hunter in the arson. Hunter is on his way home and I have to warn Damon so he can get out."

Silence. Stefanie had expected Val to say something.

"Stef, if Damon is at Hunter's house, he isn't planning to get out. He's waiting there to kill Hunter."

With shocking clarity Stefanie knew it was true. There was no journal. No desperate plan to bring Hunter to legal justice for murder. Just revenge.

"Damon killed Trisha, didn't he?"

"Oh, no, Stef. He wouldn't, he couldn't . . ."

Then another truth hit Stefanie. Val had suspected or known this all along, yet she had said nothing. Because of her love for Damon she had been willing to let him get away with murder, willing to protect him with her silence, willing to encourage Stefanie's suspicions of Hunter.

Willing to let me go to trial, even conviction, for the murder Damon had committed!

Now Damon was waiting to ambush Hunter. Stefanie dropped the phone and ran for the door.

29

Stefanie skidded the Toyota out of the driveway and raced along the back road to Hunter's house. It was the same route she'd taken the night she ran from the house with the feel of the gun still hot on her hand.

A new thought struck her. Perhaps Trisha really did leave a journal. But the person it incriminates is not Hunter but Damon himself . . .

Her heart plummeted as she spun into the circular driveway. Hunter's Porsche was already parked near the double front doors of the house. He was nowhere in sight.

She squealed to a stop on the concrete. The big house, once so familiar, now looked alien; a peculiar aura of abandonment hung over it. She jumped when one of the automatic outdoor lights came on. Was Hunter already dead and Damon gone, his vengeance complete? Or was Damon hiding inside, waiting for Hunter to stumble into his trap?

Yet surely Damon must know he couldn't

get away with another murder! A bone-chilling wave of fear slammed through her. After he killed Hunter, Damon couldn't leave her alive to incriminate him.

With shaking hands she started to turn the key in the ignition. She'd call Ben. It wasn't her responsibility to try to save Hunter.

But with a sinking feeling she knew that her conscience wouldn't let her run. She couldn't abandon Hunter to a deathtrap. And there wasn't time to get to a phone and call Ben for help.

Stefanie slid quietly out of the car. She hadn't taken more than a step toward the house before another vehicle roared into the driveway. She stopped short. It looked like Ryan's Blazer. A man and dog jumped out.

"Stef, what are you doing here?" Ryan yelled. "What's going on?" Sherlock flew across the concrete and stuck his nose in her hand.

Stefanie desperately wanted to throw herself into Ryan's arms and hide, but she didn't do it. Neither did she waste time asking how he and Sherlock had gotten here bare seconds behind her. "We can't let him hear —"

"Can't let who hear? What's going —"

"Damon killed Trisha. Now he's set up an

ambush to kill Hunter. I think they're both inside the house."

Ryan shoved her toward the car. "You wait here. I'll —"

"No! I'm coming. You don't know the house."

She saw Ryan hesitate. Not, she suspected, because of apprehension about his unfamiliarity with the house, but because he knew she'd follow him no matter what he said. So he grabbed her hand and pulled her with him. They ducked low as they passed the kitchen windows.

The back door opened with smooth silence when he turned the knob. They eased through the mudroom and into the kitchen. They paused by the refrigerator. The house was eerily silent. Stefanie felt a flutter of doubt. Was Val mistaken about Damon's intentions? Perhaps he'd already found the journal and left the house without waiting for Stefanie's warning signal.

Then a calm voice spoke from the living room. "Fancy meeting you here, Blackwell."

A grunt of surprise from Hunter. "What the —"

Stefanie saw a pile of mail scattered on the kitchen counter. Hunter must have stopped in the kitchen to open it before going on to the living room. Where Damon patiently waited for him.

"Can we get in there without Damon seeing us?" Ryan whispered.

"The living room is open all along this side. If he's facing this way, he'll see us the minute we open the door."

Hunter swore as he apparently recovered from his surprise. "What are you doing in my house? Get out of here!"

Cynical laughter from Damon. "You're not the one with the gun this time, Blackwell. So I don't think you're in any position to give orders."

An unintelligible sound of outrage from Hunter. "You can't —"

"Sit down, Blackwell. Right there on the sofa, right where you killed her." Hunter apparently didn't comply quickly enough, because Damon reinforced the words with a deadly sounding, "Now!" A crash followed.

"And now," said Damon, again in that dangerously calm tone, "we're going to talk about justice."

"This is crazy!" Fear turned Hunter's voice hoarse. "You're out of your mind! You can't force me to confess to something I didn't do —"

"I really don't care if you confess or not. All I care is that you don't get away with murder. Look at the gun, Blackwell. The way Trisha had to look at it before you killed her."

"You can't get away with this!" Hunter's voice turned shrill with panic. "You — you can't murder me and get away with it."

"Murder? No, not really. It's justice, Blackwell. Justice."

Stefanie felt confused. If Damon was there to wreak his second act of vengeance on Trisha and Hunter for what they'd done to him, why was he accusing Hunter of the murder?

"For the first time in my life," Ryan whispered to her, "I wish I was a gun-toting kind of guy." He held out his empty hands.

"What about a kitchen knife or a rolling pin?"

Ryan nodded and Stefanie eased open the drawer where she'd kept her old wooden rolling pin, but now the drawer held an assortment of bottle openers, caps, and corkscrews. Knives — knives had been over in that drawer! Spices now. She looked in dismay at the many drawers she'd had built into the kitchen cabinets.

Ryan shook his head, telling her not to bother searching further. "I'll stand over there by the door," he whispered. "When I wave my hand, you knock something to the floor. Make a big crash. Damon will have to come to investigate. I'll grab him from behind when he comes through the door."

Ryan crept into position by the door. Stefanie wrapped her hand around a wooden stand holding a half-dozen coffee mugs. At Ryan's signal, she shoved stand and mugs off the counter so hard they flew across the room and crashed into the kitchen range.

Then . . . silence. No voices, no running footsteps, nothing.

Stefanie felt as if she stood there for minutes, poised like some child in an old game of "statue." Then the door cracked open. A hand, an arm —

She saw Ryan press his body against the wall, every muscle tensed for attack. She yelled just as she recognized the knit shirt on the arm.

"No, don't! It's —"

Too late. The door burst open. Ryan's open arms encircled the man and pinned his arms to his body. They crashed to the floor together. They rolled back and forth, smashing into the cabinets and the refrigerator. A toaster crashed to the floor. Stefanie dodged a flailing leg and broken pottery crunched under her feet.

Then Ryan was on top. He was breathing

hard, but his hands spread-eagled Hunter's arms against the floor. Ryan looked into the face of the man he had subdued, and his head jerked back in surprise. Hunter lay on the floor with his eyes closed. His shirt was ripped and his chest heaved in gasps.

Ryan lifted his head. "What?"

"He — he made Hunter come through the door first," Stefanie said, looking at the kitchen doorway.

Damon stared down at the men on the floor. The gun in his hand now targeted both. His gaze flicked to Stefanie. She saw an unexpected flash of hurt on his face.

Confused explanation flooded out of her. "I thought *you* killed Trisha —"

"I wouldn't kill her. I loved her!" Raw pain rose in Damon's voice. "She was going to leave him. We were going to get back together. But he killed her!"

The watch. I always knew only Hunter could have planted it. But I lost sight of that in a rush to condemn Damon for the murder.

Stefanie looked at Hunter still spread-eagled on the floor. His head was turned, his neck strained and eyes bulging as he tried to focus on Damon.

"Get up, both of you." Damon, suddenly impatient, toed Hunter with his foot. With the gun he motioned the men to their feet.

"We all know you killed her, Blackwell. We also know the law is never going to get you for it. Not," he added with a scornful twist of mouth, "because you're so smart. Because they're so stupid. But I'm here to see you get what you deserve."

"I didn't kill her!" Hunter said wildly. "You've got it all wrong! She was dead when I got home." He lifted an arm and pointed to Stefanie. "She did it! Finger-prints, stocking cap with her hair on it, mo-tive . . ."

Stefanie stared at him in disbelief. He'd tried to frame her with the authorities for the murder he'd committed *and* he was desperately trying to turn Damon Hal-stead's murderous anger on her to save himself.

But it wasn't working. Damon simply laughed, as if he enjoyed seeing Hunter squirm like a bug on a pin. "Stop sniveling, Blackwell. It isn't going to get you any-where. You killed her, and you're going to pay for it the same way."

"You can't get away with killing me!" Hunter made an awkward, sweeping tilt of his head, as if afraid Damon might shoot if he moved his arms. "You're crazy! There are witnesses . . ."

Damon blinked. His blue eyes flicked

back and forth between Stefanie and Ryan. A slight frown cut lines between his eyebrows.

"In the other room, all of you." Damon grabbed the door and held it open. He motioned with the gun for them to go through ahead of him. Ryan grabbed Stefanie's hand as they passed through the door. She brushed so close to the gun that she could almost feel a cold aura of death around it.

In the living room, Damon motioned Hunter to the sofa. Hunter started to sit, but Damon motioned with the gun again. "No, not there, on the end. Where Trisha was when you killed her."

Stefanie shivered, certain that Damon had crossed some mental threshold of obsessive psychosis.

"You two, in the middle of the sofa." Damon's gaze jumped erratically between his prisoners. His eyes glittered, as if surging adrenaline had his system on overload.

Desperately Stefanie tried to reason with him. "Damon, think about this! You can't get away with killing all three of us. If we work together we can prove to the authorities that Hunter murdered Trisha. The law will handle it!"

"The law is full of loopholes and slick lawyers."

"What about Trisha's journal? Did you find it?"

"I don't know if there ever was a journal."

So Val was right. Damon had planned simply to ambush and kill Hunter. "We can prove it some other way. Let the law take care of it!"

Damon dismissed her pleas with an indifferent shake of his head. "This way there are no loopholes. I know for certain he gets what he has coming."

"You can't get away with it!" Hunter repeated hoarsely.

"Oh, I think I can. But it won't matter to you, will it? Because you won't be around to see whether I get away with it or not."

He leveled the gun at Hunter and made a clicking sound with his tongue. He smiled again as Hunter's skin went from pale to pasty.

"Although I'd have planned things a little differently if I'd realized how this situation was going to turn out today." He tossed Stefanie another accusing look. "I had it all figured to look like self-defense. I just came here to talk to Hunter. When he became angry and violent I had to defend myself."

Stefanie felt sick to her stomach as she realized how she'd so naively cooperated with his plan. *Oh, Lord, why did I do it? I knew from the beginning it wasn't right. Yet I rationalized myself right into this.*

"But I can make this work!" Damon continued. "I did it once in a book. Three murders set up to look like a double murder and suicide. Just what we have here."

Stefanie shivered at the sudden note of glee in Damon's voice. It was no different from figuring out a difficult plot twist. He was enjoying himself.

Damon stepped back. He studied the three of them on the sofa as if he were arranging a formal photo. He stepped forward and placed the gun against Hunter's temple. Sweat ran down Hunter's jaw. Then, without removing the gun, Damon glanced over at Stefanie and Ryan and frowned slightly.

Stefanie clutched Ryan's hand. *He really is going to kill us.* Her head reeled and perspiration wet her hand gripping Ryan's. Her breathing felt strange, as if she couldn't drag in enough air. Was she going to have one of her strange episodes? Maybe it would be easier if she did . . .

No. She swallowed and stiffened her back. *If I'm going to die, I want to spend these last moments fully aware and as close to Ryan as I can get.* She inched along the sofa and pressed her shoulder into the strength of his. Blood oozed from a cut on his jaw and a bump swelled just above his temple, where he'd hit his head on the floor. She longed to reach up and give it a tender kiss.

There's something I have to tell you, Ry. Now, before it's too late.

30

"I love you!"

Somehow, despite the danger, Ryan smiled. It was the sweetest smile she'd ever seen. "I love you, too."

Damon shot them a warning glance. He repositioned the gun at Hunter's temple and lifted Hunter's hand to the trigger. *He's setting it up to make it look like suicide. Grab the gun, Hunter!* But Hunter just sat there, his expression glazed and numb. Damon glanced over at Stefanie. His expression was calculating, like Trisha's when she'd been deciding whether to shoot.

Three murders made to look like two murders and a suicide, he'd said he wrote in a book. Could he get away with it in real life? It was insane . . . irrational!

Out of the corner of her eye, Stefanie saw Ryan's fierce concentration on the gun. Was he calculating whether he could make a lunge for it? Then he glanced at her and risked a different movement. The kiss on her cheek was tender.

"God is with us, Stef," he whispered. "No matter what, God is with us."

God is here? I don't see any sign of him. All I see is that we're going to die here.

Ryan squeezed her hand again. "We're right with the Lord, Stef," he whispered. "That's all that really matters."

I'm not right with the Lord!

He read the doubt in her eyes. "You gave your heart to Jesus once. He doesn't hand it back."

Damon laughed, apparently overhearing the whispers. "Praying, Harrison? I wouldn't count on much help from God if I were you. Will your God stop a bullet?" His finger played with the trigger.

Stefanie listened with muscles as tight as if she'd run a marathon. Yet as she watched Ryan face the gun with quiet dignity, she knew the Lord was just where he always was, and Ryan was drawing strength from him. If the time had come for the end of their days on earth, God was waiting to draw them into his eternal arms. Just as he had drawn her mother.

"Our citizenship is in heaven," Ryan whispered. "Philippians, I think."

"A Bible verse for every occasion."

"Every single one."

Her heart still thundered in fear and panic

even as that truth of "citizenship in heaven" penetrated her soul. With almost fussy little gestures, Damon was arranging his death scenario. Straighten the coffee table. Replace an overturned vase and flowers. Remove a cushion from behind Hunter.

Ryan was also not without fear, Stefanie knew as they watched Damon. She felt it in the pressure of his hand on hers.

But beneath her own fear she also felt a serenity and peace stealing into her heart. She and Ryan both had the Lord, and they had each other. She squeezed his hand, and a thought occurred to her.

"I'm sorry we never had a chance to see if that green flash at sunset really exists," she whispered.

He smiled. "God has much more than a green flash waiting for us. But don't give up yet."

Damon had the gun back against the side of Hunter's head, and Stefanie saw Ryan eye the distance between the coffee table and Damon's hand. Measuring. Calculating. Could he overturn it on Damon before Damon pulled the trigger?

An unexpected rush of cool air fluttered the pages of a magazine on the coffee table. A voice came from the direction of the open door to the kitchen.

"Damon!"

Damon's head swiveled toward the kitchen, but the muzzle of the gun didn't waver from its target on Hunter's temple.

"Don't do it!" Val begged from the doorway. Her auburn hair was disheveled. Her baggy sweatshirt hung over scruffy jeans, as if she'd been housecleaning when she dropped the phone and ran to the car. Her feet were bare. The scarlet of her toenails matched the rubies at her ears.

Talk to him, Val! If anyone could talk reason into Damon's short-circuited mind, surely it was Val. Val moved slowly toward him, like someone approaching a wild animal.

"Everything's going to be okay. You don't have to do this, hon. Everything will be fine," she crooned. She stretched out her hand. "There now, you can just give me the gun."

The plea didn't earn so much as a moment of vacillation from Damon. He moved the barrel down to Hunter's ear, as if trying it on for size. "No," he said flatly. "He deserves to die, and I'm going to kill him."

"No, please, Damon. You can't do it! There's no way you can get away with it. They'll catch you . . . you'll be in prison for the rest of your life. Or get the death penalty! Please, I couldn't stand that — I love you!"

As Val desperately pleaded with Damon, Stefanie realized with sick amazement that her best friend didn't care about Hunter's life. Her concern was only for Damon. She wanted Damon not to kill Hunter only because committing murder put *him* in jeopardy. In her strange, helpless love, only Damon and what happened to him mattered.

Her fears and desperate declaration of love had no effect on Damon. "He killed her. I'm going to kill him."

"No, he didn't kill her." Val took a deep breath. "I killed her."

Val blinked and swallowed. She touched her hair as if she felt some incongruous need to rectify her unkempt appearance.

"I don't believe you." Damon turned furious. "Don't lie for him, Val. Don't try to protect him. He doesn't deserve it."

"I — I didn't plan it. I didn't even mean to do it! I saw you and Trisha together at the restaurant over in Dutton Bay that night. I was afraid she was going to try to get you back. I was afraid I'd lose you again!"

Which was exactly what was going to happen. Damon had said it. He and Trisha were getting back together.

"I went home. But then I came here. I thought —" Val turned her palms up. She was talking only to Damon, as if she'd forgotten Stefanie and Ryan and Hunter were in the room. "I'm not sure what I thought. The front door was open, and I came in. I saw a broken lamp on the stairs. I thought she'd had a big fight with Hunter. I broke down and pleaded with her about you. She was so superior . . . she laughed! She said she'd taken you away from me once, and she could have you back any time she wanted. And maybe she'd do it, because Hunter's problems were getting so tedious. She was so . . . casual about it. As if she was deciding whether she wanted to take back some old piece of clothing she'd discarded. She was on the sofa —" Val motioned to the spot where Hunter was sitting. Her eyes lost focus, as if she were back at that night. "I was standing over there by the stairs. I saw the gun lying on the bottom step . . ." Val's gaze turned to the stairs. She shook her head, as if she still couldn't believe what had happened. Her gaze flicked back into focus. She took a step toward Damon. "I didn't mean to shoot her! I picked up the gun thinking that if pleading with her wouldn't work, maybe I could scare her into staying away from you. And then she was dead."

No one said a word. Val suddenly turned her outstretched hands to Stefanie. "I had no idea you'd been here! No idea anyone would think *you'd* done it." Her eyes suddenly blazed as her gaze swiveled to Hunter.

"I thought they'd blame *him*. He deserved it, after what he did to you, Stef! That's why I took the ring, so it would look like he did it."

Stefanie felt a spiraling sense of dizziness at Val's twisted view of loyalty and justice and logic. She remembered how Val had tried to convince her Hunter must have taken the ring as some kind of symbol.

"You killed her?" Damon said. The gun dangled limply against Hunter's temple. "*You* killed her!"

"It was a mistake, Damon." She held out her hands again in a gesture of apology and reconciliation. "But if it hadn't happened and you'd gotten back together, she'd only have hurt you again. And ruined everything for *us!* You know that. I love you —"

The gun in Damon's hand blasted. A startled look of surprise leaped into Val's eyes. Her hands clutched disbelievingly at the hole in her chest. Then, with incongruous grace, she slid silently to the floor. Stefanie stared at the crumpled form on the carpet.

Val's beloved ruby earrings shone like

jewels of blood on her ears. Her auburn hair fanned gently across the pale carpet. *So much blood . . .*

Damon looked at the three people still frozen to the sofa in shock. "She killed Trisha," he said. The gun dangled loosely at his side, a dark appendage at the end of his limp arm. "She should have known I'd kill whoever did that."

Ryan stood up cautiously. Soothingly he said, "It's all over now." He held out his hand. "You don't need the gun anymore."

Stefanie stood up too, to go to Val. One part of her knew Val was beyond help, but some stubborn part still hoped. *Maybe, if we can get medical help here fast enough . . .*

Panic suddenly flared across Damon's face. He took a step backward. "No!" The limp arm came to life. He lifted the gun so that with a flick of his wrist he could target any of them. "Get back on the sofa, both of you."

Stefanie and Ryan exchanged glances. Ryan's slight nod told her to comply. Reluctantly she slumped to the blue cushion, but Ryan remained standing. Hunter looked as if he had taken root and become a part of the sofa.

"I can work this out." A strange glee danced in Damon's eyes. "Yes, why not?" he murmured as if talking to himself. "Even better than what I originally wrote. Movie material here! A successful triple murder and suicide . . ."

Damon really thinks he can kill all of us and get away with it. He was walking rapidly back and forth, his eyes glittering with a dark vitality. He paid no attention to Val's body even when his feet passed within inches of her spread hair. His plan was deadly plain: Add Stefanie's and Ryan's bodies to Val's, then make it look as if Hunter had killed himself after murdering all three of them.

Damon became aware that Ryan had not followed orders. "You —" he snapped. He took a menacing step toward Ryan, gun hand outstretched. "Back on the sofa —"

The cannonball of yellow fur shot out of nowhere. It hit Damon in the middle of the back, and he crashed forward. The glass of the coffee table shattered. The gun flew across the room. Ryan snatched it up.

Damon sprawled facedown on the carpet. Around him lay slabs of broken glass, and a crumpled silk rose covered his hand. Blood trickled from his broken nose. Sherlock stood over the groaning man. A teeth-bared growl transformed his usual good-natured expression of doggy friendliness to a savage warning not to move. A cool breeze of evening air signaled how Sherlock had gotten inside — Val hadn't closed the back door when she rushed in.

Stefanie rushed to Val. She put fingers to her wrist, then her throat. A pulse? A thread of life? No. Nothing. Blood pooled around her chest. *Oh, Val, no . . . Did you really kill her? He wasn't worth it! I don't want to believe you did this. . . . Don't be dead!*

Stefanie ran to the phone on a nearby end table. She dialed the three numbers. "A — a woman has been shot here. 1420 Ridgeview Road. I think she's . . . dead."

Then she called Ben at home and said simply, "I'm at Hunter's house. Something terrible has happened. Please come."

Stefanie went upstairs for a blanket to put over Val. Val was beyond needing it for warmth or protection, but Stefanie couldn't let her just lie there with her bare feet so exposed and vulnerable, her body so obscenely disfigured. How had love gone so desperately wrong both in what Val did and what had been done to her? "Oh, Val, Val," she whispered brokenly as she covered the body, "I'm so sorry . . ."

Ryan helped a dazed Damon to the sofa and Stefanie got a towel for his bleeding nose. Hunter huddled in his corner of the sofa, as if trying to stay as far away from Damon as possible.

Then they waited. Ryan squeezed Stefanie's shoulders reassuringly, but he never loosened his hold on the gun. Stefanie didn't want to look at Val, but even when she looked the other way, she kept seeing the startled, disbelieving look on Val's face when the bullet hit her.

Val had killed Trisha. Now Val was dead. But what about Hunter?

"Why did you plant my watch by Trisha's body and try to make it look as if I'd killed her?" Stefanie demanded of him.

Hunter lifted a trembling hand to his ear, as if to check to make sure the muzzle of the gun wasn't still embedded in it. "I came home after the barbecue in Eugene. I found her dead. The house was a mess." Defensively, he added, "It was just like I told the police."

"The watch," Ryan reminded him.

"I really thought Stef had done it." Hunter didn't look at Stefanie; he kept his eyes on his hands.

She could only stare at him in wonderment. "You really thought I was capable of murder?"

He looked at her. "You thought I was!"

"But I didn't try to frame you."

437

His gaze went back to his hands. "It didn't look like a robbery. I didn't notice then that Trisha's ring was missing. So I did think maybe you'd done it," he repeated stubbornly. "I also knew if I didn't come up with something, I'd probably get blamed. Isn't the boyfriend or husband the first one they always suspect? So I figured I had to make it look like someone else did it. I didn't know then I didn't need to put the watch out there, because your stocking cap and hair and fingerprints were all over upstairs."

"And you didn't care if I was convicted of murder, whether or not I'd done it?"

"I knew *I* hadn't done it!"

Good ol' Hunter, always looking out for himself. He'd cared more about his own neck than in finding out who really killed Trisha. Stefanie turned away in disgust.

Ben arrived first. His momentary shock at the scene was quickly replaced by efficient attention to duty. He relieved Ryan of the gun and checked Val's vital signs. He recovered her with the blanket.

"Who is she?"

"My friend, Valerie Halstead. Damon shot her."

"He's Damon?" Ben glanced toward Damon sitting on the sofa. His hands were folded in his lap. His gaze was vacant, as if he'd drifted into another world.

"Damon Halstead," Ryan said. "Val's ex-husband."

"Okay, we're going to need a statement from each of you."

The local ambulance arrived with a blare of sirens. The emergency medical technicians raced in with a stretcher, but Ben waved them to a halt. "She's dead. Gunshot. The medical examiner's going to have to look at her before she's moved."

A little later more sirens announced the arrival of deputies from the county sheriff's office. Ryan locked his arm around Stefanie's shoulders and guided her to a far corner of the living room. Sherlock padded along with them.

Stefanie knew the tears would come, but for now shock kept her dry-eyed. Which was harder to believe? That Val was dead, or that Val had killed Trisha? She asked a question of Ryan that was of little importance in the bigger scheme of things, perhaps because the bigger things were too terrible to face.

"How did you get here right behind me?"

"I turned the corner at the bottom of the street just as your car tore out of the driveway. Sherlock was running along behind it. I opened my car door and he jumped in. Then I just followed you."

"I must've left the house door open when I ran out. Hunter was there earlier. I'd given Damon a key to this house before that. And then Val said Damon hadn't come to look for a journal, that he intended to kill Hunter. And I thought I had to warn him . . ."

Stefanie started shaking. Ryan gathered her into his arms and let her bury her head against his shoulder.

The medical examiner had not yet arrived, but when Stefanie's shaking dwindled to an occasional spasm, Ryan said, "I'll go ask Ben if it's okay if we leave now."

She drew back. "You're leaving again?"

"Not leaving you," he assured her with a quick kiss.

"When do you have to be back at work?"

Ryan's smile was rueful. "The company made me an offer I definitely *could* refuse. So I am, I fear, gainfully unemployed. Which is not much of a recommendation for a man about to propose marriage to the woman he loves, is it?"

"The man *this* woman loves has enough to recommend him for a lifetime, job or no job."

31

Twila held up her needle. "My dear Stefanie, if you don't stop wiggling, what you're going to get here is acupuncture, not seam repair."

"Sorry."

Stefanie clutched her bridal bouquet. Twila Mosely returned to her last-minute needlework on the seam of the wedding gown in which Stefanie's mother had been married. From the sanctuary, Stefanie could hear soft strains of organ music and the shuffle of feet. Outside the window, a branch of maple flamed with fall colors against a cloudless blue sky.

Stefanie looked down at the diamond ring shimmering on her hand. She thought of another ring, the engagement ring that had eventually been found hidden in Val's condo. *Oh, Val, Val . . . I wish things had been different. I wish you were here with me today.*

It had been three months since Val's death. But even though that day still haunted her, it couldn't destroy Stefanie's joy.

Is Ryan as nervous as I am? Surely not! There's no need to be nervous. She was marrying the man she loved, the man who loved her, the man she believed God had intended for her from the day they first met back in junior high.

"Is Ryan here?" she asked Twila.

"I would imagine so. Unless he's chasing around investigating someone."

There was a new sign on the formerly unused portion of the Fit 'n' Fun building. In discreet lettering it read "Harrison Investigative Services." On a wall inside hung Ryan's new license as a private investigator. The phone wasn't exactly ringing off the hook yet, but Ryan had located a missing heir and had done several background checks on potential employees for Volkman Laser Systems. The insurance company for which he had formerly worked had hired him to investigate a fire in Coos Bay. They'd tried to entice him to return to full-time work for them, but he'd firmly said he worked for himself and would accept only occasional freelance assignments.

Stefanie fingered the cameo necklace at her throat as Twila's nimble fingers restored the seam on the old ivory satin. It wasn't the jade cameo her mother had given her, but it was equally precious. Ryan had given it to her, and someday she hoped to pass it on to a daughter of their own. Hunter, before he had left town, had finally admitted he knew what happened to her mother's jade cameo. Trisha had flushed it after they came home from the incident at the Singing Whale.

Hunter. Nothing could tie him to the man who set the fire at the mill. If Trisha's journal had ever existed, it hadn't been found. The insurance company had paid off a month previous, but little was left after cleanup costs and paying off the company debts. She and Hunter had agreed that he could take the remaining cash, and she would keep the property where the mill had once stood. She doubted if Hunter would ever return to Julesburg, unless he was subpoenaed for Damon's upcoming trial.

Tina, Stefanie's matron of honor, cracked the door and peeked inside. "About ready?"

Twila gave her a thumbs-up sign and knotted the thread. A minute later Betty Higgins's authoritative hand on the organ crashed into the strains of the wedding march. Swallowing hard, Stefanie stepped outside. Ben was waiting to give her away. He lifted his elbow, and she wrapped her hand around his arm.

Then she was marching down the aisle. She had a blurry view of Ryan waiting for her at the altar. The distance seemed, strangely, both too short and too long. One part of her wanted to take it in gigantic, unladylike leaps, the way she and Ryan had leaped from rock to rock on the beach when they were kids. Another part of her wanted to take a leisurely pace and savor the sweet miracle of the day.

She stopped at the end of the aisle and looked up at the cross on the wall, right where she had first accepted the Lord. *I'm sorry I tumbled from that mountaintop, Lord. But thank you, thank you, for bringing me home again. Thank you for bringing Ryan back into my life. And I pray for your blessings on this marriage.*

The music ended. Pastor Gordon spoke, his tone appropriately sonorous. "We are gathered here today. . . ."

Stefanie intended to listen to every word. She wanted to absorb and remember and treasure each one. But looking into Ryan's loving eyes, all she could hear was the thunder of her own love for him. He squeezed her hand hard, and she managed to whisper, "I do," at the proper time. Then the pastor was saying, "You may now kiss the bride."

Ryan smiled and lifted her fragile veil. He gathered her into his arms. Their eyes met for a moment, and then he dipped his head to hers. Other kisses had been sweet and passionate and glorious. But none could compare with the meaningful depths of the very first kiss as husband and wife.

And then she felt it, deep inside her.

Who needed a beach or a sunset? Because here it was in all its glory, rising not out of the sea, but out of her heart. The green flash!

Or perhaps it wasn't green, she thought dreamily as it filled her heart and senses. It didn't matter. No mythical flash of any color could ever compare with the most glorious explosion of light and dazzle ever to cross any horizon! And wasn't that just an angel or two singing sweetly in the background?

Stefanie leaned back in Ryan's arms and smiled. "I suppose you have an appropriate Bible quotation for the occasion?"

Ryan looked momentarily perplexed, but Pastor Gordon smiled.

"From Malachi," he said. " 'Has not the Lord made them one? In flesh and spirit they are his.' "

And it was so.